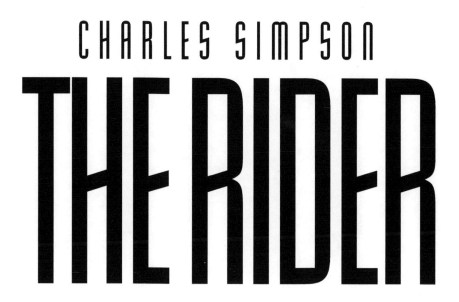

CHARLES SIMPSON

THE RIDER

Print ISBN: 978-1-09830-343-3

eBook ISBN: 978-1-09830-344-0

I WOULD LIKE TO DEDICATE THIS BOOK TO MY FIERCEST SUPPORTER, SELF-PROCLAIMED BIGGEST FAN, AND LOVE OF MY LIFE AND DESTROYER OF MY SANITY—JESS. WITHOUT YOUR SUPPORT, WORK, AND MOTIVATION, THE RIDER WOULD NEVER HAVE MADE IT TO WHERE IT IS NOW, AND FOR THAT, I WILL BE ETERNALLY GRATEFUL.

CHAPTER 1

OCTOBER 31, 1915

8:00 A.M.

THE FIRST RIDE

"JANUSZ"

Four strangers watched Janusz Zalewski die.

As death overtook his body, he realized it was nothing like when his wife had passed away. All of Marzehna's loved ones had surrounded her and had held her hands. He, with their children, had said a tearful goodbye as their priest administered the Last Rites.

Janusz exhaled a ragged breath as he thought about the two situations. Although he was alone when his life slipped away, he was at peace with it. He had lived a decent life, married a good woman, raised three children, worked an honest job and believed in God.

In fact, only one thing bothered Janusz; he could not recall how he had ended up on the sidewalk so far away from his house. He ignored all the people around him who asked if he was all right and concentrated on remembering. He probed his mind and saw himself waking up. He took another shallow breath, concentrated harder, and finally remembered taking his daily walk.

He smiled as he recollected walking down the stairs and marveling at the beautiful day. As the images of the trees flashed back into his head, he thought about how most of the leaves had fallen, but the ones still clinging to the trees caught his attention the most. Former shells of themselves, they were all but dead and would be ripped off forever by the next wind only to fall to the ground and rot.

Janusz recognized the irony. He managed to produce a weak laugh through his labored breaths, and he realized he was now one of these leaves. He was hanging on to life, but soon death would blow just like the wind and rip him from the tree of existence. Yes, that was the reason for being so far away from his house; he kept walking to see how many leaves still clung to the trees.

But the leaves were not the only things that kept him walking earlier that day as he continued to ponder. He thought about the man, the man with a pipe, who sat on the porch of one of those new houses that were everywhere now. Janusz almost had the memory of the man with the pipe until another blinding flash surged through his head.

Janusz no longer saw the people standing around him.

He could not open his eyes, but darkness had not completely engulfed him yet. His time was coming though, only a matter of minutes. The pain in his head disappeared, and excitement started to build for the next journey.

Janusz still heard the people around him talking, but he had no interest in their words. He wanted to drift off; he was comfortable in this place. The man with the pipe still bothered him though. Janusz needed to know who he was, and then he would drift off forever. He fought the urge to let go and tried to focus on the man's face in his memory.

Janusz knew that he had stopped and looked at the man, but could not remember why. The man had a look Janusz recognized and for some reason it made him smile. Then, all thoughts of the man with the pipe vanished, and Janusz tried to take a breath, but couldn't. The pull towards the comfortable was too powerful, too welcoming, and Janusz let himself go.

Janusz heard no more voices around him. He felt weightless and most of all, good. He realized he was leaving, and soon St. Peter at the

Pearly Gates would meet him. Soon he would see his beloved wife; soon he would see his parents. As he drifted off into oblivion, happiness filled him with the thought of spending eternity with his loved ones.

CHAPTER 2

OCTOBER 31, 1915

8:31 A.M.

THE SECOND RIDE

"ROY"

Janusz opened his eyes, unsure of his location or what had happened. He was no longer in the street surrounded by strangers looking down at him, but in a bright room with many people talking and what sounded like a woman screaming. Chaos filled the chamber, and none of it made sense to him. He now questioned if he had not died, but instead, had survived. Had one of the people taken him from the street into one of those nice houses?

He tried to say something but couldn't. The room buzzed. Too many people talked at the same time, and nobody listened to him, so he started to scream. He tried to move, but somehow, his arms and legs would not work how they should have. The confusion now grew into something else--fear.

Although something was different than it had been on the sidewalk, he was confused, but not debilitated. His thinking was clear but somewhat limited. His tongue would not work, and he couldn't form words. He could only scream, and he wanted to go back to the peaceful serenity. Janusz noticed the people in the room were much quieter now; the woman had stopped screaming, and the other voices talked in softer, almost soothing tones.

Janusz did not care about the sudden quiet in the room. He continued to scream. He wanted to make them understand, but the more he shrieked, the more the people talked in calming voices. Suddenly somebody moved him and picked him up. In addition to his jumbled thoughts, his vision was blurry, he couldn't see very well. It was like when he would accidentally put on his wife's glasses instead of his. As he thought of his wife, images of her calmed him a bit, and he stopped screaming. He still breathed rapidly, but at least he did not scream.

He was not being moved anymore; instead, a woman held him. Janusz looked up at her and tried to make out her face. His vision cleared as she held him close to her. He had never seen this woman before, and he did not know why she held him.

Janusz no longer thought of his wife and calmness crumbled, which made him want to yell out again. As he tried, no sounds came out. The energy had left his body. All at once he was tired and exhaustion like never before cascaded down his body, and he started to drift off to sleep. He wondered if sleep really pulled him or if it was death coming to take him for good.

He tried to fight, wanted to stay conscious. He needed answers to questions such as who these people were and why they had brought him here. Unfortunately, all strength to fight dissipated. He slipped into sleep, and before everything went black, a man appeared to him through his blurred vision.

The man put his hand on Janusz' head and said something he did not understand, but it comforted Janusz. Although he couldn't see the man clearly, he believed he recognized him. He struggled to recall why the man looked so familiar, but sleep overtook him before he could remember and he drifted off into a deep slumber.

31 OCTOBER 1915
10:30 A.M.

Janusz woke up refreshed. The weird dream about dying and waking up in a strange house lingered for only a few moments, but the realism of it jarred him. He shook his head.

Silly old man, he thought.

He pushed the memory out of his mind and figured it high-time to get up as there was no use in dwelling on childish things like dreams.

He tried to get up, but something was wrong. He couldn't move; his body didn't work the way it should. Getting out of bed always took Janusz a fair amount of time because of arthritis, but this was different. There was no pain, but he couldn't move his arms and legs properly; it was as if they were made of rubber.

Something else was wrong too; he noticed he was not in his bed. Walls surrounded him; he could feel them as he flopped his arms around. He stared up at the ceiling, and it was different too although he couldn't see it very well. He needed his glasses. Janusz started to breathe heavy again as he thrashed his body around; he tried to lift his head, but it was so heavy, and he didn't have the strength.

He could move his head a bit though and that allowed him to look down toward his body and he froze--everything was wrong. Terror poured over him, knocking him over like a strong current in the river and he cried out in shock. This was not his body; it felt like his own, but it did not look like it. At that moment Janusz suspected he did not dream the previous events, but he still didn't understand. He could not get up, could not talk, and could not see well. So he did the only thing he could do: he screamed.

Out of nowhere, a woman appeared and picked him up. It didn't make sense to him how a woman could lift and carry him, but she did. He tried to fight her but failed, as he did not have the strength or coordination. Through his teary eyes he saw the woman, but not the woman who had held him before. Now the woman stopped; she didn't carry him anymore.

Janusz now heard the woman speaking to another woman, but he cried so hard, he couldn't understand the conversation. He moved again, and the woman passed him to the other woman. She was the one from earlier that had held him close, the one that had a strange, comforting effect.

Janusz stopped screaming for a moment to look at her, she smiled and warmth emanated from her. He was tired again, but wondered how. He had just woken up. He thought to himself that it might be better to remain calm and relax until he could get his strength back, and then he would figure everything out. That was his plan, at least until the woman with the warm smile did something unspeakable.

The woman pulled the sheet that covered her aside and exposed her breast to Janusz. The sight shocked him, and for a moment he couldn't make a sound. He asked himself why the woman did this and wondered if she was a whore. Janusz was a God-fearing man, and he had only seen one pair of breasts before in his life, and those belonged to his dear wife. The sight overwhelmed him, and he remained motionless with his mouth agape.

The woman then did something even more horrifying; she began to pull Janusz' head towards her breast. He screamed again and did everything to fight against being pushed into this strange whore's breast. He struggled and fought for minutes until the woman passed Janusz to the other woman and once again she carried him and placed him back down in the strange little bed.

He now found himself too tired to scream anymore, and he rested, trying to catch his breath. Thinking and thinking, struggling to figure out this situation, the strange exhaustion took over again and once more Janusz closed his eyes and drifted back into a deep sleep.

31 OCTOBER 1915
12:30 P.M.

Janusz awoke less shocked and disorientated. He still had so many questions, but most of all he was still scared. He told himself, at the very least, that counted for something. Also, the sudden exhaustion that kept overtaking him seemed to be gone, at least for the moment. *Good*, he thought, this could give him a chance to think about what was going on. Unfortunately, there would be no thinking for him because he had another problem… hunger.

As he thought about it, hunger did not adequately describe it; he was famished and tried to remember the last time he had eaten. The hunger consumed him, and he could think of nothing else. The speed of the feeling of emptiness in his stomach surprised him. He couldn't remember ever feeling a burning in his stomach like this before. He had never been this hungry, not even in the years before coming to America from his native Poland, where food had been scarce.

Janusz now started to worry and thought he might starve to death. He dwelled on this point over and over in his head. Getting up was impossible, and if he couldn't get up, he wondered how he was going to feed himself. He wondered what it would be like to die of hunger. He imagined it would be horrible, especially if how he felt at that moment was any indication.

The sound of voices jarred Janusz out of his worries of dying of hunger. He couldn't see the people talking, but he knew the voices to be those of the two women. Back and forth, he thrashed his head. He flailed his arms to try to get their attention. He then tried to yell the word "help," but only managed to produce a few gurgling sounds.

The sounds caught the attention of one of the women. The voices stopped, and soon, the woman who always picked him up appeared over his strange bed. Like before, the woman carried him to the woman with the warm smile who had shown her breast to him earlier. Janusz tried with all his might to squeeze some intelligible words out and ask for something, some soup or warm bread. He didn't care; he just wanted to stop the pain of hunger growing in his stomach. He needed to let them know he was hungry, and since he couldn't speak, screaming was his only outlet.

Soon he found himself in the arms of the woman with the warm smile, and once again she produced her breast to him. The sight of the large full breast was no less shocking than it was before, and she tried to force his head to it again. Janusz couldn't believe the strength of this woman. No matter how hard he fought her, the woman overpowered him and forced his mouth to her breast. He struggled and moved, but the woman held his head to her breast firmly. She said something to the other woman, and this caused Janusz to stop crying to try to listen. His hearing still was not great, but he heard the woman standing say, "hungry."

Yes! Janusz thought, that's right, he was hungry. While he paid attention to the women speaking, he did not notice that his mouth was now pressed against the woman's nipple. As soon as the realization hit him, he almost protested again until something strange happened. Warm liquid splashed across his lips. He involuntarily opened his mouth, and the liquid ran across his tongue, which caused the greedy hunger to be in total control of his actions. He couldn't help it, but he started to suckle on the woman's nipple, and the more he did, the more the warm liquid came out. Soon he found himself swallowing it, and the burning hunger in his stomach began to die down.

Disgust washed over him, but he kept suckling. It was as if some internal force drove him, and he kept drinking from this woman's breast. He closed his eyes and asked God for forgiveness and continued to quench the hunger in his body.

CHAPTER 3

1 MAY 1916

Sunshine painted and warmed Janusz' face as he awoke in the morning. He could see it clearly through the window as he lay. The beautiful sun made him forget what had happened to him. Janusz felt the energy from the sun filling him, and he sat up.

He tried to remember the last time he had seen the sun, but couldn't. It seemed to him the winter had dragged on for an eternity and then the rain had followed with months of cloudy skies. Not today though. The sky boasted a crisp blue, and the beautiful yellow orb hanging above spoke to him. As he basked in the warmth of the sun, Janusz noticed something; he was sitting up.

He stopped thinking about the sun and looked around from a new perspective. For the first time since his death, he was able to sit up, so he tried to move his arms. Every day they worked a little more, but today they functioned better than ever. He lifted both hands up and slowly brought them to his face. He caressed his cheeks and felt the heat the sun had left from its kiss.

"I did it," he tried to say, but the only thing that came out was non-sensible gibberish. *Ok, one step at a time*, he thought, and he started to laugh.

The sound of his laughter sounded so funny to him that it made him laugh even more, and soon he couldn't stop himself. He laughed and laughed until he felt a presence in the room, which caused him to stop.

The familiar looking man stood in the doorway and Janusz turned his head, and the two made eye contact. Janusz wanted to tell the man and share his excitement, "Look at me, I can sit up again. I can move my hands."

He couldn't though, and only continued to make the gibberish sounds, but the man looked like he was in no mood to share in the joy. He stared at Janusz with wide eyes.

Janusz thought the man looked scared, or at least a bit shaken, and Janusz couldn't understand why. So he made some more gibberish sounds to make him realize how grand this moment was. Nothing worked, and the man started to walk backward out of the room. Strange energy emanated from the man, and then the woman's voice rang out.

"Peter, what are you doing?"

The man jumped as if hit with a bolt of lightning. "Jesus, Mary, you startled me."

She looked at him as if he were silly. "What has you so fidgety?"

Peter said nothing; he only pointed over to Janusz who still sat up, enveloped in sunlight. Mary looked in the direction where the man pointed and saw Janusz and shrieked with joy. "Good Lord, would you look at that, little Roy is sitting up."

Now Janusz jumped and thought about the name, "Roy." He thought he had heard this before, but couldn't be sure. Now there was no doubt; Mary had called him Roy. Janusz knew she spoke of him, as the familiar man's name was Peter.

No, he thought, *Janusz, my name is Janusz.*

She ran over to Janusz' strange little bed, picked him up and said, "Look at you growing up so fast, Roy, already sitting up."

Once again Janusz tried to say, "Not Roy, Janusz," but out came the gibberish words and this time he did not find them funny, they angered him. He moved his head away from the woman's chest, which allowed him to get a good look at the room with his seemingly newfound eyesight, and glanced at the strange little bed. Only it wasn't a strange little bed with walls, not really; it was baby's crib.

As Janusz pondered this new revelation, Mary spoke again to Peter. "What are you doing way over there in the corner? Come over here and tell your son how much of a good boy he is."

Peter said nothing; he stood and looked at Janusz with suspicion.

The woman stomped her foot and raised her voice. "What's wrong with you, Peter? You're acting like there is a rattlesnake in front of you; come here."

Peter shook his head. "I'm sorry, Mary, I guess I'm just surprised." He took a deep breath as he looked out the window and turned back to Mary. "You know, since it's such a fine day, let's take little Roy out for a walk."

Mary squealed and clapped her hands together in front of her chest. "Peter, what a great idea."

Peter cracked a small smile at his wife's excitement and said, "I'll wait on the porch while you get him ready."

* * *

Janusz soon forgot about the strange feeling between him and Peter. After Mary fed him, all he thought about was being outside in the beautiful sunshine. He longed to feel the wind on his face and to smell the spring fragrances. Janusz had not been on a walk for a long time, and he missed it dearly.

Mary dressed him with great care and carried him to the door and placed him down in something. For a moment, he was puzzled, but when he started moving, he realized he was in a baby carriage. He shook his head and cursed in his thoughts. How was he supposed to walk without being able to stand up, he asked himself.

He pushed this disappointment aside; even though he couldn't walk outside as he had for so many years, at least he would be outdoors, and that would have to do for now. As the woman pushed the carriage, he heard her call out to Peter and the door opened. Once they were outside, the air patted his face and happiness filled him. *Finally*, he thought, he was out of that damn house.

Something else hung in the air too, other than the scents of spring. It was a pungent odor with a sweet overtone in it, and Janusz tried to place it as he knew the smell.

"Are you ready?" Peter asked Mary.

Janusz looked over in Peter's direction. He suddenly remembered the smell along with other things. Janusz saw Peter standing over him, smoking a pipe.

Janusz gasped and tried to say something, but couldn't even make the normal gibberish sounds; all he could do was scream.

Peter was the man with the pipe, the man Janusz had seen on his walk on the day he died.

Peter pulled back at the sound of Janusz screaming and looked at Mary. "What's wrong with this child?"

Mary's face tightened, and her eyes narrowed. "Nothing is wrong with your son."

Peter looked at Janusz as if trying to see something beneath the surface. "That's not normal; the boy cries too much."

"Well, maybe he doesn't like the smell of that wretched pipe."

Janusz turned his head away from Peter. He couldn't look at the pipe without sending himself into a panic because it made him realize some things. He knew he was still in Port Walden, but most of all, he knew that he hadn't died and that somehow, he was *in* the baby that the man with the pipe had been waiting for on that day.

CHAPTER 4

Janusz loved apples. He ate them every chance he got. Every morning he discovered a fresh new plate of the red fruit, and every morning he went straight for them. Mary usually insisted on cutting them up for him, but he always tried to grab one before she saw and would take a bite. The feeling of sinking his teeth into the firm sweet flesh was something he missed terribly. By the time he had turned 40, he had lost most of his teeth, and that pleasure was gone. *Not today,* he thought as he swallowed the mashed up apple and licked his new shiny teeth.

While Janusz marveled at the fact that he had teeth again, Peter walked into the kitchen and said, "I've never seen a child like apples so much."

Mary smiled but kept looking at Janusz. "I know. I love watching how he savors every bite."

"Well, he better enjoy them while he can, because those are probably the last until next season."

Janusz snapped his head towards Peter, which caused the man to step back a bit. *Next season,* thought Janusz, which made him wonder what the date was. He had been so caught up in making his body do more things like walking and getting his tongue to work as it should that he had forgotten almost everything else.

Now thinking about the date, he turned and looked at the calendar on the wall. The date was October 31—exactly 2 years after his death. His stomach no longer accepted any more food, and he only stared at the calendar.

In the background, Mary said, "Peter, look, I think he knows it is his birthday today."

"Nonsense, Mary, the child is only two years old; there isn't a damn 2-year-old in the world that can read a calendar." However, the tone of Peter's voice suggested he didn't believe his statement.

Janusz heard them talking, but he was more focused on the date rather than their discussion. Two years kept flashing through his mind. Janusz wondered for a moment if he should think of himself as 67 or as two. He shook his head and tried to push this out of his thoughts, which was something he did a lot. Dwelling on what had happened did nothing but get him spun up, and he needed to concentrate on developing, then he could figure out what in the hell had happened.

The sound of the door slamming shut bumped Janusz out of his pondering and he looked around the kitchen. Peter had left as he always did in the morning. Janusz thought Peter was a strange man for a few reasons. He never really said goodbye to Janusz when he left unless Mary forced him to, and the man would never touch or hold him either. Although it did not bother Janusz, he found it strange. When Janusz' children had been born, he couldn't get enough of them. He hated to go to work because he would have to spend the entire day without seeing them, especially his little girl Agata, his little Button.

Most of the time, he didn't like to think about his little girl. The memories caused his stomach to twist up, and he would slip into depression. Today though, he had a feeling his daughter would be thinking about him, and he hoped she would not be too sad. The one thing Janusz could never stomach was seeing his children sad, no matter what age they were.

He would do anything to see Agata again, to put his arms around her and give her a great big giant hug.

Janusz didn't notice the tears escaping out of his eyes until one of them rolled off his cheek and splashed onto his hand. Mary saw it too and asked, "What's wrong, Roy? Did you bite your tongue, little one?"

He almost said aloud what he was thinking at that moment but didn't. He didn't want to scare Mary or make her think there was something wrong with him, so a discussion about feelings from a two-year-old was out of the question. Janusz knew it was bad enough that Peter thought he was strange, so he took a deep breath and smiled at Mary.

Mary kept looking at him and smiled. "Oh dear, are you sad because your poppa left without saying goodbye?" She picked him up and carried him into the other room where she sat him down. "Now don't you worry about that, he just gets busy with work and forgets things." She then bent down and squeezed his cheeks. "Just like you will when you grow up and have babies."

Janusz looked up at her and again stopped himself from saying what he wanted to say.

His look caught Mary's attention, and she asked, "What, Roy, do you want to say something?" Mary got down fully on the floor and sat in front of him. "Come on, Roy, you can do it." She pointed to herself and said, "Momma."

Her eyes were wide, and she wore a big smile as she repeated, "Momma." Janusz figured he should take pity on the poor woman and give her something, so he said, "Momma."

A little gasp fell out of her lips, and she said, "That's right, I am your momma."

Janusz' stomach lurched a bit as he thought, *no you are not*, but he just smiled at her.

Mary looked around the room and motioned to a chair and said, "Chair."

Janusz said, "Chair" and the two continued this game, much to Mary's delight.

Mary leaned in and hugged Janusz. "Look at my big boy, such a smart big boy."

The words angered Janusz as she said them. Janusz did not think of himself as a big boy; he was a grown man. A grown man that had worked hard and raised a family and now he was being treated like a child by this damn woman, who from what Janusz could see, didn't know her place. Janusz had noticed how she would sometimes talk back to Peter and even though Janusz didn't care for him, he was still the man of the house, and his wife should respect that.

Mary kept talking, but he didn't pay any attention to her until she poked him in the chest. "Can my big boy tell me his name? Huh, can he?"

"Janusz," slipped out of his lips. The word came so fast that it took him by surprise. But that was his name, and Janusz needed this woman to realize this.

"You silly boy, you know your name now, come on, tell me," she said, and laughed.

Janusz gritted his teeth as the phrases "big boy" and "silly boy" crashed around in his head, making him want to rage. Mary prodded once again. "Can the big boy tell Momma his name?"

All of the shackles that bound his tongue broke free at that moment, and Janusz spoke clearly, "Yes I can tell you my name. My name is Janusz Zalewski."

Mary's head snapped back almost as if someone had slapped her. "What did you say?"

"I said my name is Janusz, not Roy. My name is Janusz Zalewski."

Mary scuttled back on her hands and feet until she hit the wall behind her and sat there and stared at Janusz.

CHAPTER 5

4 AUGUST 1918

Janusz listened to the preacher tell the congregation about the dangers of sin and how a non-righteous life would ensure eternal damnation. The man continued and explained that going to church and praying to God would grant entrance into heaven. When he heard these words, his jaw tightened and he clenched his fists.

Janusz wanted to stand up and shout at the preacher. He wanted to ask the man if that was the truth, then why was he sitting here listening to him instead of enjoying heaven with his wife? Janusz blocked out the rest of what the preacher said and silently said his own prayers, his Catholic prayers. This church always felt strange to him, and he wished they could go to a Catholic church sometime, but in the end, he told himself at least it was a house of God, even if they were not worshiping correctly.

Still deep in his thoughts, someone tugged on his arm. He turned to look, and Mary said, "Roy, dear Lord, I said your name twice."

Janusz looked around and noticed the church service had ended and most of the people were now getting up and leaving. He shook his head, turned back to Mary, and smiled. "Sorry, Mother, I was thinking about heaven."

Mary smiled back at him and put her hand on his head. "Roy, you have nothing to worry about, as long as you do what the preacher said, you will go to heaven."

Janusz fought the urge to tell her that may not be true, but he didn't want to scare her. Ever since the time he had told her his name was Janusz, he had been careful not to do anything like that again. After that incident, she was distant with him for a few days, and that was something he couldn't risk; he needed to have at least one of his caregivers like him.

Mary kept smiling at him and caressed his head. "I tell you what. Since it is such a nice day, why don't we ask your father if we can walk to the sweet shop to pick up a little treat?"

"I would like that, Mother."

As the three of them left the church, Janusz thought of nothing except what the preacher had said. His mind would jump back and forth from being angry to wondering more about why he was there. He briefly suspended his thoughts as one of those new automobiles drove by. Janusz hated those things and every day he noted more and more of them, and this made him realize that the longer he stayed on this earth, the more of them he would see.

Thinking about the cars made Janusz wonder for the first time how long was he going to live. He wondered what else he might see and experience, as he figured he had another 60 years on this earth if all went well. He shuddered as he thought of seeing the year 1978 and all the damned foolishness people would create.

Thoughts of automobiles, the expanding town, and being stuck in this world without his wife for many more years bounced in his head. He barely noticed that Peter and Mary were talking to somebody until something snapped his attention back into reality. The next moment happened so quickly that he didn't have time to stop it, and the words came flowing out of his mouth like the current of a mighty river.

Two women were talking to Peter and Mary, one older and one younger. Later, when Janusz would have time to think about it, they seemed to be a mother and daughter. Only the younger one spoke to Peter and Mary though. What grabbed Janusz' attention was when the older woman said to the younger one, "Zapytaj ich, jak nazywa się dziecko," which meant in Polish, *ask them what the child's name is.*

Before the younger woman could translate the words into English, Janusz said, "Nie musisz ich pytać, mogę ci powiedzieć. Mam na imię Janusz" which meant, "you don't have to ask them, my name is Janusz." The old woman's head snapped back as did everybody else's and the younger woman spoke in Polish to Peter and Mary, but it was obvious they did not understand.

"How is it that your child speaks such perfect Polish?" she asked. Peter did not answer, instead, he abruptly grabbed Janusz' arm and dragged him in the direction of home.

* * *

Even though it was still early, Mary put Janusz in his bed as soon as they arrived home. Peter was upset, and Janusz knew he had made a mistake by talking to the women. Through the closed door, Janusz heard Peter and Mary talking.

"That's not normal, Mary. How could he know how to speak Polish, and did you hear how easily it rolled off his tongue?"

"We don't know anything, Peter, and besides he probably picked it up from somewhere. You know how children are."

Peter's voice elevated with his reply. "Picked it up from where? Nobody he has contact with speaks Polish. Also, I heard the damn name again, Janusz."

"Please don't be upset. When you get upset, I get upset, and that is not good for me right now," Mary said, as she began to cry, which made Janusz feel bad.

Janusz thought about her statement for a moment and wondered what it meant. Peter continued, "We have to put a stop to this nonsense; you will not have time to worry about his silly games when the baby comes."

Janusz pulled his head back from the door and understood; Mary must be with child. Just then, he heard heavy footsteps walking towards the room, and he rushed back to his bed as he heard Peter say, "This foolishness stops today."

Peter swung the door open and made his way towards the bed. Janusz scooted back in the corner as far as he could and brought his knees up to his chest. Peter had crossed a bridge, his eyes full of determination as he grabbed Janusz by the shoulders and shook him. "Where did you learn that? Where? Tell me, goddamn it!"

Mary cried harder, pleading for Peter to stop when he hit Janusz across the face. Janusz stared with his mouth agape, as did Peter. The only sounds coming from the room were the sobs of Mary. Peter still held Janusz by the shoulders and looked back at Mary. "You see, he doesn't cry! What kind of child doesn't cry when smacked?" Peter turned his head back towards Janusz and screamed, "Your name is Roy. Do you understand? Your damn name is Roy."

CHAPTER 6

15 AUGUST 1920

Janusz held his breath as he watched Mary tend to the baby. His hiding place behind the door was perfect. He could fit in the corner with no problem, and there was a gap between the door and the frame, which allowed him to see into the kitchen. Ever since the baby had arrived, Mary had been overwhelmed. So Janusz had more opportunity to be alone or get into slight mischief here and there.

Mary milled about the kitchen, getting things ready for what Janusz assumed was a baby feeding. As she turned her back away from him, he looked out the window and smiled. He could not have asked for a better day, the sun shone bright, but there was also a slight breeze that kept it from becoming too hot.

He told himself he would only go to the porch, but then he saw the lush grass out front and decided he would sit there and enjoy the day. Earlier he had asked Mary if he could go outside and read his picture books, but she had told him no. Janusz wasn't sure why she had said this, but it probably had something to do with her not being able to focus on him outside as well as the baby. Or he thought, maybe she did not want him talking to people without her.

Janusz knew Mary's attitude had changed toward him. It wasn't only because of the baby, either; it had started the day when he had spoken Polish to the women outside of the church. He had scared her, and unlike the time when he said his name was Janusz, she never really bounced back. Janusz could not complain though. She treated him well, even if there was a distance between them now. One thing was for certain; he never spoke Polish in front of her or Peter again.

He turned his head back from the window and saw what he had been waiting for. Mary was seated with her breast out feeding the child. He backed up without making a sound, always keeping an eye on her until he reached the door.

He waited, holding on to the handle until he heard the sound he needed. Like clockwork, Mary started singing to the baby. She always did this as she had with Janusz. He waited for a few more moments, and when she began the second verse of the song, he turned the handle and slipped outside. As he walked out on to the porch, he could still hear her voice, so he continued down the stairs and out to the lawn.

When he came to the spot where he planned to sit, he looked up to the trees above and saw the wind gently moving the leaves. He took a deep breath and felt his skin prickle as a smile broke out on his face. Before he knew it, his feet began to move, and he found himself walking down the sidewalk.

He knew he shouldn't, but he went anyway, almost as if he did not have a choice. Janusz figured he could be back before Mary finished feeding the child, so he didn't worry. Also, Peter was not there, and Janusz wondered if the man would even care if Janusz disappeared. It wasn't that Peter was a bad father; on the contrary, he was close and tender with baby Samuel.

The walk woke something up in Janusz, something that he had been trying to push down for the past few years. Janusz had been careful as to what he did or said ever since the day with the Polish ladies, and as a result, he had begun to wonder if he had made everything up in his head. There had been times in the past few years where he had gone weeks without thinking about who he was and just concentrated on being "Roy."

Not this day though. With every step he took he remembered the walks he used to take and the sense of freedom opened a door for him. He still had no idea why this was happening to him, but at that moment he didn't care. He stopped walking, looked up, closed his eyes, and took in a deep breath. When he opened his eyes, he decided he better get back to the house before Mary noticed he was gone.

As he turned to walk back to the house, he saw her.

The woman was crying as she looked at the house and the instinct to act took over his body. He darted up to the woman, grabbed her hand and said, "Oh Button, don't cry, close your eyes and take three deep breaths and everything will be ok."

The woman yanked her hand out of Janusz' grip and reeled back. For a moment she didn't say anything; she just stared with her jaw open at Janusz. Once again, not thinking about the circumstance and acting on emotion, Janusz asked, "What's wrong, Button? You can tell me."

The woman stomped her foot and glared at him. "Stop it."

Janusz took a step back and did not understand why his daughter was so upset. "It's ok; it's me."

"Who are you?" The woman's voice began to grow louder, and her tone sharpened as she moved closer to Janusz. "Where did you hear that name from?"

"You know I always called you that ever since you were little because you were as cute as a button."

"Stop saying that name."

Janusz hated to see his daughter upset; he could never stomach it. He was always a "fixer" and would do anything to make things right. So he tried to think of something to calm her down and was having trouble until he looked to his right.

He couldn't believe it; he was standing outside of his old house. It was his home. As he looked at the house, images of his previous life bombarded him, and he forgot everything about his current situation. For a moment, he could have sworn he saw his wife inside the house with the children, getting dinner ready. That moment, when he would walk through the door after work was his favorite. The smell of dinner cooked with love would hit him, and the children would rush to the door to great him. It was only the voice of his daughter that jerked him out of his reminiscing. "Why are you doing this?"

Janusz turned and looked back at her. Even though she was in her 40's, all he could see was his baby girl. Then he turned his head back to the porch and pointed towards it. "Remember when you and I would come out and sit there, just the two of us, and talk about everything that bothered you?" As Janusz remembered, he smiled and thought of those times.

The smile left his face when his daughter slapped him. It was hard, and it hurt, and Janusz could feel tears starting to well up in his eyes either from the pain or the disappointment, or maybe a combination of both. The blow knocked him to the ground, and as he sat there, he looked down at his body, which was not the body of a 70-year-old man.

He wanted to say something, but the thoughts in his head started to collide with each other and speech was impossible. So Janusz did the only thing his body was capable of and got up as quickly as he could and started to run.

Janusz sprinted towards the house where he currently lived. He had no plan; he also had no idea how long he had been gone. He just wanted to run and get away from his daughter who was beyond upset.

As soon as he made it to the steps, Mary barreled through the door with Peter close behind. She grabbed him and with a fear-strained voice asked, "Where have you been?" Janusz didn't get the chance to answer as Mary pulled him close to her and squeezed tight.

There was also another voice, and this voice was also upset. It was his daughter.

"Is this your son?" his daughter demanded.

Mary jumped at the woman's voice but said nothing as she continued to hold on tight to Janusz. Peter then walked farther out onto the porch and asked, "What is this all about? Who are you?"

Janusz' daughter responded with a question. "Who are you people, and what kind of monster are you raising?"

Peter took a step back, and the color drained from his face. "What are you talking about?"

Janusz' daughter recounted the story of what had happened only moments before. His heart broke as he saw how upset she was. He wanted to comfort her, reach out and hug her while cradling her head and telling her, "It's ok; it really is."

But there was no way to reach her in that moment. Although his daughter was upset, there was something different about the way she looked at him. Janusz still hoped he could reach her maybe someday in the future.

Janusz was torn out of his thoughts when he heard his daughter's voice grow even louder and break with sobs while she said, "My father was a kind, gentle, and loving man. Anybody that would put this little boy up to something like this clearly is a sick person." His daughter stormed off, and Janusz' first impulse was to go after her, but Mary was holding on to him too tightly.

The next moments were uncertain for Janusz; Mary's grip tightened even more, and now she placed herself between him and Peter, who had lost the scared look, and now it was replaced by anger. "Move out of the way, Mary." Janusz started to become frightened, and while Mary did not move, he could feel her body trembling.

Peter did not repeat himself; instead, he slapped Mary across the face and she stumbled off to the side. He then grabbed Janusz and shook him while he yelled. "What the fuck is wrong with you?" Peter pushed Janusz backward, and he fell on the floor. Something clicked in Janusz, and he knew he had to get out of there, so he quickly got up and ran to his room.

* * *

Janusz heard them talking through the door of his bedroom. "Come on, Mary. You know there was something wrong with that boy the moment he was born. He has never been right."

Mary replied without too much conviction. "Peter, he is a little boy. He could have picked up those Polish words anywhere, especially in this city, and he could have overheard people talking about that old man."

"You know that's not true, Mary. The boy is either evil or sick in the head, and I've let this go on too long as it is."

"What do you mean?"

"What I mean is that we have to think of our other son, the normal one. He still has a chance, and we can't let anything or anyone endanger him."

As soon as Peter finished, Janusz heard footsteps approaching his room. The door flung open and slammed against the wall. Janusz could not bring himself to look at Peter, let alone say anything, but it did not matter; Peter was not in the talking mood and grabbed Janusz by the arm, dragging him across the room much like a child drags a doll.

Once they were out of the bedroom, Peter continued to drag Janusz toward the front door. Mary was there, holding the baby and sobbing with tears running down her cheeks.

Peter stopped for a moment and pointed his finger in her face. "Move out of the damn way, Mary." There was an icy tone in his voice that Janusz had never heard before.

Mary moved away from the door, and Peter pulled Janusz through it. Unbeknownst to Janusz, that would be the last time he would ever go through that door.

As they reached the sidewalk, Peter did not drag Janusz anymore, but he still had a firm hand on his arm as they walked briskly down the street and away from the house. Peter said nothing as they walked, but he didn't have to--Janusz knew where they were going.

As they entered the church, everything was silent. All that could be heard were rushed footsteps as they headed towards the altar. Once they reached the first pew, Peter stopped, motioned for Janusz to sit down, and without a word continued walking toward the back of the church towards the pastor's office.

Once Peter was out of sight, Janusz' body relaxed a little bit. At first, thoughts swirled around in his head like a hurricane, but as he sat in silence, they slowly began to settle, and Janusz reflected on the events that had happened that day. He started to think about the situation at the house with Peter and Mary. He was confident that he was now at a point where the damage was irreparable. He also knew that Peter did not like him, or, at the very least, the man was uncomfortable around him. Mary, on the other hand, was much nicer, but there was also a distance. Maybe deep down inside Janusz had always known that, but one could see it as plain as day when the new baby came. Mary was just closer to the new child than she had ever been with Janusz.

The situation at the house, the rift with Peter, and the distance with Mary were bad… but none of that bothered Janusz. What broke his heart was the situation with his daughter. Janusz prided himself on being a good father and seeing the state his daughter was in was unbearable for him, and he was the reason for her distress.

As his despair about his daughter grew, Janusz looked up at the altar and pondered his relationship with God. He had a sudden urge to want to be in his church; he wanted to be looking at an altar with a depiction of Jesus on a cross. In the end, Janusz concluded that God probably was not just in the Catholic Church, but also everywhere. So he decided to pray to St. Jude.

Janusz prayed so profoundly that he blocked everything out around him. He did not hear the pastor come into the church. It wasn't until he had sat down next to him that Janusz became aware of his presence. Janusz stopped praying and looked at him. The pastor said nothing, so Janusz decided to break the silence. "Where is Peter?"

The pastor lowered his gaze to look Janusz in the eyes and said, "You mean your father."

Janusz contemplated for a moment; it was such a simple statement, but he struggled to respond. After all, he sat in a house of the Lord, and he could not lie. He knew the answer the pastor wanted, but in Janusz' heart, he could not say it. The reason was because Janusz' father was not that man who had brought him here. Janusz' father had died more than 50 years ago in Poland. So Janusz' remained silent and turned his head back towards the altar.

The pastor asked another question; this time Janusz could answer it and not lie in church. "Are you praying?"

"Yes."

"So you believe in Jesus Christ?"

"I do." After Janusz answered the question, the pastor remained silent for a few moments, but Janusz could still feel his gaze locked on him. The silent pause worried Janusz; he did not know what the pastor wanted, or what he was going to say. So he decided to try to absolve himself. Even though the man beside him was not a Catholic priest, confession might be the thing to do so he said, "I'm praying to St. Jude."

Out of the corner of his eye, Janusz could see the pastor's eyebrows rise. "Why are you not praying to Jesus?"

"Because St. Jude is the patron saint for grief and despair."

The pastor replied with a sharp, clear voice. "I am well aware of that, young man, but we don't pray to saints; they are not something to be worshipped."

"I know that, but praying to the saints can help God answer your prayers."

"Who told you this?"

"My priest."

"Son, you don't have a priest; I am your pastor, and you know this. I've been your pastor since the day you were born."

Janusz paused before replying. He thought carefully about what to say and how to say it. The circumstances he found himself in were dire, but Janusz wondered if there could be away out of this. Maybe now was the time somebody would listen to him and maybe, just maybe, the pastor could tell him what was going on. "Then you will know the truth, and the truth will set you free," Janusz said meekly trying to muster up the courage to continue.

"John 8:32," replied the pastor. "Go on, boy."

With that, Janusz took a deep breath and told his story. He told the pastor about coming from Poland, his children, and about the day he died. He explained his confusion when he woke up an infant. Throughout the whole story, the pastor never once interrupted Janusz, but rather, let him continue. When Janusz recounted the incident that had happened earlier, he let out a deep sigh and slouched his shoulders and returned his gaze towards the altar.

The two sat for a long time, neither one speaking a word. Then, the pastor exhaled and put his hand on Janusz' knee and gave it a gentle squeeze before standing up and walking back towards his office.

Janusz sat alone in that church for almost an hour. He did not mind in the least bit; he felt relieved. For the first time, someone had listened to him, no anger, no doubting, just listening. Janusz felt like he could breathe again, almost as if he had been trapped under something heavy and now that burden was gone.

Now the question remained, what would happen next? Would the pastor tell Peter and Mary? If so, would they go to his daughter and tell her what happened? Was this some sort of miracle? Janusz knew none of these answers, but for the first time since his death he felt hopeful, and he felt a smile beginning to form on his face. This situation could be a new beginning for the simple immigrant from Poland.

When Janusz heard footsteps coming from the pastor's office, he thought at first that it might be him. He imagined the pastor had spoken with Peter and explained everything. Janusz thought they would go back to the house and figure out how to deal with this new situation. He told himself it would not be easy, but at least they could work out some solution until Janusz was old enough where he could take care of himself.

When Janusz saw the owner of the footsteps, it was not Peter but rather, the pastor. Janusz' face gave way to the shock that he felt, and the pastor calmly said, "It's ok, Roy, there is nothing to worry about, we are going to get you taken care of."

Roy, Janusz thought and immediately became worried when the pastor called him that instead of Janusz. The previous hope of a new start and understanding started to fade. The pastor explained to Janusz that he had told Peter everything and how he was not an evil child, but instead had a malady of the mind. Upon hearing this, Janusz became agitated, but the pastor grabbed ahold of his arm firmly and said in a caring voice that it was not his fault.

"Roy, your father has given me permission to take you to a place where you can get some help and pretty soon you will be able to come home again."

Panic started to spiral in Janusz, and it was making it difficult for him to think. "What place? Where? I thought you understood me?"

"Calm down now, child. You are a sick boy, and we need to fix the sickness so you can lead a productive life."

"I'm not going anywhere," said Janusz, and as the words left his mouth, the pastor slapped him across the face with enough force to knock him to the ground. Janusz sat stunned, feeling the coppery taste of blood in his mouth while he looked up at the pastor from the ground.

"Now child, you listen to me good. You are going to come with me and not give me any problems, do you understand?"

Janusz said nothing, but nodded his head in affirmation. After a few more moments, the pastor helped him up and escorted him out of the church.

After leaving the church, the two did not speak much. Janusz decided not to make any trouble for fear of another slap--or worse. There was no way he could do anything in this situation. To the world, he was a five-year-old boy and nothing he said or felt mattered.

The two walked for a short distance before they reached their destination. Janusz noticed they were at the train depot as he looked at the sign. He began to wonder why they were there, but a small part of him was excited; he had never ridden on a passenger train.

A sharp tug on his arm pulled him out of his thoughts and the pastor said, "Come on now, boy."

Janusz continued walking and followed the man up to the ticket office where the pastor said, "Two for Detroit."

"Round-trip or one-way?"

"One round-trip for me and the other one-way."

Janusz jerked his head up. "One-way? Am I not coming back?"

"Boy, I told you to be quiet."

Janusz hung his head low as the pastor paid the man and then the two of them made their way to the platform. Only silence passed between the two as they boarded the train and found their seats. Janusz sat and looked out the window; he had a thousand questions but did not dare ask any of them.

Soon, he heard the release of the brakes and the train began to move towards their destination. Janusz watched his beloved city move by him until everything was a blur. The worry that he felt began to fade, and that left anger--anger at this pastor, anger at Peter, and most of all, anger at God.

He wanted to know why God was punishing him. Even if he did deserve it, he wanted an answer. But Janusz received nothing, only silence.

When Janusz felt the train slow down, he broke out of his thoughts. They were pulling into Detroit, and Janusz marveled at the city. It had been many years since he had seen it and much had changed. As the train fully stopped, the pastor said, "Stay close to me and don't wander off, we only have a little ways to go."

Janusz nodded his head and obeyed by staying close to the pastor. As Janusz took in the sights and sounds of Detroit, he was amazed. There were so many automobiles, many more than he had ever seen before. It seemed like everyone was in a hurry and had no time to stop. They walked past shop after shop of tailors, butchers, and various other places which made Janusz wonder how they all stayed in business. He thought, *there couldn't possibly be that many people here in Detroit, could there?*

After the short walk, they arrived at the streetcar station and boarded. They were not on the streetcar for nearly as long as the train, but it was still enough time for Janusz to observe many people get on and off. As they slowed for the next stop, the pastor said, "We are here."

Janusz got off and walked with the pastor until they came to the gates of a place that Janusz had never seen in person before, but knew it well by reputation: Oakbrook Asylum. Janusz panicked and tried to run, but the pastor grabbed hold of his arm and pulled him into the entrance.

Janusz screamed as they entered through the doors, and two men wearing all white came up and grabbed him. They carried him away, kicking and screaming while Janusz caught one last glance of the pastor, who spoke to what looked like a doctor.

They left Janusz in a room for what felt like hours. He was scared and hungry, and he had to go to the bathroom. Just when he thought he might wet himself, he heard the lock of the door being opened from the outside and in walked the same two men in white that had put him in there, but now the doctor who had been talking with the pastor was with them.

Janusz trembled as he looked at the three men. The two assistants said nothing, but the doctor asked, "Are you calmed down, son?"

Janusz nodded his head.

"Do you need to use the facilities?"

Once again he nodded his head.

The doctor looked at the two men, who then approached Janusz and took him by the arms. They brought him to a room that housed a toilet and Janusz was able to relieve himself at last. When he finished, Janusz tried to open the door but discovered it was locked. So he knocked on the old wooden door, and a moment later the door handle moved, and the guards once again took him by the arms and escorted him down a hallway.

This time, they did not go back to the room he was in previously, but rather to what looked like an office. They placed him in a chair that faced a large oak desk and the guards stood on both sides of him. A few moments later, he heard the door open from behind him, and the doctor came around and took a seat on the other side of the desk.

The doctor looked at him for a few moments, studying him in a way, before he leaned in across the desk. "Roy, do you know why you are here?"

Janusz gritted his teeth as his hands clenched and said, "My name is not Roy."

"And why do you say that?"

"Because my name is Janusz, and I want to leave this place."

"Roy, that's not possible right now, your parents want you to get help."

Something exploded in Janusz, and he screamed. "Peter wants to get me out of the way because he can't accept the truth. My name is Janusz Zalewski, and I died five years ago only to wake up like this, so if you want to help me, then tell me what is happening."

When the last word left Janusz' mouth, he felt the sting of the needle in his arm. Moments after that, his vision started to blur, and he collapsed.

With the help of the men in white he was kept on his feet only to see the doctor's face as he said, "Don't worry, son, it's not too late for you, we will get you fixed right up."

That statement was the final thing he remembered before everything faded into darkness.

* * *

Janusz woke up strapped to a bed in a room next to another room separated by an open doorway. It only took a slight turn of the head and he could see all the people in the room. The first was the doctor, the second Peter, and the third was Mary, who sounded as if she were crying.

He closed his eyes slightly in case one of them looked over, and calmed his breathing the best he could so he could listen to their conversation.

Peter and Mary sat across from the doctor as he explained to them what the course of the treatment would be. "Your son has a severe mental condition, and I fear if we don't aggressively address the problem now, he could be untreatable and unfortunately confined to an asylum for the rest of his life."

Mary sat up a bit and began to say something, but Peter threw her a sharp glance, and she remained silent. Then the doctor said, "Actually sir, I think it's best if we continue to speak alone."

Peter turned his head and said, "Mary, wait in the hallway."

Mary knew better than to put up any further protest and left without saying a word.

The doctor continued as soon as the door closed. "Your son has fanatical delusions that he is somebody else who has died and since returned into another body, but with the consciousness of the person from before."

Peter looked at the doctor without blinking as he processed the information and said, "I've always known something was not right with that boy, I could feel it the day he was born."

"I just want you to understand that this treatment comes with some risks and due to his young age, the risks are even higher."

Peter did not hesitate, not even for a moment. "Whatever you need to do, do it. I have another son to think about, a normal son, and I can't have a lunatic running around endangering him."

"I understand," said the doctor as the faintest hint of a smile splashed across his face.

Although Janusz didn't know it, the doctor was finally going to be able to test his procedure out on a child.

* * *

Shortly after, the doctor came into the room with a group of different people. Janusz began to ask questions, but nobody would answer him. They just prepared instruments of sorts and checked his restraints. Finally, one of the men all in white tightened the straps to hold him to the table. Next, they inserted an object into his mouth with a strap tied around his head. He could neither close his mouth nor could he talk. All he could do was squeeze out muffled screaming sounds.

He thrashed about and tried to pull his hands free, but it was useless. He was immobilized. The only saving grace, albeit small, was a tender caress of a nurse who was at his side and looking at him. Her face was pretty and in a way, seemed to glow. He moved his head to get a better look at her and could see she had a large stomach although she was not an overweight woman.

This woman was with child.

He looked back at the doctor and saw him pick up a needle. The sight scared Janusz, and at that time his bladder failed him. One of the big men all in white mentioned this to the doctor, who looked at it with a mild annoyance. Janusz glanced back at the nurse, the one with the kind, glowing face, and kept looking at her. For some reason, her face calmed him a bit, so as he drifted out of consciousness, she was the last thing he saw.

21 AUGUST 1920
8:57 A.M.

Janusz remained strapped to the bed and unconscious for days, but while his body was immobile, his brain was anything but. Janusz dreamed non-stop, but to him, they were not dreams, but living relics of his life where he experienced moments of his past, which felt real. He could feel things, taste food, and smell fragrances. Before he woke up, he dreamt of his wife.

It was a warm spring day in the dream, and Janusz and his wife were on the bank of the St. Agnes River, looking out across to Canada. They would do this all the time when they were young and even after their children had been born, although not as often. This place was their spot, and it was his favorite place in the world.

"You have to go now," his wife said.

"What do you mean? We haven't eaten."

"You have to go, you're too hot," and he noticed that he was hot. He was sweating, and it was difficult for him to think. He tried to get up but he couldn't, something was going on. He called out to his wife, but she was not there. In fact, he was not there.

He opened his eyes, confused; he was in a hospital, surrounded by people. At first he did not recognize them, but after a few moments, clarity returned to him, and he knew the people and the place. He was in Oakbrook, the big men in white were there, once again holding him down. He couldn't understand why, because he was already tied. He turned and saw the doctor as everything began to shake.

Janusz frantically looked around for the nurse with the kind face but did not see her. He tried asking the doctor where she was, but the thing in his mouth prevented it.

He could hear the doctor say, "The fever is too high; he is starting to convulse." Janusz began to shake uncontrollably, so hard that it was difficult for him to breathe. Inside of his head, it felt like a vice was putting increasing pressure on his brain until, finally, it broke.

Everything was still.

No more shaking and no more heat--just stillness, silence, and blackness.

And at that moment, Janusz died for the second time in his existence.

CHAPTER 7

21 AUGUST 1920
8:58 A.M.
THE THIRD RIDE
"ELIZABETH"

Not far from where Janusz died for the second time lay a woman named Mildred Adler. In fact, she was in the same building, but just in another wing. And at that moment she gave birth to a healthy baby girl. The delivery was not particularly difficult, but she longed to see her husband and was told he was not available.

"What do you mean he is not available?"

The midwife looked at the nurse who said, "Mildred, there was an emergency in the ward."

"What kind of emergency?"

"The boy, Roy, his fever began to rise, and he started to convulse."

Mildred felt a pang of fear for the boy as she had felt sorry for him the day they brought him in. Really, she was not supposed to be working anymore but would sometimes come in with her husband to kill the boredom, and when she saw the small child, she decided to help, even if it was against her husband's wishes.

"Now Mildred, don't you be worrying about that nonsense, you need to get some rest because there is a baby girl who needs her mother now," said the midwife.

Mildred nodded her head, gave the baby to the midwife and rolled over and immediately fell into a deep sleep.

When she awoke, her husband was next to her holding the baby. "You've rejoined us; how do you feel?" he asked.

"Better. Is everything alright with that child, Roy?"

Her husband looked at her for a moment. "That's nothing for you to worry about; you shouldn't have been in there the other day."

"John, tell me what happened, please."

Slowly, her husband looked up from the baby and shook his head. "He didn't make it. The fever took him over, he went into a full seizure, and his brain couldn't take it."

Mildred was silent for a moment; she could feel tears welling up in her eyes at the thought of the poor child with those sad, soulful eyes.

* * *

Janusz knew he had died. The first time it had happened, he was pretty sure, but now, the second time, he was positive. The blackness lasted about the same amount of time, and while everything was dark, he felt at peace. He was happy and relieved. That was until right after the darkness came the light, the familiar screaming from a woman and that sense of newness accompanied with the inability to control his limbs and the blurry vision.

This time he didn't scream, not right away. It was only after a woman held him close to her chest and he could see her face clearly. It was the woman with the kind face from when he was brought in, the pregnant one. Then the realization hit him, and he screamed and screamed until he exhausted himself.

It had happened again.

When he woke up the next time, the woman did not hold him, but rather a man, and this was a man he knew. Janusz stared into the face of the doctor who had tied him down and injected the chemicals into him.

This time when he started screaming, it was more out of fear than anger or shock.

CHAPTER 8

21 AUGUST 1933

Janusz woke up on what everybody else would consider his thirteenth birthday, but to him, his birthday was actually three weeks prior on July 31st, and he had turned 83 years old. Although that was something, he had never told anybody and didn't ever plan on telling anybody. Janusz had learned to play a sort of game and fit in as best as he could and judged that he had done a pretty good job. This "Ride," as he had come to call it, was different, but some things were the same. Janusz still had problems connecting with people. There still seemed to be a sort of distance between him and everybody else; he knew people said, "There is something off about that one, and I can't quite put my finger on it."

Janusz shook his head and tried to think about today, but it was tough as he felt strange and just wanted to lie in bed all day. He had never put much stock in his birthday before and didn't see the sense in it now. Plus, he felt terrible having gifts thrown upon him, especially now with so many people out of work and so many families that couldn't even feed their children due to what Hoover called a "depression."

He sighed as he lifted himself out of bed and thought, *not that Mildred and John would know anything about a depression.* It seemed that locking up people and calling them crazy was quite profitable. Janusz shook the thought out of his head and told himself there was no use in getting all riled up. So he sat down in front of his mirror and looked at himself.

The image he saw before him was not the image in his head. Most of the time he avoided mirrors as they caused him to panic at the absurdity of what he saw. But he knew he could not hide from it too much longer; just because he didn't look in the mirror, it didn't mean this body he was in was not changing into a young woman.

He ran his finger along his face, turning to each side to get a better look--not just a young woman, but a beautiful young woman. He wished the opposite. He wanted to be ugly, so men would not look at him. He hated their looks, and it had been happening more and more. Some of the men that looked at him had a sort of hunger in their eyes that was neither respectful nor sane.

He feared what some of them would do if they had the chance.

A dull pain shot through his breasts. His hand dropped from his face and clasped around them as he hunched over. The feel of the weighty, dense masses still felt foreign to him and even more so as they continued to grow larger. Janusz did not like to touch his breasts, and only did so when he bathed himself. He couldn't help it now, though; the pain took him by surprise.

Janusz also had a stomachache with a thudding headache that seemed to grow stronger as the morning passed. He looked over at the bed and noted how welcoming it appeared. He asked himself if it would be that bad if he crawled back into bed and tried to sleep the day away.

He knew that was not possible, as Mildred would make a big deal out of his birthday today. For weeks she had pestered him about gifts, and he had finally relented, giving her a list of books he wanted to read. Janusz knew Mildred thought reading so much and, particularly, these types of books, was a waste of time. Mildred wanted Janusz to concentrate on blossoming into a well-rounded young woman who could find a husband.

Janusz shuddered at the thought of having a husband. He whispered in the mirror, "There is no way a man is ever going to touch me in that way, and if he does, he is going to wish he hadn't."

Janusz tossed the thought from his head and took solace in the fact that at least John approved of the books. Of course, he took all the credit for his brilliant daughter and said things like, "Well you know, the apple does not fall far from the tree." Janusz felt like vomiting and telling the man to shut up every time John said this, but Janusz also knew he might be able to use the man's pride in the future.

He took a deep breath, stood up, walked over to the window, and looked out at the beautiful day. He wondered why he was procrastinating to get ready. He grabbed his stomach again as a mild pain coursed through it and told himself it was because he felt ill. That was a lie though; in his mind, he felt that by getting ready and celebrating the birthday, he would be accepting that he was growing into a young woman.

The list of books that Janusz had given Mildred did not satisfy her, so there had to be something else. So after much thought, Janusz had told her he would like to go to Port Walden for the day and have a picnic along the river. To his surprise, both John and Mildred thought this was a grand idea. Janusz' face darkened for a moment as he knew the only reason John was so excited was that it would be a chance for him to show off his new convertible.

Janusz scolded himself for letting his thoughts go dark. He should be happy today as he was going to be close to his wife, or at least the place they had once enjoyed together. As Janusz started to pull clothes out of his closet, though, he wondered if this was such a good idea after all.

He was dressed by the time he heard the knock on the door. It was Mildred, and she came in beaming and singing *happy birthday,* carrying a package of wrapped books and a dress. He backed up when he saw the dress and groaned. "Mother, I thought you said I did not have to wear a dress today."

Mildred sighed as she stood in front of him. "Elizabeth, I said you did not have to wear a *fancy* dress today, and besides, this is not for today, this is for the summer dance."

As soon as she said those words, Janusz felt himself start to panic. Mildred had been talking about this dance for weeks, and Janusz had pushed it out of his mind and figured he would try to find a way out of it later. Mildred was excited, though, and kept making stupid little comments about how maybe a boy would ask her to dance and other nonsense. He wanted none of it and he damn sure wasn't going to dance with a boy.

Although lately, he had been starting to think about others in ways he hadn't in years. Nothing terrible, but he had started to notice how people looked and last week when he looked at somebody, he got that old, long forgotten feeling like he used to get when he looked at his wife in his youth. There was one problem, though, and it was a big one--he would only get the feeling when he saw a pretty girl.

Janusz figured this whole situation was going to be an issue later on, but right now he did not have to think about it and decided to focus on the trip back to his beloved Port Walden, where he could lay his eyes on the river again and relive some pleasant old memories.

* * *

The wind blew across Janusz' face and through his hair. He closed his eyes and enjoyed the moment. The fresh air eased his headache a little bit, and he took solace in that even though his stomach and breasts still hurt. He put his hand to his abdomen and opened his eyes. The area between Detroit and Port Walden was beautiful, and it showed none of the decay one saw in Detroit.

The closer they got to Port Walden, the more nervous Janusz became. He hoped the city hadn't changed too much, although he prepared himself for the possibility. He heard a rumor that they were going to build a bridge connecting Port Walden to Canada, and he scoffed at the idea. He wondered why people needed a damn bridge when the boats and ferries worked just fine.

He muttered, "Nothing is ever good enough for people. Once they get something, they want more." Then he looked right at John driving the convertible with his stupid hat and dark glasses.

As they crossed the city limit, Janusz read the sign "City of Port Walden." He sat up, and the excitement now overshadowed the discomfort in his stomach and head. At almost the exact moment they crossed into the city, Janusz turned his head to the right, and he could see the river. Janusz had seen this river thousands of times in the past, but he felt like he was seeing it now for the first time.

Janusz' excitement paused, however, when he felt the car begin to slow. The spot where he wanted to picnic was still almost a mile down the road. Janusz was confused and more so when the car started to pull into a driveway connected to a house that sat on the riverbank.

Janusz looked at the house and over to John. "What are we doing? I thought we were going to have a picnic on the river."

"We are darling. This is a colleague of mine, and his house sits right on the bank."

"But I wanted to go to the park down the street."

John waved his hand in dismissal. "I honestly don't know how you know about that place, but I've been told it is full of ruffians who are too lazy to work and good for nothing drunks. It is no place for a proper young lady to be."

Janusz clenched his fists and wondered what would happen if he smacked John up along side of the head. He had brought his wife to that spot countless times, even when she was young, and even though Marzehna was not rich, she was a proper young lady. Janusz thought about protesting some more or sitting in the car and refusing to leave. He had this overwhelming urge to be spiteful, although he had no clue as to where it came from.

Mildred sensed his disappointment and said, "Darling, trust us, this place is much better. You can see the park from the house, and John's colleague has a delightful young daughter you can chat with."

Janusz sat in the back seat of the car with his arms crossed, but he could feel his wall of stubbornness starting to crumble. His legs began to move as the door opened and next he stepped out of the car. He glanced in the direction of where he used to sit with his wife, and the memory filled his head in an instant, and for a moment he thought he might start to cry. This emotion angered Janusz; he hated to cry--only women cried--but there he was on the brink of tears, and he could not figure out what the hell was making him act so crazy.

He managed to compose himself as they walked up the path to the front door of the house. Just then another spiteful thought crept into Janusz' mind, and he told himself he may have to eat here, but he sure as hell was not going to sit around and chat like a damned school girl with this guy's daughter. He was going to sit by himself and look out at the river and to hell with the whole lot of them.

The moment they reached the stairs, a slender, well-dressed woman came out, followed by a middle-aged, balding man. The woman rushed out on the porch and threw her arms around Mildred. "Oh, Mildred, my God, it has been way too long."

"Oh Betty, well, you know how the time goes with raising children and keeping up the house."

Janusz looked at the two women with annoyance. The way they talked to each other was fake, and the way they made their lives out to be such a struggle was ridiculous. He found himself wanting to scream in their faces, asking them what in the hell did they know about struggling as they stood in front of the fancy house, wore their custom tailored clothes, and prepared to eat like kings while the rest of the country would probably end this day with nothing in their stomach.

The woman, Betty, turned her attention to Janusz and said, "Good Lord, is this Elizabeth?"

Janusz bit his tongue to stop himself from saying something he would regret and smiled. Betty turned to Mildred again and said, "My God, Mildred, she is beautiful." The woman lowered her voice. "She is going to snag herself a fine husband when she gets older."

Wanna bet, thought Janusz but held his tongue.

Janusz just wanted to get into the house. His headache raged, and his stomach still hurt, but most of all, he was so unbelievably hot. His discomfort drowned out the noise of Mildred and Betty talking to an unintelligible drone. He looked over past the two women and saw John speaking with the other man, but could not hear a single word and for that, Janusz was grateful for the headache. Then, all sound was drowned out, the pain in his head and stomach temporarily forgotten, and his breath taken away.

Through the door walked a young woman, and if Janusz did not know any better, she could have been the sister of his dear wife. The resemblance was uncanny, and Janusz began to feel things he had not felt in a long time as well as some feelings that were foreign to him. He watched the young lady walk towards him as her long blond hair swirled ever so softly around her neck. She smiled at him, and when Janusz looked into her blue eyes, he thought his knees were going to buckle.

The shrill voice of Betty ripped him out of his stupor. "Mildred, you remember Peggy?"

Mildred smiled and returned the same hollow compliments that Betty had given Janusz moments before.

Then Betty turned to Janusz and said, "Elizabeth, this is my daughter, Peggy." Janusz could not formulate words, so he smiled and looked at her while at the same time hoping his mouth was not hanging open.

Betty turned to Peggy and said, "Dear, why don't you take Elizabeth out back and let us grown-ups talk a little while before we eat."

"Yes, mother," Peggy replied, and the beautiful young woman grabbed Janusz' hand and led him through the house out to the back yard. The feeling of her skin on his drove him mad. Janusz felt his head spin and wondered if he might pass out. He looked around the back yard, but paid no mind to it; he was happy to be outside, away from the suffocating heat inside.

Peggy led him to the edge of the yard, which overlooked the river, and said, "Elizabeth, why don't you have a seat and I'll get you something cold to drink. You look flushed."

"Thank you," was all Janusz could say, but at least he said something.

Peggy turned and went back inside the house and Janusz looked out over the river. He could see Canada on the other side, but that didn't interest him much. He leaned forward in his chair and looked to the left and smiled. He could see it. Although they were not there eating, at least he could see the spot where he had sat with his wife so many times over the years.

His smile quickly disappeared, though, when he thought about Peggy. He tried to figure out what kind of thoughts and feelings were running through his head, but knew, in the end, that he was having sexual thoughts, and they were not about his wife.

"You damned old fool," he said to himself as he realized he was thinking about a young woman decades his junior.

He decided he would no longer think about this nonsense, but almost the instant the thought slipped into his mind, it slipped out and was replaced with the thought of Peggy. He pictured her breasts, which were much more significant than his and although he could not be sure, he could have sworn he had seen a trickle of sweat roll down her chest and between her cleavage.

He shuddered at the thought, and then he thought of her lips. They were so full, and in perfect proportion to her face. Janusz wondered what it would be like to kiss her. Nothing dirty, he told himself, a soft kiss on the lips with a moment's linger to smell the freshness of her breath.

Janusz felt a hand on his shoulder and jumped. It was Peggy, and she looked at him with a strange look he could not read. For a second he was mortified at the thought of fantasizing about her and getting caught, but he told himself she could not possibly know that.

Then, Peggy leaned in close to his ear and whispered, "Come with me upstairs, and follow me very close."

Janusz sat in the chair, unable to move. But, Peggy grabbed his hand and lifted him out of the chair. They walked at a brisk pace with Janusz following close behind her. Peggy led them upstairs to what he assumed was the young lady's bedroom, and farther, to an adjoining bathroom.

Thoughts of what could happen swirled in Janusz' head. What were they going to do? He hoped he would get the chance to kiss those lips he had fantasized about only moments earlier. He knew he should think about his wife, and maybe that would cool the fire burning inside of him, but it was too intense. Janusz could not explain the feeling, it was like he was in a speeding locomotive and the brakes would not work.

Janusz was shaking by the time they entered the bathroom. Peggy saw this and smiled softly and caressed his cheek.

The young woman turned around and closed the door and resumed her position right in front of Janusz and asked, "Is this your first time, sweetie?"

Janusz racked his brains for an answer. Of course, it wasn't his first time, but he couldn't exactly go into detail. Then a strange thought hit him: even though he thought and felt like a man, his body was female. He bit down on his tongue as he wondered how that situation would work.

Peggy spoke again, "It's ok, it happens to all of us, and it is nothing to be ashamed of, no matter what some people think."

He looked at her and tried to figure out what she meant. "What happens to all of us?"

Peggy's face softened more, and she pointed to the back of Janusz' dress and said, "You're becoming a woman."

Janusz twisted around in front of the mirror and gasped when he saw a rusty red stain. The sight of the blood did something to him, and he found it hard to breathe. His pushed his hands down to the spot and felt the wet stickiness of it, and he tried to back up farther, but only managed to bump into a shelf containing various cosmetics and other feminine items, all of which tumbled to the floor.

He tried to apologize, but couldn't seem to speak. Peggy remained calm and reached out her hand, putting it on his shoulder. "Elizabeth, it's ok; this is nothing to be ashamed of."

Janusz stood motionless and stared at her with horror. Once the initial shock wore off, Janusz began to feel stupid and embarrassed. He thought Peggy had brought him in here to kiss him, but it only turned out he was bleeding like a damn stuck pig. He scolded himself, and he wished he could disappear.

Peggy's calm way of speaking soothed him a bit, and she asked, "Has your mother told you about this, what you need to do?"

Janusz only shook his head.

Peggy smiled and nodded her head. "Ok, well you can't go downstairs like this, so let me show you what to do."

"Ok."

"I'm afraid this dress is probably ruined, so go ahead and take it off along with your panties."

"What?" The word slipped out like a bullet. Janusz wasn't sure he had heard correctly.

Peggy smiled again. "Elizabeth, it's ok. Us girls have to take care of each other. I'll grab you one of my dresses and some panties, and I'll show you how to use a sanitary belt."

"A what?"

This time Peggy giggled, but it was not meant to be demeaning, only a giggle at his naivety. "Yes, a sanitary belt," she said as she reached into a cabinet and pulled out what resembled a small oblong cushion along with a weird contraption that looked like two belts connected to each other at perpendicular angles. Peggy held up the object and said, "The blood is going to keep coming for a few days, and this will contain it."

Janusz shook his head in disbelief. He wondered if his wife had ever used this, or what she did each month. Obviously, she had a menstrual cycle too, but that was something they never spoke about. "Can...can you tell me how to use it?"

"Of course, darling, but first clean yourself up. While you are doing that, I'll go get you some new clothes."

Then the strangest thought hit Janusz; what was he going to tell John and Mildred? He worried about what they would say when he went back outside wearing different clothes.

But then Peggy said, "Don't worry about our parents, our fathers are too busy trying to impress each other. I doubt they will notice, and if our mothers say something, we will tell them you spilled something on your dress, ok?"

Janusz nodded, and Peggy left him to clean up as she went to get new clothes. Janusz took off his dress and panties, being careful not to touch any of the blood or look at it for that matter. The sight disgusted him, and it dawned on him that he was going to have to deal with this situation every month. It just didn't seem fair.

Janusz had cleaned himself by the time Peggy came back. She walked in holding fresh clothes neatly folded into a square and set them down next to the washbasin. Janusz felt extremely vulnerable standing mostly naked in the bathroom with Peggy, but at the same time, it excited him.

Peggy picked up the belt and a pad and explained how it worked and how often it had to be changed. She showed him where it went and how to secure it. In doing so, one of her fingers lightly brushed Janusz' inner thigh. The sensation caused him to gasp, and he started to become hot and sweated more. He prayed Peggy did not hear the gasp and closed his eyes, chastising himself for being so damn foolish.

When Peggy finished, Janusz pulled the dress over his head and said, "Thank you."

"Oh, it's nothing, but you are going to have to tell your mother about this when you get home. You will have to change the pad."

Janusz shuddered at the thought of having this conversation with Mildred, but knew it would be necessary and said, "I will."

Peggy smiled and asked, "Now, what do you say we get back downstairs and enjoy your birthday?"

Janusz smiled and followed the young woman out of the bathroom to join the others.

CHAPTER 9

26 AUGUST 1933

Janusz sat in front of the vanity mirror in his bedroom with his hands holding his head. All of his attempts to avoid the social had failed, and now his last act of defiance was procrastination. He wondered if he waited long enough if Mildred would get frustrated and give up on this damned foolish idea of making him go to this dance.

A sharp rap on the door caused him to jump, and moments later Mildred walked in wearing a smile that stretched from ear to ear and holding a dress. As soon as Mildred's eyes locked on Janusz, her smile disappeared. "What are you doing? Why have you not done your hair and make-up? If I didn't know any better, I'd think you don't even want to go tonight."

"I don't want to go tonight."

Mildred scoffed and waved her hand at him. "Now don't be silly, I know you want to go, you are just nervous. But don't worry, momma is here to help you out."

Now Janusz felt like kicking himself. At least if he hadn't procrastinated, he could have done the minimal girl things, but now Mildred was going to help and go over the top on everything.

Janusz shook his head and muttered, "Stupid old man."

Mildred set the dress down on the bed and turned to Janusz, pulling him up by the arms. She lifted his shirt over his head, and Janusz quickly brought his hands up to cover his chest.

Mildred laughed as she looked at him. "Now there you go being silly again." She looked him up and down, examining his chest for a moment. "Besides, now that you are a real woman, there are a lot of things I need to teach you."

Janusz looked at her and prayed she would not start talking about the menstrual stuff again. It was bad enough that he'd had to tell her when it first happened, but she had to harp on it constantly. Janusz could not believe how happy the woman had been when he had told her; all in all, he thought the whole damned thing was ridiculous.

Fortunately for Janusz, Mildred was all business about this dance. She slipped the dress over his head and stood beside him as they both looked in the mirror. Mildred gasped and said, "Oh my."

Janusz felt like backhanding her, but of course, didn't. In his 83 years of life, that was one thing he had never done, and he wasn't about to start now. Janusz held the firm belief that real men did not hit women; they took care of them, they didn't beat them. He knew that everybody felt like smacking a woman at some point in life. He knew a man couldn't control how he felt; he could only control his actions.

So he stood there and looked in the mirror with her. But Janusz did not see what Mildred saw, at least not entirely. Mildred looked at a 13-year-old girl rapidly transforming into a beautiful woman, and Janusz saw an old man wearing a dress. Janusz could see the girl too, but to him, it was only a mask, and a transparent one at that. A bolt of shame coursed through him and for some reason, he wondered what his father would think of him now, standing in this room wearing a dress.

"Let's get your hair done and some color on those cheeks," Mildred said.

Janusz forced a smile and said, "Ok." Although he protested about many things and could be stubborn, Janusz did let John and Mildred have their way when it was necessary. His last "Ride" had taught him some valuable lessons, and he had no intentions of repeating those mistakes.

"Ouch," blurted Janusz and jerked his head to the side as Mildred got a little too rough with the hairbrush.

"Sorry dear, but if you'd let me brush your hair more often, it probably would not look like a rat's nest."

Think about the plan; think about the plan, he repeated in his head over and over before he answered, "Yes, mother, you are right."

Mildred smiled as she continued brushing and talking about some nonsense that Janusz could not have cared less about. Now his thoughts wandered to his plan. The ultimate goal was to get out of this house unscathed and away from this family. Not just away, but far away, and an image of Paris, France, danced in his head. In Paris, he would not be locked away in an asylum for liking women.

Even after all these years, every time Janusz looked at John, hatred bubbled to the surface, and all he could think about was being strapped to the bed as John did his "experimental" treatment on him. Janusz had learned to control his emotions, but most of all, he had learned how to control John.

Janusz kept his hatred towards John in check. He also had to admit that John did have attributes which were not all bad, although most were borne out of the man's narcissism. One of John's positive characteristics was his support for education. He spared no expense when it came to Janusz and his schooling. 13 years into this ride, Janusz had already learned more in the way of academics than he had in his entire existence.

Of course, Janusz knew that the more he learned and excelled, the more John could brag about his "bright" daughter. Sometimes, though, Janusz found it difficult to remain silent in certain things, one of those being language learning. Janusz was currently learning French, and John had been giving him advice and telling him things such as, "learning another language is hard." Janusz knew all about this since he spoke zero English when he had arrived in America from Poland.

Pick your battles, Janusz kept telling himself.

"There, now every boy is going to want to dance with you tonight, look how beautiful you look," Mildred said, admiring Janusz' reflection.

"What?"

"Look at yourself in the mirror, darling; you are going to have to beat the boys off with a stick."

Janusz looked in the mirror but still saw an old man dressed up as a young girl and sighed. He looked over at Mildred and said, "Thank you, mother" all the while thinking to himself that there was no way he would be dancing with any damn boys, and if they tried, they were going to be going home with a black eye.

* * *

When Janusz walked into the dance hall, he could feel eyes on him. He had been noticing this type of thing more and more, and when he did, he usually would look down and not make eye contact. He was halfway across the hall when he found his spot in the corner, out of sight, and a great place to "hide" for the rest of the night. Once he was in position, he felt better and not as exposed. So with the combination of his hiding spot and being "standoffish," hopefully nobody would ask him to dance.

His plan worked perfectly, and he was pleased with himself. He glanced up at the clock on the wall and saw that an hour had passed and felt he could get through the night, and at the very least, the music was good, and that helped pass the time too. When he looked away from the clock, a young man was standing in front of him, smiling with a dumb look.

The boy said nothing, just stood there, and the situation started to become awkward.

Janusz lost his patience. "Can I help you, young man?"

The boy's smile fell off his face, he slumped his shoulders, and looked down at his feet. But somehow he mustered up the courage to ask, "Um… hello Elizabeth, I was um…wondering if you would care to dance with me?"

Elizabeth, thought Janusz, wracking his brain as to how this boy knew his name and it hit him--he was the son of one of John's pals from the yacht club. Janusz groaned as this was another one of those "pick your battle" type of situations. If Janusz refused, and told the kid to bug off, John would probably hear about this and be embarrassed because of his "rude" daughter.

After a moment of deliberation on the pros and cons of angering John, Janusz said, "Sure."

The smile returned in an instant to the boy's face as soon as he heard the words and he reached out, took Janusz by the hand and led him to the dance floor. The boy's hand felt like a warm slug, and it took all of Janusz' willpower not to jerk away and run. The dance was just as torturous, and Janusz could have sworn the band played the extended version of the song as there seemed to be no end to it.

The boy was a young gentleman, kept the proper distance, and made small talk during the song. Janusz tried his best to be nice, but he hated the feel of the boy's hands on his waist and shoulder, and he hated the feel of his own hands on the boy. Janusz was as stiff as a board during the song and did not look at the boy once. He could not be entirely rude, though, so he answered all questions with short "yes" or "no" responses.

After some time, which felt longer than the 83 years Janusz had been on the earth, the song ended. Janusz thanked the boy and then made a beeline back to his spot on the wall. Once he was back in his position, he looked out on the dance floor and saw that the boy was still standing in the spot where he had left him. Janusz could tell that the boy was confused, but God intervened at that moment as a pretty little blond girl made eye contact with the boy, and now his attention was focused on her. Janusz breathed a sigh of relief, closed his eyes, and leaned his head against the wall, trying to forget the fact that he had danced with a boy.

When he opened his eyes, he noticed a girl looking at him with a peculiar smile. Quickly, Janusz looked away and stared at the ground. After a moment, he looked back up and now the girl, who was maybe two years older than he, approached. Janusz started to get a rumbling feeling in his stomach and could not figure out why she was coming over here. Also, he found the way she smirked at him odd.

Before he knew it, the girl was in front of him and said, "I don't think you could have been more uncomfortable dancing with that boy if you had been naked."

"Excuse me, but what are you talking about?"

The girl smiled, grabbed Janusz' hand, and led him away. Janusz felt he should say something, protest, but she was in control of him, and he followed her. They were walking so fast he had a hard time keeping up. He felt mesmerized by this girl and her long dark hair and slightly olive skin. She was beautiful, and she moved so gracefully, like one of those jungle cats that Janusz had seen at a circus once.

They stopped around the corner in what was not quite a room, but more of a little enclave. They could still hear the music, but really, all Janusz could hear was the thumping of his heart in his ears. The girl gently pushed down on Janusz' shoulders, sitting him on the floor while she looked around the corner to ensure nobody had followed them.

Once the girl was confident they were alone, she sat down on the floor across from Janusz and said, "You are different." Her accent was peculiar, and Janusz could not place it.

Janusz looked at her and thought about getting up, but he was curious. "What do you mean?"

"I've been watching you all night. You never look at any of the boys, and when a pretty little fresh flower of a girl comes by, you look at her, trying not to be caught." The girl smiled at him in a way that was unclear if she was mocking him. "And when you were dancing with that boy, it looked stranger than a horse trying to ride a man."

Janusz began to protest but found that his words kept getting stuck in his throat. The young girl reached out and lightly put a finger on his lip to calm him, but as soon as she touched him, she pulled her hand back quickly as if she had touched a pot cooking over a fire. The girl's eyes widened, and Janusz immediately felt embarrassed, as he was sure she was going to be repelled by him as so many others were.

He stood up to leave in order to save himself from the awkward situation but the girl's eyes returned to normal, and she smiled. Something clicked in Janusz when he saw this smile; it wasn't a smile of happiness per se, but a smile of someone who had just discovered a secret.

"I think we should go back to the hall before somebody finds us here," said Janusz.

The girl smiled and looked around and answered his question with one of her own. "How long have you liked girls?"

Janusz froze and stood there looking at the girl, unable to speak. Now the girl was even more interested and grabbed his hand, pulling him to the floor again. She leaned towards Janusz until their faces were mere inches apart. "What are you doing?" he asked.

"Do you want me to stop, or do you want me to come closer?"

Janusz only nodded his head, not sure if he was saying for her to stop or to keep going. His eyes closed and soon he felt her lips on his, which sent a shock through him. He pulled away and asked, "What if we are caught?"

The girl pulled back and smiled. She then produced a rolled cigarette and struck a match, inhaled deeply, and blew the smoke up in the air. Janusz looked at her for a moment as the smoke circled around her. She appeared not to care about anything, and she owned absolute confidence that he had never seen in a woman before.

The girl puffed on the cigarette one more time and handed it to Janusz, who took it cautiously in his right hand. "Give me your left hand," she said, and without consciously doing it, he watched his left hand reach out to her.

She took it, turned it over, and started to trace the lines in his palm with her finger. Janusz tried to pull his hand back, but she was strong and held tight. "What are you, some kind of gypsy?" he asked.

The girl smiled but did not look at him and kept tracing the lines of his palm. "You don't belong here," she said, now looking at him with even more curiosity.

"What do you mean?"

The girl was about to say something when a sharp voice beside them broke Janusz out of his trance. "Young ladies, what are you two doing back here?"

Janusz looked to where the voice came from and saw that it was one of the dance chaperones, and he thought his heart was going to seize. His thoughts were frantic, and he wondered what the woman thought. Did she see the kiss? What was going to happen now?

Janusz turned back to look at the pretty young gypsy girl with the big confidence, but he only caught a fleeting glance of her as she turned the corner towards the back entrance.

The chaperone grabbed Janusz' hand, jerked him off the ground, and rushed him out of the dance hall to the front entrance. Once they were outside, the chaperone said, "Young lady, the only reason you are not in more trouble is that you have a fine family, and I don't want to embarrass them."

Janusz stood outside the hall with his back to the wall and his head hung low. He was not quite sure what was going to happen. The chaperone left and went back inside. He had no idea what he should do now. He wondered if he should stay or run, or just go home. If he ran, where would he go? If he went home, Mildred would first wonder why he was not at the dance and then be upset about his walking home alone. So he decided to wait there against the wall for what came next.

Soon, the chaperone returned, her face stern as she said, "Stand up straight, young lady. A woman must compose herself and never slouch." So Janusz stood up straight and tried to quell the fear building in his stomach.

Janusz remained there for what seemed like hours until he saw John's Cadillac turn the corner. His heart sank as the car pulled up to the curb and the chaperone went to the window. She started to talk to John, and Janusz could also see Mildred in the car as well. Janusz could feel his stomach wrap around itself, and he chastised himself for letting the gypsy girl lead him to that back room and for letting her kiss him. It was stupid, and now he had no idea what John was going to do to him. For sure, John's ego would not allow any daughter of his to be the type to kiss other girls. Would he kill him?

No, he thought to himself, that would be too much and above all else, John thought about his career. Would he lock him up in Oakbrook? Janusz had heard rumors of women being locked up for doing perverted and sinful things with other women. But Janusz doubted that as well because that also would not look good for John, having his daughter locked up in the asylum where he was in charge.

When the chaperone walked back towards Janusz, she said, "Your parents are waiting for you now."

Strangely, the first thought that skipped across Janusz' subconscious was, *my parents have been dead for more than 60 years.* He said nothing, though, and walked toward the car much like a man walking toward the gallows, getting ready to meet his maker.

He got into the car, and nobody said a word. John drove and Mildred sat silently in her seat. Janusz was mildly relieved when he noticed the path they were taking was toward their home and not toward Oakbrook or any other place. After John parked the car, all three walked up the sidewalk to the house.

Once they were inside, Mildred spoke, but only to say, "Go upstairs and prepare yourself for bed. Your father and I will be up shortly to speak with you."

"Yes, ma'am."

Janusz wasted no time and prepared for bed, but John and Mildred did not come up for a long time. He took that time to try to figure out what to say. It was agony trying to think of a thing that would not land him in hot water. One thing was for sure though; he would speak nothing of his "Rides." He knew exactly where that would land him.

Maybe, he thought, he should just come out and tell them that he liked girls and kissing the gypsy felt good. That scenario would not end well, but at least it was better than the whole truth. Janusz had pretty much settled on that course of action when the door to his room opened up, and John and Mildred came in. Mildred sat on the bed next to Janusz and John stood next to the bed in front of the nightstand.

Janusz looked at them and decided to jump in and tell them about liking girls and get it over with, but Mildred cut him off and said, "Look, dear, your father and I know that the world is changing and becoming more modern or whatnot."

Oh God, Janusz thought, *here it comes.*

Mildred swallowed and took a deep breath. "But it is still not appropriate for a lady of our class to be smoking cigarettes, especially in public."

Janusz' eyes widened, and Mildred continued. "No proper young man is going to want a woman who does that because he might think you are a prostitute or, at the very least, loose."

Janusz looked at Mildred and could not believe this was the thing they were worried about. Had the chaperone not seen the kiss?

And then John spoke, "Also, you must watch who you consort with, it is not acceptable to be seen with people like that girl. Her kind travels from city to city, taking advantage of people and stealing what they can. They are no better than animals."

Janusz felt a pang of anger at this statement because he didn't believe the gypsy girl was an animal. In fact, she was the first person in years he had actually felt comfortable with, but he said nothing.

Mildred took Janusz' hand in hers and said, "Everything you do affects this family, and we all must be careful. Your father's work is important, and if people think badly about you, then they think badly about him, and his career suffers."

Janusz shook his head. Of course, this was about John and how it would affect him. He wanted to scream at both of them. He knew though, that would achieve nothing. He had to think about Paris and the plan so he said, "I understand, and it will never happen again, I would never want to do anything to hurt the family."

John nodded, seemed content, and left the room. Mildred stayed for a moment and said, "Don't worry, soon you will be grown and we will find you a good husband who you will give a family, and you will understand."

Janusz replied, "Thank you mother, you always know best."

Mildred's face lit up. This obviously pleased her. She then stood up and left the room, leaving Janusz with much to think about.

CHAPTER 10

12 JUNE 1943
7:00 A.M.

Janusz and Beatrice lay naked together on the bed of their dormitory room in silence, the kicked towards the bottom. The still, heavy air made it too hot to have anything on their skin.

At the foot of the bed stood packed suitcases, which served as a reminder of the end of freedom. Janusz hadn't wanted to pack the night before, but he knew that John and Mildred would wish to return home right after the graduation ceremony. Those two had planned a big party and invited half the town to show off their daughter's achievement.

Janusz did not feel too upset though; after all, it was John's narcissism that made everything possible. Janusz had managed to feed John's ego enough to make him feel it was a good idea to go to university. Janusz sighed and looked over at a still sleeping Beatrice; he would miss waking up to her every day and did not know how he was going to cope with being under John and Mildred's control again.

Janusz got up off the bed slowly so as not to wake Beatrice, and made his way to the bathroom. He looked around the room and noticed how bare it was, compared to what it used to look like. All of their items were already gone except a painting of the Eifel Tower. He decided to leave the painting and not take it with him. The picture used to serve as a symbol of his future, but now he only felt disappointment when he looked at it, as Paris was out of the question now with the war going on.

Janusz turned his head away from the picture and walked into the bathroom. When he finished, he walked back toward the bed. Instead of getting back into it, he pulled a chair out, sat down and looked at Beatrice sleeping. Janusz knew what they were doing was wrong. Women did not sleep together. The Bible stated that very clearly, and it was against the law, but above all, Janusz felt guilty that he was lying with another woman who was not his wife.

He sighed and imagined he would have to answer for that to St. Peter when the time came, if it ever came. But he could not help himself, and the feeling of attraction he felt to Beatrice was something he could not control. Janusz had never questioned God's judgment in the past, but questions as to why God would put these feelings in him if they were so wrong had started to develop.

At that moment, Beatrice sighed and turned a bit. Janusz froze, and hoped that she would not wake up; he wanted to savor this moment for a bit longer. He watched intently as Beatrice took a deep breath and continued to sleep, and soon produced ever so slight snores. Those snores were the exact type his wife had once made, and that comforted him.

He reached out and lightly stroked her hair and noticed how warm it was from the sun beating down on it. He thanked God for Beatrice, even if what they were doing was a sin. Before Beatrice had moved into his room two years ago, Janusz had not realized how lonely he had been. Before her, he'd had no friends on this "Ride" or the last one, but it didn't matter, he was used to people finding him weird by now, plus school kept him busy. But then, "Beatrice from California" came along, and he felt a connection similar to the one he had felt with the Gypsy girl all those years ago.

Beatrice had brought him the first little slice of happiness he'd felt since this whole damned situation of the "Rides" had started. They did not become lovers right away; in fact, it took over a year, but once they did, it opened up everything for Janusz, and he knew he could not lose her. At first, Janusz thought Beatrice was a "Rider" too, but she had shown no signs of that over the past two years.

He had tried to talk to her about the future, but Beatrice always said, "Things will work out." Janusz had been trying to figure out a way for them to be together, but every avenue he turned to was blocked. He thought about moving to California, but how would he support himself? Even with most of the boys off to war, it still was not easy for a woman to support herself.

Janusz became so frustrated with the social situation that he wanted to rage. In almost every aspect of his being, he could out-perform any man except for strength. He was even named valedictorian, but somehow that did not carry much weight because it was a "girls' school." It was not fair, and Janusz wanted to scream in people's faces at times.

It was not only the men, though; many of the young women here at the school also did nothing to change the situation. Most of them had the primary goal of going back home, finding a good husband and starting a family. Janusz shook his head and wondered why any of them came to the University if they were going to throw all of their knowledge away.

Not Beatrice though, she was different. She had dreams, and she made Janusz feel like anything was possible. He smiled at the thought and realized that was why he loved her. He still loved his wife, and always would, but Janusz had to admit that his wife was gone, and he was still here, and Beatrice was here.

Janusz heard a noise outside of the window, turned to look, and saw a bird flutter above a nest in the tree. He smiled as he saw the bird and felt envious at how free it seemed. When he looked back, Beatrice's eyes were open.

She smiled at him and said, "Good morning. Why didn't you wake me?"

"You looked so peaceful; it seemed a shame to ruin that."

She yawned, stretched her arms and said, "Well, we better get up. The last thing we want is for one of our parents to show up here while I am naked in bed."

10:00 a.m.

Janusz could not concentrate on any of the speakers. All of them spoke in the same monotone voices, and if it were not for Beatrice sitting next to him, Janusz believed he might have drifted off. Out of the corner of his eye, he could see the sleek outline of her body, and he longed to touch her. He thought about sliding his hand over and placing it on her leg and wondered if anybody would see.

He never got the chance. Right before he decided to go for it, he heard the dean announce, "And now, ladies and gentlemen, please extend a warm welcome to our valedictorian, Miss Elizabeth Adler." Janusz remained in his seat for a moment, not wanting to get up, but finally, Beatrice put her hand on his shoulder and urged him on.

To look at him, one would have thought he was on his way to face a firing squad rather than to give a valediction. The entire place stood and clapped, filling the air with a deafening roar. As he made his way up to the stage, he made eye contact with no one. Even when he shook hands with the dean and the other administrators, he made a point to look through them and give a false smile.

Once he was at the podium, he looked out over the crowd. He saw a lot of young women that had put in a tremendous amount of work and study. The thought made him proud, but he knew that most of them were going to go home, find a husband, and have children as soon as possible. Janusz wondered how many of them wanted that life, and how many of them were pressured into it, sometimes without realizing it. He wanted to tell them the measure or worth of their life did not depend on their husbands.

Janusz took a deep breath and fought a mental battle in his head. He had two speeches, and the one he wanted to give would take courage.

It would require going against society's norm, and angering a great many people. But he wanted to say it all; he wanted to say how many of these young women had brilliant minds, how any of them could do any job of any man, or how immediately getting married and then raising children might not be the path for everybody.

He looked out and saw potential CEOs, lawyers, and doctors. Janusz began to open his mouth to tell all these young women that they could have a career or do anything they wanted, but then he saw John and Mildred. Anybody else who looked at them would have thought they were a couple of proud parents, which in a way, they were, but Janusz knew different.

The problem was that John was proud of himself, and not of Janusz. He saw everything that Janusz did as a direct result of himself and used it to his advantage every chance he got. Although, to be fair, Janusz had used John through manipulation to get what he wanted, also. So now Janusz wondered what would happen if he spoke the words in his heart, and what he felt to be true.

Upon hearing something that went totally against the grain of society, John would be embarrassed. He would be angry, and the times of Janusz manipulating the man might be over, which meant no plan, and no plan meant no Beatrice, and in the end, it all totaled up to no happiness. After another moment of deliberation, Janusz closed his eyes, took a deep breath and said, "Dear classmates, many years from now when we have married and raised families, we will look back on this time with a special sentiment."

* * *

The crowd gave Janusz a standing ovation once he finished the speech. He smiled and waved to everyone, but deep down inside, he was ashamed of himself and had a bad taste in his mouth, which he was sure would be there for a good while. As he stepped off the stage, not only John and Mildred, but also Beatrice and her parents, greeted him.

Janusz stopped and looked at the two families. For a moment he worried that they might know what Beatrice and he had been doing, and now wondered what he should say. Janusz imagined he looked somewhat stupid standing there with his mouth open, but he could not help it. Fortunately, John and his ego came to the rescue, and he said, "You did not tell us how much of a big shot in Hollywood Beatrice's father is."

Janusz grinned and thought, *why would I talk about her father, she is the one I love.* But instead said, "Oh Father, I am sure I mentioned something about it."

Janusz waited for a response, but none came, and the two men started to brag subtly about the people they knew, how much one made in their professions and a multitude of other mundane topics. Then, as if on cue, the two women slipped into their roles about motherhood and supporting their husbands' careers and aspirations.

As Janusz followed the two sets of parents, it struck him as being odd that nobody spoke of the accomplishments their daughters had achieved. Janusz shrugged and looked over at Beatrice, who smiled as well, and the two enjoyed the short time they had with each other in silence.

After the two families said goodbye and parted ways, Janusz felt as if part of his soul had gone too. Today was different than leaving for spring or summer break. There would be no return in a few weeks or months, and Janusz feared that not only was he saying goodbye to Beatrice, but he was also saying goodbye to his freedom.

It was Mildred who broke Janusz out of his deep pondering. "Dear, wait until you see the party we have planned for you."

"Mother, can't we celebrate quietly with just the family?"

"Oh, don't be silly, plus we have a surprise for you; a certain young gentleman by the name of Grant is dying to meet you."

Janusz' body tensed. "What?"

Mildred lowered her voice and smirked. "He is a senator's son."

Then John chimed in. "Yes, and poised to far exceed his father in the political arena."

Janusz did not like the sound of that one bit.

6:00 p.m.

Janusz sat in his room in front of the mirror with his head in his hands. He could hear the commotion of the party downstairs and knew it was a typical over the top production by John and Mildred. He slammed his hand down on the table and wondered why they could not leave him alone, just for one night. He missed Beatrice, even though only a few hours had passed.

Finally, Mildred had enough of it and she barged into the room. "Dear, I know you are nervous about meeting Grant, but if you stay up here any longer, you are going to appear rude."

Janusz sighed as he stood up and allowed Mildred to escort him downstairs almost as if they were presenting him to the King at court. He felt ridiculous, and he also felt the whole party was ridiculous. He hadn't made it five steps past the stairs and already three people had told him nonsense such as, "Such a great achievement, especially for a young woman," followed by, "You know, in this day and age a man is looking for a smart wife," and "How lucky are you to have such a smart and successful father to look up to."

Janusz wanted to punch every single one of them in the face.

Luckily, Mildred was anxious to introduce her to this Grant guy, so they did not loiter too long in one spot, which made it easier to dismiss the comments. He wished Beatrice were there. She had a particularly calming effect on him, and he could use it.

His thoughts of Beatrice were cut short, though, as he saw John standing next to a man and a woman as well as a younger man. He assumed this was Grant. John wore a stupid grin on his face as he sometimes did when he was proud of himself.

Right before they reached the group, Mildred leaned in and whispered in Janusz' ear, "Isn't he so handsome?"

Janusz didn't have an opinion on it; as far as he was concerned, the guy looked normal. He could not see the beauty in men as others did, but if Mildred said so, Janusz would agree. "It appears so," he said.

When they were standing in front of everybody, John made the introductions. "Senator and Mrs. Jones, I would like to present my daughter Elizabeth."

Everybody smiled, and Grant took Janusz' hand and kissed it. Janusz' skin crawled, and he fought the urge to yank his hand back. He directed his thoughts back to Beatrice and how he would somehow be with her and about the life they would have. Grant said, "It is so lovely to meet you."

"It's nice to meet you too, young man," Janusz forced the words out of his mouth as he could feel the hard glare of Mildred.

Then the senator said, "My God, John, you didn't tell me your daughter was this beautiful," and slapped John on the shoulder.

Janusz ignored the comment and kept the fake smile pasted on his face. As the conversation went on, Janusz could not help but feel like he was some sort of horse being sold at auction.

Suddenly, John said, "Senator, I would like to show you my private stock, and I'm sure the women have much to talk about."

The senator nodded his head. "Why yes, and that will give these two a chance to talk."

Janusz could tell that Grant was on his best behavior, but that didn't matter. Janusz didn't like him at all. He got the sense that Grant was like a shark circling prey in the water, waiting for his chance to strike. During the conversation, Grant only asked one question about Janusz--which had to do with being relieved that school was done--and the rest of the evening was all about Grant.

Janusz could see why John liked this young man; aside from the potential political possibilities, this could be a young John. Janusz never believed he would meet anybody in love with himself as much as John, but he had, and he was standing in front of him.

* * *

Janusz was happy the night finally was ending because it meant he would not have to listen to Grant talk about himself anymore. He had started to get a headache from the whole ordeal and wanted to lie down to escape the world. So he was glad when goodbyes started to be said along with the usual pleasantries.

Then, something made his head hurt even more.

"So, your parents tell me you are free tomorrow evening, and I was thinking about picking you up at 6," said Grant who didn't wait for Janusz to reply before he continued, "I'll see you then."

Janusz told himself there was no way he was going to go out with Grant. He couldn't bear another minute around this man.

CHAPTER II

13 JUNE 1943

Janusz woke up in the morning expecting to see Beatrice but was disappointed when he opened his eyes and she was not there. That feeling usually happened to him the first days after spring or summer break. He would be slightly disappointed, but he always knew it would not be long until they saw each other again. This time was different because there was no going back to school.

The "Paris plan," as he liked to call it, still bugged him from time to time, but he figured it best not to dwell on things he couldn't change. So Janusz put all those thoughts out of his head, got dressed, and went downstairs to eat breakfast.

He wondered what time it was as everybody sat at the table, eating. "Good morning, sleepy head," said Mildred.

"How long did I sleep?"

"Not too long, darling. We figured with all the excitement, you needed your sleep."

As soon as Janusz sat down, John set his paper on the table and looked at Janusz. "So are you excited about the night out with the senator's son?"

God, Janusz thought, he had completely forgotten about that.

Janusz groaned and said, "Father, I don't think he is the type of person for me. Besides, I am not sure I will have time for courting because I have to think about the future."

John slammed his hand down on the table, which startled everyone in the room. "Elizabeth, enough with this nonsense. You've gone to university, you are 23, and now it's time to find your husband. *That* is your future."

Janusz clenched his fists and poised his body for attack; this was one of the battles he would fight.

Before he could say anything, though, Mildred took his hand in hers. "Look, dear, I don't know if you have noticed it, but there is a war going on, and the choices for suitable men are getting slimmer every day. If we don't find you somebody now, you will be a husbandless spinster before you know it."

John stood up to leave, but before he did, he said, "Grant is assured to take his father's Senate seat soon, and that is the very least. This young man could go to the White House in the future, and that means you as well. So you WILL go out with him, and you WILL be a perfect lady and then, hopefully soon, you will receive a proposal."

CHAPTER 12

Janusz stared out the window as the snow blanketed everything in sight. Christmas Eve was usually a magical time for Janusz. As a boy in Poland, he would love the feel of the air on this day. Even on his last "Ride" with Peter and Mary, Christmas Eve was special; it was the only day of the year in which he did not feel like an outsider.

Today was different.

Janusz had begun to worry a lot about Beatrice. He had heard from her less and less, and on the rare occasion he did talk to her on the telephone, she was evasive and always had an excuse as to why she couldn't speak.

Then there was the whole courting situation with Grant, which Janusz began to dislike more every day. Aside from the fact that he was a man and Janusz had no desire for him, or any man to speak of, there was something about him that Janusz just did not like. For the most part, Grant acted like a perfect gentleman on all of their dates, and he always acted like a gentleman in front of the parents, but there was *something* underneath the façade.

Janusz had seen it the previous week at the end of a date when Grant had had a little more to drink than usual and tried to kiss him. When Janusz pushed him back, there was a flash of malice in Grant's eyes, albeit fleeting, but nevertheless, it was there. At that moment, Janusz decided it was time to end it and all he had to do was figure out a way to tell John and Mildred.

He sat there going over all possibilities in his head when he heard a knock on the door and in walked Mildred. "Good morning, dear, this came for you yesterday, and I thought you would like to read it before breakfast." She held an envelope in her hand, and the sight of the familiar handwriting sent his heart racing as he could see it was from Beatrice.

Janusz leaped off the bed to grab the letter, but at the last moment, Mildred pulled it back out of his reach. "Also, your father and I need to speak with you, so please hurry and get dressed and meet us downstairs." Janusz watched her leave the room and noticed she was acting strange. He had no idea what they wanted. It didn't matter though, because he was too excited to read the letter from Beatrice.

He tore the letter open and devoured the words.

Dearest Elizabeth,

I sincerely hope this letter finds you well. I have been thinking about different ways to say this to you for a long time and no matter which way I try to say it, all are difficult. In short, I have met someone. His name is Richard, and he is an actor, who, incidentally, you will see in upcoming movies. In addition to that, I have decided to be an actress, too, and that has taken up so much more of my time than I ever could have imagined. I know these words will be hard for you to hear, but I was a very confused girl during university. After talking with my father and Richard, I now see what we did was not right. Richard has told me it is a sickness that I must deny, and after thinking about it, he is right. Please try to be happy for me, Richard is a wonderful man, and he loves me. I'm sorry, Elizabeth, but this will be the last time you hear from me. Please do not call or write to me anymore.

I will always hold a spot for you in my heart, but we must grow up and move on.

Beatrice.

Janusz' mouth hung open after he read the last sentence. He looked at the letter again, not reading it, but just staring at it. Soon his hands began to shake, and he felt sick to his stomach. When he looked up from the letter, he decided to go downstairs to the telephone. He thought surely if he could talk to Beatrice, he could make her understand.

Janusz slowly folded up the paper and slid it under a drawer before he made his way downstairs. Paris was already ruined, and Janusz didn't want to think about how he would feel if there was no Beatrice in the future either.

Once he was downstairs, he reached for the telephone but did not dial. He knew what he wanted to say, but wondered what he would do if she still said no? He gripped the receiver harder and decided if it came to that, he would go out to California and deal with this face-to-face.

The receiver felt heavy and he closed his eyes, took a deep breath, and started to move his finger towards the dial. When his finger entered the hole in the dial, he heard Mildred's voice.

"Elizabeth, are you finally down here?" she called, "Come to the kitchen right away; your father and I have some exciting news."

Janusz grunted as he put the receiver down and walked into the kitchen. He had completely forgotten that Mildred had said that she and John wanted to talk about something.

As he sat down at the breakfast table, John spoke first. "Elizabeth, Grant came to speak with me yesterday and asked for your hand in marriage."

The breath left Janusz' chest, and his head snapped back. Out of the corner of his eye, he could see Mildred squirming in her seat with a huge smile on her face. After a moment's pause, John said, "Tonight we are having dinner at the senator's house, and the young man will propose to you."

A thousand things swirled around in Janusz' head, but the only thing he could manage to say was one word, "No."

Now it was Mildred who looked like she had been hit with a hammer. "What do you mean, 'no'?"

Janusz had to think; the next few words he said could well determine his fate. "It's just that, I was thinking about continuing with school."

"What do you mean, continuing with school?" asked John.

"Well, I was thinking about maybe going to medical school."

John rolled his eyes. "Nonsense, you have a perfect opportunity here, and I will not let you squander it because of some fantasy you have in your head."

"It's not a fantasy. During university, I read about more and more women becoming doctors, especially now with the war going on and so many of the men gone."

This time John shouted. "Stop it! Stop it right now! This is preposterous, YOU are not going to be a doctor. YOU will marry Grant, and YOU will take advantage of this opportunity put out in front of you."

Janusz said nothing, as now the situation was lost. He had hoped that he could spin it to make John realize that having a daughter who was doctor would look good for him, but he didn't see it that way. He saw Grant and his family's political options as a better path and nothing was going to distract him from that.

Then John added, "Elizabeth, nursing is the only role for women in the medical field and even then, that is really only a pathway to meet a doctor. So tonight you will accept the proposal and act as you should because if you don't, I will cut you off from this family and no amount of education will save you. You will just be a woman with no money and worse, no husband."

Mildred reached out and grabbed Janusz' hand softly and said, "Elizabeth, dear, sometimes we must do things that are not in our heart for the good of the family."

"What about love?"

"Oh dear, love is not what you see in the movies or read in those books of yours. Love is something you learn, and I promise you that after a while, you will love Grant."

Before leaving, John said one final thing. "So this is settled. Tonight you will accept and act surprised. It is time to grow up, accept your place in society, and be of service to this family."

5 p.m.

Janusz lay face down on his bed and punched the mattress.

It seemed no matter what he tried to do, he was blocked at every turn. He thought about what John had said, about being cut off, and truthfully, that did not sound entirely bad. He had no illusions as to how hard it would be to survive on his own, but there was also that fear in the back of Janusz' mind about John. He doubted John would ever let him go and what would happen if Janusz did try to leave? Would John have him committed? Would he find himself back at Oakbrook or another asylum to be "cured?"

Janusz shivered at that thought. He never forgot what John had done to him on his last "Ride." Was he willing to spend out the rest of his days in an asylum or end up dying again? This thought stuck with Janusz…dying again. He wondered what would happen. Then he took the idea further: what would happen if he died on his terms?

Janusz got up and went into the master bathroom and opened up the medicine cabinet. He looked at the multitude of tablets, some of which Mildred took, of course, given to her by John for when she needed to relax. Janusz picked up a bottle of Benzedrine and shook the bottle. It was full, and he did some quick calculations as to how many he would have to take to end it all.

The realization of what he was about to do hit him. He knew what happened to people who killed themselves; they burned for eternity. Janusz thought about suffering in Hell for a moment. Often he thought he was already in Hell, having to continue to live on in another body but still be himself. The situation was more than he could take at times, so he asked himself if he wanted to chance eternal damnation. He closed his eyes and took a deep breath and thought.

Then he opened his eyes, put the bottle back in the cabinet, returned to his room, and started to prepare for the dinner.

24 DECEMBER 1943
7 P.M.

Janusz sat at the table and looked around at everybody. At least there were no surprises, he told himself as the dinner went precisely as he had expected. John and Mildred put on the perfect show, and no one could even tell there had been a big altercation earlier that morning. Janusz felt like a man standing at the gallows with a noose around his neck, wondering when the lever would be pulled.

Every time one of the members of the senator's family spoke, Janusz was sure the proposal was coming, and he would brace himself. He made a point not to look at John, but that didn't matter. All John cared about was that the senator was impressed, so he paid no mind to Janusz anyway. Mildred, on the other hand, constantly annoyed Janusz. One would almost think she was sitting on a mound of fire ants by the way she kept squirming around.

Once everyone had eaten dessert and the servants had brought out drinks, the senator grabbed his lead crystal wine glass, stood up and tapped it with a fork. "I'd like to make an announcement."

Here it comes, the lever was thrown, and now Janusz fell towards the earth waiting for his neck to snap with the abrupt stop of the rope.

Mildred now looked like she was no longer sitting on fire ants but rather on a pile of venomous snakes.

The senator continued, "As you know, the Allies are beginning to advance against the Axis powers in Europe. But this alone is not enough, and the war department has just given the Senate word that they will be increasing troops for a major offensive."

Everyone fell silent and followed his every word, and now Janusz had a glimmer of hope; maybe there would be no proposal tonight.

The senator took a deep breath and looked around, drawing out the tension. "Unfortunately, this means members of Congress in the House and Senate are being scrutinized for having able-bodied sons not fighting in the war." Janusz' head jerked up, and now he paid attention to the words of the senator. "If I have any hope for a continued political career, or even more important, if Grant has any hopes to succeed me, I can no longer shield him from the war." The senator paused to take a drink and make sure everybody hung on his words. "Therefore, Grant will be commissioned in the Army and leave for the European front next spring."

The room was silent except for a slight gasp from Mildred, but for Janusz, he felt like this was a stay of execution. The senator looked over at Mildred and said, "Not to worry, young Grant will not be on the front lines and will never be in danger. I have personally seen to this."

Once his father finished speaking, Grant stood up. "Thank you, Father, as you know it will be a great honor to serve the country in any capacity that I can, but now I would like to say something." Janusz, with hope sinking into the pit of his stomach, looked at Grant. "Elizabeth, yesterday I asked your father for your hand in marriage, and today I would like to ask you to do me the honor of being my wife."

Janusz' head spun, and he thought he was going to lose consciousness. He could feel the hard stare of John boring into him, so he took a breath, nodded his head and said, "Yes."

The senator then let out a cry of excitement. "Well, we have a lot of work to do if we are going to get these kids married before Grant ships out."

Ships out? Janusz thought. It hit him then; they were going to marry him off before Grant left.

Snap! Just as the rope cinches and breaks the neck of the condemned, so did it for Janusz as his fate was sealed at that dinner.

CHAPTER 13

1 APRIL 1944
9 A.M.

Janusz sat in front of the vanity mirror on his wedding day feeling disgusted. He felt disgusted wearing a wedding dress, felt disgusted he was about to marry a man, but mostly he felt disgusted at himself because he was not able to stop this tomfoolery. Growing up during his first "Ride," which he imagined was the original, he always believed if one worked hard, believed in God, and was honest, then one could achieve anything.

He hadn't been able to stop this, so he felt like a failure. He tried to think what he could have done different but was at a loss. Maybe, he thought, he hadn't worked hard enough, or perhaps he hadn't prayed hard enough. So that is what Janusz did: he prayed to God, not to intervene and stop this wedding, but he prayed for strength because he felt he was going to need a lot of it.

9 p.m.

Janusz could feel Grant becoming more and more agitated. He knew Grant wanted to leave the reception and go back to the room, but Janusz did everything to stall. He talked with as many people as he could, he gave Grant drinks as often as possible in the hope that the alcohol would make him pass out, or at the very least put him in a position where he would not be able to perform.

Finally, Grant had had enough. As Janusz talked with a couple he had never met before, Grant walked up, grabbed his arm a little too roughly and said, "I'm sorry, but I must steal my wife away, it is time for us to retire."

Grant said nothing as he pulled Janusz by the arm upstairs and into the honeymoon suite. Once they entered the room, he slammed the door, and Janusz was alone with a man who had hunger in his eyes. Grant wobbled, clearly drunk, but judging by the bulge in his pants, the drink had not affected him as Janusz had hoped.

Grant removed his clothes and walked toward Janusz, who took a step back for every step his aggressor took forward. Then Janusz' back hit the wall, and he had no more room for escape. Grant was now only a few feet away where he paused only for a moment to remove his pants.

Janusz stammered and said, "Grant, let's just go to sleep."

The man said nothing. He threw Janusz on the bed and forced his tongue into his mouth. Janusz tried to push him off, but it was no use. Grant was strong, and Janusz was pinned under him and couldn't move no matter how hard he tried.

The next thing Janusz felt was his underwear being ripped off. Grant had lifted his mouth off Janusz' and said something indecipherable and Janusz pleaded, "No."

The plea for him to stop only seemed to encourage Grant more, and he pushed Janusz' legs apart with his knees. Janusz started to hyperventilate as Grant began to enter him. The pain overpowered him, and when he was able to control his breathing again, he started to weep.

Grant continued with the violation while holding Janusz' hands over his head and keeping all his weight on top of him. After a few minutes, Janusz was exhausted from struggling and couldn't move anymore, so he remained still until the man finished. Once Grant ejaculated his seed into Janusz, he rolled over and almost immediately fell asleep.

Janusz lay on the bed for the better part of an hour and wept. He had no idea the violation would have been that horrendous, but it was, and he wasn't sure how to process it. When he felt strong enough, he got up and limped into the bathroom where he cleaned himself up.

CHAPTER 14

2 APRIL 1944

Janusz had not slept a single minute. He kept replaying the attack over and over in his head. Finally, the sun made its appearance and light began to flood the hotel room; not long after that, Grant began to stir. When he opened his eyes, he smiled and said, "Good morning" and put his hand on Janusz' arm.

Janusz felt only revulsion but said, "Good morning."

Grant groaned a bit as he stretched. "The whiskey has done a number on my head."

Janusz said nothing; he just looked at the man with hatred unable to believe that he was acting as though nothing out of the ordinary had happened.

Grant got up and rubbed his head. "I believe our parents will be downstairs shortly and we best get there soon."

CHAPTER 15

2 JUNE 1944

Janusz stood in front of the stove as the teakettle screamed. The high-pitched noise seemed to grow louder and louder by the second, and Janusz felt himself being transported out of the kitchen. He leaned forward and put his hands on the stove and clenched his eyes while trying to stop himself from going to *that* place.

His breath quickened, sweat began to pour down his face, and no matter how hard he fought it, he was back. He was back on the bed, on the wedding night, and Grant was on top of him, forcing himself inside Janusz. He no longer heard the scream of the teakettle; now it was his screams and cries for Grant to stop pushing and tearing.

Janusz opened his eyes and said, "Enough of this poppycock."

He grabbed the teapot off the stove and threw it across the room, hitting the wall. Decorations on a shelf fell where the kettle hit and shattered on the floor as Janusz collapsed and pulled his knees to his chest.

Janusz sobbed and started to become angry with himself for falling apart. He banged his fists against his head. It had been ten days since his last episode, and he had hoped he had finally gotten over what Grant had done to him. He wiped his eyes and concentrated on controlling his breathing as he calmed himself down.

When he thought he was back in control, he stood up and turned off the stove. After that, he looked at the state of the room and muttered, "Just look at that mess, you damned old fool."

As he walked over and started to pick up the broken pieces of glass, he told himself that at least the episodes were not as frequent as they used to be. After the incident, Janusz felt himself reliving the wedding night every day. Everything reminded him of what had happened, and he would lose control and fall apart, much like he just had.

It could have been worse, he told himself.

At least God allowed Janusz a slight reprieve by moving up Grant's ship out date. Janusz didn't know the whole story, but the day after the wedding, the senator received a phone call from somebody, and there was a lot of discussion between Grant and his father. They told Janusz little, only that Grant had to take care of some business with his father and he would have to leave immediately.

Janusz could not have cared less. He wanted Grant gone and most of all he wanted to be left alone. Janusz got his wish; for the most part, he was alone in the big house owned by Grant, the only exception being the incessant visits from Mildred.

Janusz sighed as he looked outside. The day was so beautiful, but he sat in the house feeling sorry for himself. The big oak tree stood as a sentinel with its army of leaves gently blowing in the wind. Janusz focused on a leaf and asked, "Why in the hell am I inside on a day like this?" He looked at the remaining mess on the floor and decided to clean it up later. Right now, he needed some fresh air and some wind on his face.

Janusz could not believe how much better he felt once he started to walk. He had no particular plan, he just let his feet guide him, and they seemed to know where to go. He had no idea how far walked, but he took a look at his surroundings and noticed he was in the heart of Detroit.

The city was more alive now during the war compared to the years during the depression. Things buzzed more, everybody had a sense of purpose, and there were hardly any young men around. Janusz paused for a moment as this made him think of all the boys overseas and he felt a bit of shame. Fortunately, Janusz never had to face the horrors of fighting in a war, but that was not what he felt ashamed of. He felt ashamed about wallowing in his sorrow while brave young men were facing death every day.

A sudden growling in his stomach diverted his attention away from his thoughts. *Must be around lunchtime,* he thought as he patted his stomach. He had planned on being back by lunch and eating at home, but the idea of eating lunch downtown appealed to him more. He looked around and saw nothing right away, and decided to walk a bit farther and try to find a café, and then thoughts of sandwiches with coffee and cake drove him forward.

As he started the search for the café, he window-shopped along the way, and a second-hand shop caught his eye. He stopped in front of the window and stared at an object propped up against the wall--a beat up old guitar.

Janusz stared at it for a long time as memories bombarded him. As a child in Poland, he had found an old broken guitar discarded by a band of traveling Spanish musicians and he had managed to piece it together enough to get a decent sound out of it. Once he had scrounged up some strings, it wasn't long before he had taught himself how to play, and play he did. He would play until his fingers were bloody and then play some more. Janusz had never gone anywhere without that guitar.

When he had come to America, he continued to play. His wife had bought him a new guitar shortly after they were married. He smiled as memories popped into his head of playing songs for her and the children. After the death of his wife, he had found himself playing less and less and then arthritis had taken over his hands, and he was not even able to finger the simplest of chords.

But at that moment, Janusz felt something awaken in him and although he didn't notice it, he was not thinking about what had happened on the wedding night. Like a moth being drawn to a flame, Janusz felt himself walking into the shop and heading straight to the guitar.

Once inside, the shopkeeper, an elderly man in his 70s whose hair and teeth had left him long ago, quickly greeted him, "Good day, young lady, is there something I can help you with?"

Janusz paid him no mind and reached for the guitar to pick it up. He felt energy surge through him and, for the first time in a very long while, he felt a purpose.

"Ah yes, that will make a fine gift for your husband," said the shopkeeper.

The word *husband* snapped Janusz out of his trance, and he said, "I beg your pardon?"

"A fine gift, I might say, for your husband," and the shopkeeper pointed to the ring on Janusz' left hand.

Janusz was silent for a moment and said, "Yes, he is off to war."

The shopkeeper took the guitar out of Janusz' hands. "Well, she is a little beat up, but the neck is straight, and she has a good sound."

Trying not to give too much away Janusz said, "I will take your word for it."

"With a little bit of care, she will play for many years to come."

Without asking for the price or bartering, Janusz said, "I'll take it."

Once Janusz had paid for the guitar, he walked outside the shop and looked around. He smiled and noted how different the city looked now than when he had gone into the shop; he knew it was stupid, but the day seemed brighter. He also forgot about being hungry and headed straight home in a brisk walk that was not quite a run but wasn't far from it. He barely got through the door before he threw his bag down, kicked off his shoes, and started to tune the guitar.

The shopkeeper was right; the guitar held a good sound and was in tune with itself. As Janusz fingered the first chord and strummed the strings, the feeling hit him like a train. Everything came back, and all of his old songs filled the house with their sweet harmony.

At one point Janusz noticed that the muscles in his hand were sore; he knew that was only temporary, as he needed to condition them so they would build up strength. He kept playing, though, and played well into the night until his fingers bled. When his eyes could not stay open any longer, he put the guitar down and decided to go to sleep. And as he lay in the bed, he realized for the first time that he was happy, really happy, since before his wife had died. Even his time with Beatrice could not compare to this. He fell asleep with a new sense of satisfaction and even...hope.

CHAPTER 16

8 MAY 1945

Janusz sat on the front porch as he listened to the phone ring for the third time. He knew the person on the other end of the phone was either Mildred or Grant's mother, and he knew what they had to say. The time to face what would happen approached, but now, he wanted to savor a bit more peace, while he still could.

Janusz never paid any attention to news of the war. The grueling and tedious visits from Grant's parents, as well as his own, gave him all the news he needed to know. The only interest he showed was when somebody would walk up the steps and Janusz would quickly decipher whether it was a mail carrier or a telegram boy. The mail carrier meant it was a letter from Grant, which Janusz would take and smile, and walk directly to the fireplace, where he would burn it without opening it. A telegram boy meant something else--that Grant had been killed--but sadly, the boy never climbed the steps of the house.

Today though, Janusz could not ignore the news of the war. It was all anybody was talking about because the Germans had surrendered. Grant would be returning soon, and the thought filled Janusz with dread. He was scheduled to return last month, but according to his father, he had chosen to stay to see the surrender through (sitting behind a desk far, far away from any danger, of course).

This past year Janusz had been happy. He knew the guitar had saved his life or at the very least, it had saved his sanity. After the first day, it wasn't long before he had built up the muscles in his hand as well as formed callouses on his fingertips, and his skills had returned. In fact, his playing was better than it had ever been. He tried new things, learned new chords, and created music that touched his soul.

Janusz needed to escape from the news of the war, so he went into the house to get his guitar. As he picked it up, he heard a knock on the door. When he opened it, he saw Grant's parents standing there with big smiles on their faces, and Grant's father said, "Grant will be home this Friday!"

11 a.m.

Janusz stood in front of the state capitol with Grant's parents, John, Mildred, the governor, and a multitude of other people he did not know (or care about). The only thing he wanted to do was play his guitar in solitude. Ever since Grant's father had told him the news of Grant returning, he hadn't had a moment's peace. Mildred was a constant presence in the house, along with a variety of other people helping him prepare the home for Grant's return.

Of course now, just because he was a senator's son, his homecoming was a bigger deal than it needed to be. The whole thing was a political spin for the senator as well as for Grant and his posturing into politics. There were signs and posters everywhere in the capitol with the words "Welcome Home Hero" printed on them.

Reading those signs disgusted Janusz. He wondered to himself, *a hero for what; risking paper cuts while sitting behind a desk writing reports?*

Janusz went through the motions, said the right things, and smiled when appropriate, but in the back of his mind, all he could think about was his guitar, and that gave him the strength he needed to get through this.

From out of nowhere a band started to play music, and Janusz wondered for a moment where it had come from, as he didn't remember seeing it. The thought quickly left his head as he saw a progression of cars pulling up to the front of the capitol. As the doors opened, Janusz saw Grant step out, and he suddenly had the urge to flee.

There were so many cameras taking pictures that he wondered if there were any reporters left in Michigan today. Grant made his way up the steps, greeted his father, the Governor, and finally, Janusz. Grant reached out and embraced him with a kiss and that feeling of revulsion that the guitar playing buried deep down inside bubbled to the surface.

11 p.m.

Janusz watched Grant bounce around the last few remaining guests, rehashing the same stories he had been telling the entire night. Everybody at the party swooned over him, called him brave or a hero. Janusz gritted his teeth as Grant did nothing to correct them, even though the man probably had not heard a single gunshot over there.

Finally, at the end of the night, Grant told the guests that it had been a long day and he was ready to retire.

At that point, Mildred smiled and said, "Why yes, I think these two need to get started on building a family."

Everyone laughed except Janusz.

Janusz prayed that Grant was indeed tired, too tired for what Janusz feared. This time, Janusz did not try to push drinks on Grant in an attempt to inhibit his performance as that had failed miserably last time, but it didn't matter, Grant appeared to have a taste for the drink and was inebriated when they got up into the bedroom.

As soon as the door to the bedroom closed, Grant was on him, pushing his whiskey-soaked tongue into his mouth, making him gag. He managed to push Grant off him for a moment and said, "Grant, let's wait; it's been a long time."

Grant acted as though he didn't hear anything and threw Janusz down on the bed.

Oh God, Janusz thought, it is going to happen again, and he could sense his breath becoming shallow, and his head started to spin.

Grant had removed his shirt and kicked off his shoes and was in the process of removing his pants when he lost his balance and fell.

Janusz pulled himself together and sprung off the bed, running into the bathroom, locking the door behind him. He stood there with his back to the door trying to control his breathing and tried to think of something to do. He could hear footsteps approaching the door, and then the door handle turned.

Grant began to scream for Janusz to open up the door, but he only stood there with his back against it, praying. Soon Grant started to beat on the door, causing it to shake on its hinges, and Janusz feared it was going to break. He frantically thought of what he could do when he saw a jar of petroleum jelly on the sink.

Janusz ran to the sink, grabbed the jar, opened it and placed a finger full of the substance between his legs. At that moment, the door lock failed, and Grant burst through. Janusz began to beg when Grant punched him in the stomach, and the jar of petroleum jelly flew across the floor, where it broke, and Janusz crumpled to the ground.

Grant grabbed him by the hair, bent him over the toilet and asked, "What the fuck is wrong with you? You are my wife, and when I tell you to spread your fucking legs, you spread them."

Janusz felt his underpants being ripped off and soon Grant entered him. Grant still had a handful of Janusz' hair in his fist and pushed his face against the toilet. Grant thrust in and out of him mercilessly and as he felt Grant release inside of him, Janusz stared at the broken jar of petroleum jelly on the floor.

CHAPTER 17

21 JUNE 1945

Janusz clenched his fists and wondered why it had not arrived yet. But of course he knew why; Grant had been having his way with him four to five times a week. He looked in the mirror and said, "For somebody who has been alive as long as you have, you sure can be a damned old fool."

A deep breath of air escaped his lungs as he accepted the fact that he was going to have to tell Grant. He thought Grant would have noticed the menstruation cycle had not come, but he didn't. Every night Janusz would apply the petroleum jelly between his legs, and almost every night Grant would climb on top of him for a few minutes and release.

He had stopped fighting Grant a long time ago. He was trapped and could do nothing, so Janusz would lie there with his eyes closed and imagine himself by the river with his wife, playing guitar. He found that working out chord patterns in his head made the process bearable...or at least, he did not want to kill himself after every time it happened.

Janusz walked out of the bathroom and decided it could wait until another day. Right now Janusz needed some relief; he needed to escape into the world of music, so he climbed up into the attic where the guitar was hidden and started to play.

He let the music wash over him, which immediately brought happiness. It had been a few days since he had played, which is why he probably lost track of time. He must have been playing for hours because suddenly, he heard a voice behind him ask, "What are you doing?"

Janusz jumped, stopped playing, and turned around to see Grant standing there with a bottle of whiskey in his hand. Grant did not allow Janusz to reply and he asked, "Do you have any idea what time it is?"

Janusz slowly shook his head.

"It's fucking six o'clock, and what am I supposed to eat?"

Stammering, Janusz said, "I'm sorry."

Grant walked towards him with that look in his eye. Janusz was amazed at the two sides of Grant. When they were out in public or with either set of parents, he was the picture perfect "All-American" gentleman and doting husband. Then, behind closed doors and God forbid, if the drink was in him, he was a monster.

Grant stood in front of Janusz holding a whiskey bottle in his hand, and a fire blazed in his eyes. Grant said, "I know you have been sneaking up here playing this goddamn thing instead of caring for the house as you should."

"Grant, I'm sorry; it just relieves my stress."

"Stress? What do you know about stress? You are treated like a queen while I am out trying to make a better life for us."

Before Janusz could move, Grant snatched the guitar from him and smashed it against the wall.

Janusz screamed, "No!" and stood up.

Grant raised his hand to hit him when the words, "I'm pregnant" spilled out of Janusz' mouth.

CHAPTER 18

15 SEPTEMBER 1945

"Come on, Elizabeth, the fresh air will do you good," said Mildred.

Janusz lifted his head a bit off the couch and looked at Mildred. "Mother, every time I move I feel as though I am going to be sick."

"That's exactly why you need the fresh air, my dear. Now come on; you are not the first woman to ever have a baby."

Janusz thought, as he lifted himself off the couch, *Yeah, but I might be the first man ever to have one.*

He could not believe how bad he felt. He never remembered his wife being this sick; Marzehna had always seemed to be able to do anything. At that moment Janusz realized he should have been a little more sympathetic or at least understanding to his wife because what he was going through was hell.

After he managed to sit up, he looked at Mildred and took a deep breath. "Ok, but not too far."

"Just get up, I promise you will feel better once you get outside."

Janusz got up and followed her as he knew she would not give up until he did what she wanted. Plus, he knew she was not going anywhere, because she had been a constant fixture in the house throughout the pregnancy, but this was a blessing in disguise as Mildred did have some good advice. The best thing, though, about having her around was that Grant was always on his best behavior around her. The whole pregnancy changed him a bit; the bigger Janusz became, the less Grant was interested in sex.

The second they walked out the door, Janusz had to admit he did feel a bit better. Mildred helped him down the stairs and into the car, and when they were both in, Janusz turned and looked at Mildred. "Don't drive too fast and not too much talk about the baby. The child is not even here yet, and I am already sick of it."

Mildred snapped her head at Janusz and her brow furrowed. "Oh dear, don't say such wretched things. This child is a blessing."

Janusz only exhaled as he rested his head in his hand. Once Mildred saw Janusz was not going to say anything else, she continued to talk about her usual mundane topics. Finally, Mildred stopped the car in front of a teashop, and the two walked in.

The moment Janusz entered the teashop; he knew what was happening. All of Mildred's friends were there, and this was a chance for Mildred to show off her daughter and brag to the other women. There was no way Janusz could endure this nonsense for too long, and after one cup of tea, he complained about feeling ill.

Mildred pursed her lips and looked at the clock. "Well, I guess it is OK if we leave now."

"What do you mean? Why would it not be OK?"

"Oh Elizabeth, don't you worry yourself about trivial matters."

Janusz hated when Mildred dismissed him like this. He wanted to fight back, but he did not have the strength and let it go. The two walked out of the shop, and Janusz collapsed in the car and said nothing on the drive home.

* * *

Mildred parked the car in front of the house and got out. Janusz expected her to come around and open the door for him, but she put her hand in the air towards him signaling to wait. Mildred looked at the house, and Grant walked out and waved at them to enter. Janusz found the whole thing strange. At that point, however, he didn't care as he genuinely felt ill and wanted to get into the house and lay back down on the sofa.

When they walked into the house, Janusz stopped in his tracks. Grant stood next to a grand piano and smiled from ear to ear. Janusz didn't understand what was going on and Mildred said, "Grant told me about the accident with the guitar, and honestly, dear, it's for the best that you broke it."

Yeah, I broke it, thought Janusz.

Mildred added, "Elizabeth, women don't play guitars, but if you must dabble around in a hobby to keep you busy, then a piano is for the best."

Then Grant said, "Starting Monday, I am having a teacher come over to start instructing you."

Janusz could not understand the reasoning behind this gift as he strolled around the piano and lightly tapped some keys. It did not matter though, at least it was music, and that was better than what he had now, so he would take it and he prayed it would give him some relief like the guitar did.

CHAPTER 19

1 MARCH 1946
9 A.M.

"Harder, you must push harder," ordered the nurse.

"I can't," cried Janusz, "Something is wrong; I'm going to die."

"You are not going to die, but you must push more."

Janusz tried to push the child out of him, but he did not think he could. The pain was beyond anything he had ever imagined it would be. Janusz took another breath and tried to push the child out but there was nothing but pain, and he was exhausted.

Labor had gone on for many hours, and he had lost track of time. All he wanted to do was cry. He was also angry at himself for his arrogance. The doctor had told him about a procedure called an epidural, and supposedly it eased the pain during labor, but Janusz had refused. He said he was going to have this child the way God intended it to happen. He justified this reasoning by thinking of how his wife had given birth three times and it didn't seem to be so bad for her. Janusz felt guilty as he realized he had discounted what Marzehna had gone through.

The nurse screamed, "Push, the head is almost through."

At that moment, Janusz was not afraid he might die; he *wanted* to die. He wanted the nurse that screamed at him to leave him alone. She wouldn't, though, and Janusz gave one more push so the woman would stop yelling at him. He felt another intense, ripping pain, but he also felt as if he had crossed a threshold. He was still in pain, but not as much, so he pushed again, and it happened.

He felt a release, and the nurse said, "It's a boy."

He saw the nurse take the child away, and another nurse told him to lie down while they cleaned him up. As Janusz waited for the nurses to finish their work, he thought about his wife and the way she had looked when she held their babies; it was pure love. Janusz thought maybe the child would not be such a bad idea now. He had not felt that type of love since his first "Ride" had ended, and perhaps this was God giving him a gift.

Excitement coursed through his veins as he waited for the child to be placed in his arms. The nurse washing the baby said, "Oh my, he is such a sweet little one; he is hardly making a sound."

When she finished, the woman walked over to Janusz and placed the child in his arms. Emotion overwhelmed Janusz, but it was not love, it was revulsion. He might as well have been looking at mold-covered food found in the back of the icebox; he would have had the same reaction. Janusz also noticed it wasn't just him, the child felt it too, and the little one started to wail as loud as his lungs would allow him.

Janusz did not understand why he was having these feelings towards the child. Was it because the child reminded him so much of Grant, or was it something much worse? Janusz thought something that frightened him; he wondered if the baby was like him. Could it be possible that he had passed this on to the child? Could this be a "Rider?" The thought of this broke Janusz' heart.

He would not wish his fate on anybody, even somebody the likes of Grant.

CHAPTER 20

15 SEPTEMBER 1947

Janusz woke up expecting the usual chaos that accompanied the reset or the beginning of a new "Ride." Unlike the other times, he would welcome the reset because that meant he would be away from Grant. After a moment though, he realized something was wrong. He knew he was in a hospital, but it was too quiet, and there were not a bunch of people milling around like before. Also, his senses were sharp, and he could see clearly.

He turned his head, and when he saw who sat there, he began to cry. As soon as Mildred heard Janusz' sobs, she stood up and came over to him. "Oh dear, there is nothing to worry about, the baby is fine, but the doctor said you almost died."

Janusz closed his eyes and clenched his fists. He could not have cared less about the new baby or even the other child. The realization of being still stuck in this ride hit him with full force. He was always going to be imprisoned by Grant, he had to still care for Grant Jr., and now he had to care for a new child. He thought about all this, and now anger started to mix in with the grief.

"Elizabeth, dear, now that you are awake, they will be bringing the baby in. It's a little girl, but first I must tell you something, and it is not going to be easy."

Before Mildred could continue, he heard the door open, and Grant walked in, looked at Mildred, and asked, "Have you told her yet?"

Janusz looked over to his left and saw Mildred starting to cry, but she managed to wipe her eyes and said, "Oh dear, please don't be upset, it doesn't make you any less of a woman."

Now Janusz was confused. "What are you talking about?"

Grant put his hand on Janusz' leg. "You were bleeding, and the doctors could not stop it, so they had to give you an operation called a hysterectomy or else you would have died."

Janusz thought about this for a moment and wanted to make sure he understood the situation. "So this means I can never have children again?"

Grant nodded his head solemnly. "I'm sorry, but that is what it means."

Janusz remembered turning his head after that and feeling an intense surge of joy. He would never have to give birth to any more babies from this monster.

Grant walked to the door, opened it, and motioned for someone to come in. Soon, a nurse carrying the newborn child walked in and stopped at the foot of the bed. Janusz closed his eyes and muttered a prayer under his breath; he prayed this child would not be a Rider.

As the nurse placed the child in Janusz' arms, he knew immediately. He felt the same disgust as he did with Grant Jr. and the feeling told Janusz the child was not a Rider.

It was just a child with whom he would feel no connection, just like Grant Jr.

CHAPTER 21

31 JULY 1950

"Wake up. If you think you are going to lay on your ass all day, you are sadly mistaken."

Janusz rubbed the sleep out of his eyes, propped himself up on his elbows, and looked at Grant. "What time is it? It's still dark out."

"It's time for you to get up and prepare my clothes, which, by the way, you should have done last night."

Janusz didn't move, still dazed from the deep sleep, and tried to make sense of everything. Grant grabbed the blanket from the bed and threw it across the room. Janusz knew better than to stay in bed any longer, as Grant could be just as violent when he was hung-over as when he was drunk. "I'm sorry; what do you need me to do?"

"I've already prepared my clothes for the fishing trip, no thanks to you, but I need you to make sure my suit is impeccable for the business dinner tonight."

"Ok, Grant."

The man walked over to Janusz, grabbed him by the chin, which elicited a small cry from Janusz' mouth and said, "And don't think about sending it down to the hotel laundry. YOU do it, and do it right. Also, tonight at least pretend you are a caring wife. The last thing I need is for these men to think I have a listless idiot for a wife."

Janusz didn't have a chance to answer before Grant turned around and walked out of the hotel room, slamming the door behind him. Janusz looked over at the clock on the desk and saw the time was 5:30. Grant would not be back for another 12 hours, or at least that was what he had said. Janusz had no idea how long fishing trips lasted, and he doubted Grant knew either.

A deep sigh escaped his lungs as he looked at the bed. He could climb back in bed; after all, he was in Chicago, and the children were staying with Mildred, so Janusz could sleep for as long as he wanted. He looked out the window and saw the sky changing from a deep purple to a rust orange as the sun prepared to make its appearance for the first time that day.

He walked over to the window and put his hand on the glass. He questioned whether or not he wanted to waste any time in bed as this was the first day of freedom he had had in years. And most of all--today was his birthday. Not his fake birthday which everybody would celebrate tomorrow but the day 100 years ago in which he was born Janusz Zalewski.

He decided against the bed and walked into the bathroom. As he looked in the mirror, he laughed at the absurdity of the situation and said, "For a damned old fool, you don't look half bad for 100."

When he came out of the bathroom, he noticed Grant had set aside the suit for dinner later that night. For a moment he debated whether or not he should iron it right now or put it off until later. "Better do it now," he said. The vision of what would happen if Grant came back early and the clothes were not done popped in his head, and it was not pleasant. He plugged the iron in and walked back over to the window while it warmed, and he looked at the colors the sunrise painted on Lake Michigan.

He glanced up at the clouds in the sky hanging over the lake and smiled. A few clouds always made the sky look better during sunrise and sunset, for that matter. The only thing that would make him happier was if the clouds later decided to turn into a thunderstorm while Grant was in the middle of the lake and caused some of those 20-foot waves that had claimed numerous boats, and sometimes ships, on the Great Lakes.

At the ironing board, he licked his finger and tested the iron. When it made a slight "hiss," he knew it was ready; he picked up the iron and started with the pants while he still thought about the man's death. Not today, or anytime in the future, but at some point, he would see Grant die, and Janusz would keep on living. Although Janusz didn't know who the actual winner would be, Grant or him. In truth, Grant could be gone for many years, and Janusz would still have to live with the memory of what the man had done.

Once Janusz finished the pants, he inspected them and knew they were good. He carefully put them on a hanger as to not wrinkle them and started with the shirt. He tried not to anger Grant, but lately everything he did angered the man. The change started after the second child, once Grant knew he had no chance of having another son. The beatings began soon after; although on a positive note, Grant had zero interest in sex anymore. Well, at least not with Janusz; Grant's secretary was another story, but honestly, Janusz could not be happier. She could screw the man all she wanted.

The real problems had started, however, when Grant's father decided to run for President and Grant had to take over the company. He wasn't ready for it. Grant had been given everything in his life and had never been challenged. Now that he ran the company, he was continually challenged. Then, after his father lost the bid for the presidency, tensions between the two men began to increase.

Janusz knew whenever Grant had had a bad day because he would hit him with a closed fist.

Next, Janusz hung up the pressed shirt and grabbed the shoes to give them a good shine. As he did this, he thought about how easy it should be at the company. The war had been very profitable for his father, so in reality, all Grant had to do was keep things going; but he would screw it up most of the time. Like this meeting tonight--Janusz overheard Grant's dad laying into him about not messing this deal up and how it must be done with no mistakes.

Janusz smiled as he put the shoes down and thought that maybe a beating would be worth it to see Grant fail tonight. He walked over to the window and knew it did not matter either way. The view in front of him shook the negative thoughts out of his head, and he remembered the real reason he was here...music.

Janusz had heard of the music coming out of Chicago and he was fascinated by it. He had managed to find a few records (which he had to hide from Grant), and he loved it. It reached into his soul and spoke to him. So after straightening up the room and having lunch, he made his way down into the heart of where he would find this music called The Blues.

Janusz began to notice people staring at him as he strolled through some of the neighborhoods, but he paid it no mind. His mission pushed him on and finally, even though it was a bit early, he passed a door and heard the melodies that he wanted. He stopped in his tracks, turned towards the door and entered; although he did not know it yet, his life was about to be changed forever.

A little way through the entrance, Janusz saw a staircase leading down. He could hear the music coming up from there, so he descended. The bottom of the stairs opened to a room with a bar, a stage, and space for maybe 30 people, although it was only about half full at this time. It was dark and hard to breathe as the smoke hung in low, thick clouds.

At that moment, Janusz began to feel a bit nervous as the 15 or so patrons all turned their heads and stared at him. Even the band looked a little surprised, although they did not miss a beat and kept playing. Janusz almost turned and ran back up the stairs as it dawned on him that he was the only white face in the place.

He thought about what waited for him back at the hotel, and the dinner this evening, so he forced up the nerve to stay. He walked across the bar much like someone who was walking on an old bridge that could give out at any moment. He found an open table and sat down. Everybody still stared at him, and now he wondered if this was a mistake, but then the music hit him.

No, not hit him--*smashed him*. The chords seemed to speak to him, and when the singer belted out the lyrics about the pains of life, he was all in. Janusz felt like he was part of the music. During one of the instrumental sections of the song, he noticed the singer looking over at the barmaid, making eye contact and motioning his head towards Janusz.

Within seconds the young woman came over and asked, "Would you like something to drink?"

Janusz noticed the tone was not friendly, but it wasn't hostile either, and without thinking, Janusz said, "Whiskey."

The young woman raised an eyebrow in curiosity and said, "As you wish" and turned towards the bar.

Janusz directed his attention to the stage again and dove back into the music. A bit later he looked to his left and saw the glass of whiskey there and was amazed that he hadn't seen the young girl come back; the music had taken over him.

He picked up the glass of warm whiskey, put it to his lips and took a small sip. The taste was like a harsh fire that burned all the way down. A moment later he took another swallow, this time closing his eyes and let the burning feeling mix with the music. He had never felt so alive as he had at that moment.

Janusz had no idea how long he had been listening to the music, but he was snapped out of his trance when the melodies stopped, and the singer stood up from the stool he sat on and said they were going to take a break. Almost as if a switch had been flicked, once the music stopped, he was back in the real world. He began to feel nervous and a bit out of place again, and told himself that it was probably a good idea if he left.

Right before he was about to stand up, the slightly overweight man that had been singing a few moments earlier on stage sat down on the chair across from Janusz at the table. Janusz froze and looked at the man who said nothing at first. He wore a hat cocked to one side and had a cigarette dangling out of the corner of his mouth. He also held a glass of whiskey in each of his hands.

The man set one of the glasses down in front of Janusz, took a long drag off his cigarette, and placed it down in the ashtray in the middle of the table. The man still said nothing; he only stared at Janusz with a strange look. He exhaled a thick cloud of smoke, adding to the fog that was in the room and said, "You don't belong here."

Janusz could feel all eyes on him in the room. He became more nervous and trembled. "I'm sorry; I was about to leave."

The man picked his cigarette back up, tilted his head back and took another drag while looking at Janusz with probing eyes. He exhaled again and said, "That's not what I mean. I *mean* you don't belong here, do you?"

The man picked up his whiskey and held it in the air towards Janusz. For a moment Janusz did nothing, but then he picked up his glass also, and the two knocked them together, and the man said, "To not belonging here."

Janusz took a sip while the man knocked his back in one gulp and looked towards the bar, holding up two fingers. When he turned his gaze back to Janusz, he asked, "So why does a pretty white woman with a rich husband and the eyes of an old soul know every chord progression I am playing up there?"

"I...I like music."

"Lady, don't bullshit me. Everybody likes music, but you *know* music and not the type of music a rich white lady would learn on a Saturday afternoon while her teacher taught her Mozart."

Janusz' eyes widened and not because the man had sworn at him, but because he was talking *to* him and not *at* him. Nobody had really talked to Janusz since the gypsy girl.

The man said, "I tell you what, let me introduce myself. They call me Buckets and I have 20 more minutes until I go back on, so why don't you tell me your story."

And that is precisely what Janusz did. He started to talk, and everything poured out of him, except for of course that he was a "Rider." He felt at ease with Buckets, and during the whole time, Buckets never interrupted him except for when Janusz told the story of when Grant broke the guitar. When Janusz finished, he noticed there were two more glasses in front of him, both empty.

Then Buckets said, "Well, I think we found a good name for you--*Strings*."

Strings, Janusz thought. He liked it and pondered on it for a moment. Then the music started back up, and Janusz noticed that Buckets was not at the table anymore, but back on the stage.

After the first song finished, Buckets spoke into the microphone. "Ladies and gentlemen, we have a very special guest with us tonight. She is an old soul that was born with the blues inside of her. Please give a warm welcome to Lady Strings."

Janusz' mouth dropped open, and he wondered if he had heard correctly as he sat there staring at the stage. Buckets said, "Well come on now, I have an extra old beat up six string here with your name on it."

Something awoke inside of Janusz; he felt his legs pick him up off the chair and move him to the stage. He felt his hand reach out and take the guitar from Buckets and that old surge of energy was back. Before the band started playing, Buckets said, "We'll keep the first one simple to let you get a feel for it." He turned to the band and said, "Simple blues progression in e minor."

Janusz felt all his troubles melt away; he was like a man who had been held under water until he almost passed out, only to come to the surface again, able to breathe. He jumped right in and followed the progression and added a few parts of his own. Then came the next song, and the next, and the next. Janusz played with the band for the rest of the night; the parts he knew, he would play, and what he didn't, he would skip that bar and jump in when he got the pattern down.

It was the best time of his life, and when they played the last song, he felt a pang of heartbreak.

He looked at Buckets and asked, "That's it?"

"Yup, it's closing time, Strings."

Panic set in. "What time is it?"

"It's midnight."

Janusz gasped. "Midnight, oh my God, I've got to get home," and he started to walk off the stage.

Buckets grabbed his arm and said, "Not alone you don't."

Janusz looked at Buckets. "What do you mean?"

"What I mean is that you ain't going walking back to your fancy hotel by yourself. I'm gonna have my two nephews walk you back until it's safe for you."

"Oh," Janusz said, "Ok."

Before Janusz left the bar, Buckets called out, "Hey Strings, you have a talent in you that is on fire; don't let no man or anybody put that out."

1 AUGUST 1950
1 A.M.

As Janusz walked home, the nephews said nothing to him except for a few pleasantries, which allowed his mind to run wild. Janusz could feel that he was drunk and the closer they got to the hotel, the more he began to worry. Grant was going to be angry, and he had no idea what to tell him.

The only hope that Janusz had was that maybe Grant would be so drunk that he would be passed out and he could deal with this in the morning.

No matter what happened, though, Janusz didn't care. Grant could beat him, and it would be worth it. Janusz had felt like a person with a purpose that night, and that was something he had not felt in a long time.

As soon as they reached the bridge about a half of a mile from the hotel, one of Buckets' nephew's said, "Ma'am, this is as far as we can go, you'll be fine from here," and they disappeared into the night. Janusz continued walking onto the bridge and stopped right in the middle. He looked over the edge and watched the current of the Chicago River pass underneath him. He took a deep breath and enjoyed the soft sound of the river flowing below.

He liked it here, in this spot. It was nothing like his beloved St. Agnes River back in his city, but he still liked it. Unfortunately, the peaceful moment did not last long. An angry voice from behind him rang out. "Where in the fuck have you been?"

Janusz turned around, stumbled a bit, and saw the angry, drunken face of Grant.

"Grant," he said, but didn't get to say much more as Grant punched him in the face. Janusz fell to the ground and felt his vision blur. Grant quickly picked him up and asked, "Are you drunk? What kind of mother comes home at 1 in the morning plastered?"

Janusz tried to reply but found it difficult as blood pooled in his mouth, but finally managed to say, "I was listening to music, and then they let me play." He tried to convey how good it felt to Grant, to explain himself. Then he held his left hand up and fingered a chord in the air and said, "I played the guitar again," as he smiled through bloodstained teeth.

His explanation did the opposite of making Grant understand--it enraged him. He grabbed Janusz' fingers and twisted them. Janusz heard a snap and felt pain shoot up his arm and let out a cry that echoed throughout the bridge. Grant looked around to see if anybody had heard, but they were alone.

Grant's anger grew by the moment. "I know what they do in those clubs. How many times did you spread your legs?"

"Grant, I didn't; I just played."

"Don't fucking lie to me," said Grant as he slammed Janusz against the side of the bridge. Janusz' head hit a steel beam and split open. Blood started to pour out of his wound faster than Janusz thought possible and pooled on the ground at their feet.

The blood seemed to anger Grant even more, and he shouted, "Did you suck their cocks? Huh, you whore?" When Janusz didn't answer, Grant slammed him into the side of the bridge again. Janusz' head felt like it was attached to an over-cooked piece of spaghetti and flopped around as Grant continued to slam him into the side of the bridge while screaming, "Did you suck their cocks?" over and over.

The blood at their feet created a slickness on the ground around them, and when Grant went to slam Janusz into the bridge again, he lost his footing. Grant fell on his back, but Janusz hit the rail of the bridge and felt his feet go up in the air. The momentum took him over the side, and he had no strength even to try to reach his hand out to stop from falling.

As Janusz fell, his head hit a beam on the way down, which engulfed him in blackness. When his body hit the water, he woke for only a moment before slowly sinking in the river. The water filled his lungs and he no longer felt any pain, and the familiar blackness came for him again, and he knew that this "Ride" was over.

CHAPTER 22

31 JULY 1959
THE FOURTH RIDE
"WILLIAM"

Once all the students had taken their seats after the lunch break, Janusz decided he would do it. He had chickened out in the morning, but time was slipping away, and if he didn't act now, he would lose his chance. He started to raise his hand, and the teacher turned her back to write something on the blackboard, so he lowered it again. He asked himself again if he wanted to do this, but he knew the answer; if he was ever going to put what had happened behind him, he was going to have to confront it.

Janusz took a deep breath and reminded himself that no matter what body he currently occupied, he was a 109-year-old man, and he needed to start acting like it. So when the teacher turned back towards the class, he raised his hand.

When the teacher saw whom the hand belonged to, she froze for a second, and at that moment, Janusz could see the aversion she had towards him. The teacher quickly regained her composure and asked, "Mr. Edwards, is there something I can help you with?"

"Yes, Ma'am, I'm not feeling well."

"What's wrong with you, child?"

"My stomach and head hurt; it started this morning and has gotten worse throughout the day."

The teacher stared at him for a moment too long, which made the mood in the room uncomfortable. Janusz knew the teacher did not like him and not because of anything he ever did, but simply because he was Janusz. She could tell something was off about him. Eventually though, the teacher finished with the probing look and said, "Well, you have already done all the work, so I suppose you can go. But let me tell you one thing, boy, you go straight home, because if I hear a word otherwise, I'll tan your hide."

Janusz could hear a couple of other students murmuring in jealousy as he was given permission to leave; they wanted to do the same. He was different from them though, and not just in the obvious way; he didn't need to be in summer school. He only went because he had skipped ahead two grades, and the school said it would be a good thing to prepare him. Janusz went along with it mostly because it gave William Sr. and Barbara peace of mind. In truth, he could have skipped ahead much more, but he didn't want to draw unnecessary attention to himself.

Janusz nodded his small head and said, "Yes, ma'am." He walked out of the classroom, and he could feel the teacher's eyes boring into him. He maintained this slow march until he was well out of sight of the school before he started to run. If he wanted to make it to his destination before he was expected back at home, he could not spare any time.

He ran and ran until he could see it, and then he could feel his legs slowing down until they stopped. He breathed hard, but Janusz wasn't sure if that was because of the sprinting, or what he saw. He felt as if he couldn't move, like his feet were encased in cement, and he looked down to make sure. Then he shook his head and told himself he was silly.

Even though he knew nothing was wrong with his feet, he still wasn't moving. So he made a deal with himself; he would walk ten steps and stop. So he began and counted, "jeden, dwa, trzy." It struck him as funny that he still counted and thought of numbers in Polish. Although he never said it out loud, in his mind, he couldn't change that. So he continued to ten and stopped. He found he was breathing hard again, so he closed his eyes, calmed himself, and continued to walk while counting.

Finally, he was there, standing in the middle of the bridge--in fact, on the same spot where he had died nine years ago. Of all the times Janusz had died, his death on the last "Ride" haunted him the most. He tried not to think about that night too much, but on this day it was always hard. He re-thought that; he had not just died, *he had been murdered*. He was tired of the nightmares and the thoughts of not only what had happened, but also of what had occurred during the years he was married to Grant. He became mad...no... downright furious. It was not fair that the monster kept getting to invade him. Lately, Janusz had been getting more angry than scared. Not only was today the only birthday he felt was real, but he also considered today his rebirth. Today was the day that Buckets had opened his eyes to the power of music and Janusz had had enough of Grant taking that away from him.

Janusz decided to face the demon. He looked at the railing where Grant had bashed his head in and stared at it. It was just a railing, and he reached out his hand and touched it. What he wanted to do was throw Grant out of his thoughts much like Janusz was thrown over that railing nine years ago. He could feel a surge go through him as he ran his hand over the spot and something clicked inside of him. Grant was not allowed to control him anymore. Janusz knew he would never be able to forget, but he was not going to let the memories terrorize him anymore; instead, he was going to use them as fuel to feed that fire inside of him that Buckets had started nine years ago. Janusz opened his eyes, smiled, and said, "You lose, asshole," and began to run back to his home.

While he ran, Janusz thought with excitement about the next day. Tomorrow, his "parents," William Sr. and Barbara would be celebrating his birthday (or what he considered the day the new "Ride" started) along with what he imagined the whole rest of the family. As he ran, he hoped and prayed he would get the gift that he wanted. Janusz knew it was a lot to ask for, as the family did not have much money, but if he got this, he would never ask William and Barbara for anything ever again.

In the distance, he could see the unofficial border of this neighborhood leading into the next when something struck him across the chest, knocking him to the ground. He didn't understand what had happened and struggled to regain his breath. Next, somebody picked him up off his feet and pulled him into a nearby alley where he was thrown against a wall, and a harsh voice asked, "What are you doing here?"

Janusz still could not catch his breath, let alone talk, as he looked into the hard face of a police officer standing in front of him. He felt a hard crack across his face. "I asked you what in the fuck are you doing in this neighborhood."

Janusz caught his breath, but he still wasn't able to say anything. He couldn't understand why this man, and a police officer at that, was beating on him when he had done nothing wrong.

The policeman grabbed Janusz by the shirt with his big right hand and lifted him off the ground a couple of inches and slammed him into the brick wall. "What are you, fucking stupid? Deaf and mute? Or guilty?"

Janusz' eyes widened and asked, "Guilty?"

The cop said, "Guilty, just as I thought."

"No, I didn't do anything," pleaded Janusz.

"What did you steal?"

"I haven't stolen anything!"

The policeman laughed as he set Janusz back on the ground but still held firmly onto his shirt. He repeated what Janusz had said, slowly enunciating the words as he looked at the cop standing next to him. The police officer then turned back to Janusz and asked, "Where did you learn to talk like that?"

It had never occurred to Janusz to be quiet; after all, he hadn't done anything. "In school, because in this case, one should use the present perfect verb tense."

The cop smacked Janusz across the face, which jarred the inside of his head. He was now scared; the police officer was acting irrationally. He couldn't understand why he was so angry with him. Janusz looked to the other officer; he seemed unsure and uncomfortable but said and did nothing. The second that Janusz locked eyes with him, the quiet police officer broke eye contact and looked down shamefully.

The angry police officer began to speak again, "So you learned that in one of your lessons, huh? Well, you're in luck today, because you are going to learn a lesson you will never forget."

The policeman punched Janusz in the face again, and he lost the ability to stand on his legs. The man still had a good grip on him and pinned him against the wall where he delivered another blow to the face, followed by a harder one to the stomach. After the last blow, the officer let go of Janusz and he collapsed to the ground and curled up into a ball.

Once on the ground, the officer bent over and kept punching him. Janusz thought he was never going to stop, but after the fifth punch, the younger policeman grabbed his arm and said, "Enough."

The older cop pulled his arm out of his grip but didn't hit Janusz anymore; instead, he leaned even closer to Janusz' face and said, "You maggots got to learn, this isn't your neighborhood. You need to stay with your kind on the Southside."

Janusz stayed curled up into a ball with his eyes closed, but he knew the cop was still in his face cause he could smell the stench of whiskey. The man said, "I don't give a shit if people say things are changing; as long as I am alive, your kind will never be welcome here."

Janusz was afraid that the cop was going to hit him again, but he didn't. He heard the sound of the cop spitting, and soon after, the feel of it landed in his hair. Then he heard the footsteps of the two men walking out of the alley. He didn't move; he stayed there in a ball, shaking.

When he was sure they were gone, he opened his eyes and saw that he was alone in the alley. He managed to stand up and started to make the long walk home as pain shot through him with every step.

Once he reached his house, he saw William Sr.'s mother sitting on the porch in her favorite rocking chair. Janusz had never seen the old woman move fast before, but she stood up quickly when she saw him limping up the sidewalk.

"Lord, child, what happened to you?" she cried.

Her voice was loud and shrill, and this caused Barbara to come outside. When she saw Janusz, she ran down the stairs, put her arms around him, and helped him inside. She sat him down on one of the chairs around the old table in the kitchen and immediately fetched some rags and began to clean him up.

By this time William Sr.'s mother had appeared and placed her hands on each side of Janusz' face. "What did you get yourself into, boy?" Janusz said nothing, but he did feel tears forming in his eyes.

A moment later Janusz saw William Sr. come into the room, rubbing his eyes, obviously waking up from the usual afternoon nap he took when coming home from work. When he saw Janusz, he stopped dead in his tracks. "Jesus, Jr. What in God's name happened to you?"

Janusz dropped his head into his hands. He felt a gentle touch on his shoulder and guessed it was William Sr's mother. "It's ok, child; you're safe now."

After a moment he lifted his head and told them everything. During the whole story, William Sr's mother never took her hand off his shoulder, and this seemed to comfort him and gave him the strength to continue. When he finished, Barbara looked horrified, but William Sr. looked annoyed. The look puzzled Janusz; why would William Sr. be annoyed with him?

William Sr. let out an audible breath. "Boy, what in the hell were you doing way over on that side of town?'

"I only wanted to see the bridge. I did nothing wrong and had every right to be there."

William Sr. paced back and forth in the kitchen and said, "You know, you are going to be the death of me."

Barbara spoke up and said, "William, please, he is upset."

"Yeah, well he should be upset." The tone in his voice must have told Barbara this was not the time and she said no more. William Sr. stopped pacing and turned to Janusz. "You know, Jr., you walk around in this world like you are entitled to things or at the very least, you forget who you are. You are a young black child, and if you don't start learning the ways of the world soon, you won't be long in it."

Janusz didn't want to say anything, but he couldn't help himself. "I didn't do anything wrong."

William Sr. took a deep breath like he was going to say something but stopped, shook his head, and walked out the door. Barbara walked over to Janusz, pulled out one of the other chairs, and sat in front of him. She took his hands in hers and said, "Look, baby, your father worries about you. You need to understand that it doesn't matter if you were doing anything or not; you were in a place where some people did not want you to be."

Janusz stared at her.

Her face turned serious, and she said, "Some people are going to hate you because you have dark skin and you always need to remember that."

Janusz nodded his head, and Barbara kissed him on the forehead and said, "Why don't you go lie down for a bit, and I'll come to get you when dinner is ready."

Janusz said nothing, he just nodded and went to his bed and collapsed. He didn't get any sleep, but he did think... a lot.

CHAPTER 23

1 AUGUST 1959
8 A.M.

Janusz sprang out of bed and could not believe the day had finally arrived. Once his feet touched the floor, he winced, and soon pain flowed through his entire body. He then remembered the interaction with the cop and the beating. He shook off the pain as much as he could, and the events of the previous day faded as the excitement of the present day flooded through him.

Normally he hated these birthdays, especially in the Edwards house. Every single relative in the Chicago area would be at the house for the entire day, and each would want to talk to him no matter how uncomfortable anybody was.

Today was different, though, today he might get *it* and if that meant talking to people that felt uncomfortable around him, so be it.

He wasted no time putting his clothes on and heading downstairs. Barbara had already been up for what Janusz guessed to be an hour cooking and preparing things for the party. As soon as he walked into the kitchen, she turned around, and her face lit up.

"Happy birthday, Jr." she said, and proceeded directly over to hug him.

Next, William Sr. came over and put his hand on Janusz' shoulder. "Happy birthday, son, how does it feel to be 9?"

Janusz smiled, but not because of the sentiments they gave him, but because he wondered what their faces would look like if they knew he was a 109-year-old man. "I feel good."

William Sr.'s face turned serious, and he said, "Son, sit down, I want to talk to you while you eat."

Janusz did as he was told and prepared to meet William Sr.'s words with the response that would appease him.

"I want you to know I wasn't really mad with you yesterday, but I need you to understand the dangers we face out there." William Sr. paused and looked out the window and Janusz wasn't sure if he should say something now or not, but William Sr. continued. "It's just I worry about you. Maybe someday we will be able to walk in any neighborhood without the fear of somebody attacking us for our skin color, but we are not there yet." William Sr. leaned in and took Janusz' hands in his own. "I need you to understand that."

Janusz knew now was the time to speak. "I do, sir."

William Sr. kept ahold of his hands for a few moments longer than Janusz cared for while looking into his eyes and said, "Good, now enough of this sad talk. We have a birthday party to get going, and you know your relatives are going to show up with their appetites."

2 p.m.

Janusz squirmed in his seat as he waited for the moment William Sr. would tell everybody to quiet down, and then make an announcement, and give him the gift. He could not hold out much longer. Every time he thought it would happen, Barbara brought out some new plate of food or something. He was sure she had prepared enough food for the entire Southside of Chicago, and they had shown up. There was so much talking, laughing, and games; it was overwhelming. After a while, he found a place to hide so he would not have to talk to anybody.

While he hid, he eavesdropped on other peoples' conversations and listened to them say, "Why don't that boy have any friends of his own here, that's not right" and "That boy is strange, there is something about him that is off, he doesn't act like no 9 year old I ever met." Of course, this would be out of earshot of either William Sr. or Barbara as this would have upset them. In reality, they agreed with everybody; they just couldn't admit it to themselves yet.

It didn't bother him, though; by then Janusz was used to it and all things being equal, William Sr. and Barbara were good people. They were honest, hardworking, and they treated Janusz well, and that was all he could ask.

Finally, the cake was brought out and after they ate it, the time he had been waiting for arrived--the gifts. Not many people had brought gifts, but that was fine with Janusz. He only wanted one, which he hoped would come from William Sr. and Barbara. Finally, after Janusz accepted some small trinkets from his family, William Sr. stood up and got everybody's attention.

"Ok, everybody, as you all know, Jr...well, he can be a peculiar child." William Sr. paused for a moment as everybody laughed, and then continued. "And every year since this child could talk, all he asked for was a guitar."

Here it comes, thought Janusz. He felt himself begin to sweat and tremble as William Sr. continued. "So, not because we are so nice, but because, well, we can't stand him asking anymore...Jr., here is what you have been asking for."

William Sr. produced an old acoustic from behind the table, and Janusz' knees shook. He ran up to grab the guitar, but William Sr. pulled it back at the last moment. "Jr., this was the best we could do, and hear me good now, the second you start to fall behind in your school lessons is the second you will never see this again."

Tears rolled down Janusz' cheeks, and he grabbed William Sr. in a huge embrace. William Sr. looked shocked for a moment and said, "Damn, if I knew this was all it was going to take for this child to show some affection, I would have gotten this long ago."

CHAPTER 24

1 DECEMBER 1969

Janusz sat in front of the TV with his family, as he imagined most of the country did. The man on the screen pulled little blue capsules out of a bin and read the birthdays; there was a loud sigh of relief every time they called out a date that was not 1 August.

As he sat there with Barbara and his two brothers and sister, he prayed for a high number. But that was not in the cards. On number 111 they called out the date "1 August." Barbara began to cry when she heard it, and Janusz stared at the TV. His stomach dropped, but he had to show strength for the sake of the family.

It had been three years since William Sr. had been taken from them in an accident at work, or at least that was what they were told. In the course of one day, Janusz' life took a completely different direction.

As everybody knew he would, Janusz had finished school early. He had his sights set on college no matter how hard it was going to be for a young black man. He didn't worry about it at all as he had already done it in his last "Ride" and succeeded splendidly. Janusz had told William Sr. he did not want to put the family in jeopardy just so he could go to college, but William Sr. would have none of it. He had said, "Boy, you are going to college even if it means I can't eat for the next few years or we have to beg, borrow, and steal."

Janusz had admired William Sr., despite the distance between them, which William Sr. tried to hide. It was apparent that the man was closer to the other children, but Janusz paid no mind. William Sr. had never overtly showed any favoritism and always treated him right. He had also shown such devotion when it came to his family; he would work himself to the bone, taking jobs where he got paid less than everybody or doing jobs nobody else wanted. They were a low-income family, segregated to the Southside of Chicago, but the children never went to bed hungry.

Then one day, a man with a fancy tie had come and knocked on the door, telling Barbara that William Sr. had been killed when a portion of a building collapsed on him. The man had given her an envelope with 200 dollars in it and a form to sign, and that was it.

A man who broke his back for his family went to work one day and didn't come home, and they received 200 dollars.

After William Sr.'s death, Barbara still insisted Janusz was going to go to school, but he knew that wasn't possible. In the end, he was needed there, with the family.

As Janusz watched the Vietnam draft numbers, he thought of William Sr. Specifically, he flashed back to the day when he received the guitar. Janusz took to heart the warning William Sr. had given him and never gave him any reason to follow through with it.

He had excelled in school, which he had finished early, but not so soon that he would have aroused suspicion, and he had never gotten into any trouble on the streets. Mischief was never a problem for him, as he didn't have the same urges other men his physical age had. Janusz chuckled to himself and realized he was a 119-year-old Polish immigrant with the body of a 19-year-old kid.

He had also never gotten into any trouble with girls, or better yet, gotten *them* in trouble. That wasn't too difficult, either; even though he was a good-looking kid, there was just something about him that repelled girls.

He didn't mind not having a girlfriend, though; as far as he was concerned, he doubted he would ever feel like having sex again.

As he sat there and the heaviness of the situation weighed on him, he wondered what William Sr. would tell him to do. Janusz was probably going to Vietnam next year, and there was a chance he would not be coming back…well, at least not as William Edwards Jr.

Since William Sr.'s death, he had been earning money for the family. He worked hard, never put up any fuss, and was honest. Breaking his back doing menial jobs didn't bother him in the least, as work may have owned him during the day, but music owned him at night. Janusz found himself in different clubs and bars almost every night of the week playing with his band. They had a massive following in Chicago, and there was serious talk of making a record. But it looked like that would be put on hold, and this was the fact that crushed him.

After the initial gasp when his number was called, everyone was silent for a few moments. Janusz sat there and realized that in 119 years, he had always managed to avoid going to war, but now it seemed inevitable. Finally, he turned to Barbara and said, "My number is not that low, Mother; there is a chance I will never be called."

CHAPTER 25

15 APRIL 1971

Janusz sat in the dingy Saigon bar jotting down songs in his book. Cheap whiskey and stale beer hung in the air, and the still, thick heat that enveloped everything only intensified the aromas. For a moment he put his pencil on the table and stopped writing to take a drink of his cola while he looked around. Nobody in the bar looked familiar to him, and even if he did recognize somebody in there, it wouldn't have mattered. He would still be sitting alone.

Business as usual, he thought, and he picked his pencil back up, but didn't start writing.

He listened to the young men talking in excited, drunken voices about how many days they had left, what they were going to do when they got back, and so on. Janusz never thought about how much time he had left; he only concentrated on the mission and when he had time, his music. Since there was no mission at the moment and he had a bit of writer's block, he did some math in his head and discovered he had 60 days left. The fact he had been in Vietnam for ten months surprised him a bit.

The military suited Janusz far better than he thought it would have. There was order, and as long as one conformed, everything else fell into place. Janusz had learned the hard way over the past 56 years what happened when he didn't conform. He shrugged and looked back down at his music book hoping for some inspiration. In 60 days he would be back in Chicago, back playing with his band…and that was the only thing that mattered. The music made everything else bearable. Stepping on stage and letting it pour out of him was better than anything he could think of and nothing bothered him when he had his guitar. Even when his draft number was called that night, all was forgotten when he had walked out on stage. Or when the orders came in the mail, the same thing, he acknowledged them and then went and played.

He took another drink of his cola and debated getting one more when he heard some familiar voices. Four guys from his unit walked in, and Janusz guessed they were looking to blow off a little steam. The guys saw him immediately, but all of them pretended not to. He chuckled to himself as the men took a table as far away from him as they could.

One of the guys, Pete, held a grudge against him because Janusz had been promoted to Sergeant. Pete hadn't been promoted, despite the fact that he had more time in the Army. They may not have liked him, but at least they obeyed him when they needed to, and that was all Janusz could ask.

The black soldiers shunned him too. At first, they just ignored him, but after he got promoted, they started calling him names like "Uncle Tom." Janusz had no idea what it meant, but he doubted it was a compliment.

Janusz swallowed the last sip of his cola and looked down at the blank pages in his notebook and back over to the guys ignoring him. He decided there was no use staying there making people uncomfortable, especially if he wasn't going to be productive, so he stood up to leave. An announcement on the Armed Forces Vietnam Network (AFVN) radio stopped him in his tracks though.

The DJ said, "And now, coming straight out of Chicago, the hottest new band in the country, Chi-town Boogie."

Janusz fell back into his chair when he heard this, and when the notes of the song started to play, he felt his stomach drop to his knees. Then, when he heard the voice of the singer, he had no doubt---it was his rhythm guitarist and back-up singer, Clarence. He was playing Janusz' song, the song that Janusz had written the day after William Sr. had died…and now Janusz sat in a miserable little bar in Vietnam listening to his best friend sing a plastic version of a song he had put so much heart and soul into.

His stomach turned inside of him and his hands shook. He couldn't believe it, but as he started to think about things, they began to make sense. He thought back to the night before he shipped out and the show they had played. A record exec had been there, and he had loved the songs; they talked about the future, but the problem was that Janusz was shipping off to Vietnam, so the exec said they would talk when (and if) Janusz returned.

He remembered Clarence disappearing at the end of the show and Janusz had caught a glimpse of him talking with the exec alone. When Clarence returned, Janusz had asked him what they were talking about, and he replied, "Brother, I wanted to let him know that nothing happens without you."

Janusz thought about the lack of communication with Clarence and the rest of the guys. When he first arrived in the country, he had received a few letters from Clarence, but as time went on, the letters became fewer and fewer. Now, he knew why.

So much for being brothers, thought Janusz.

The band and his music were the only thing that kept him going. Janusz couldn't bear the thought of seeing Clarence playing his songs throughout the country. The kicker was that Clarence wasn't even a great musician; he was an average rhythm guitar player at best, and his vocals were so engineered that Janusz wasn't sure how he was going to pull off any of the shows live.

Janusz felt like he could kill Clarence.

At that moment he noticed somebody standing next to the table. He looked up and saw his commander, Major Reynolds. Janusz sprang to his feet, but the other man waved his hands, telling him to sit back down and they both took a seat. The man looked over at the bar and motioned for a beer and turned back towards Janusz and said, "I know that look, the 'I just read the Dear John letter' look."

Janusz looked at the Major and started to say something, but stopped, and said, "Yes sir, something like that."

The man nodded his head solemnly. "Yeah, I've been there. First, they send you to this fucking place, and after a while, your girl finds somebody new, and when you rotate back, it's not any better because they hate us back there."

Janusz looked at the Major and thought, *As if I needed another reason for people to be uncomfortable around me.*

Then Major Reynolds said, "There is nothing back there for us, Sergeant, what jobs there are have been taken by the draft dodgers or those lucky fucks whose numbers never got called."

Janusz heard what the man was saying, but still couldn't reply; all he could think about was Clarence and the song he had just heard on the radio. After a slightly awkward pause, the Major said, "Look, Sergeant, let me be straight with you. You're a weird fucking guy, there is no doubt about that, but you are a good soldier. You do what you are supposed to, and the job always gets done when you are around."

"Thank you, sir."

"The men may not like you, but they respect the rank and in this fucked up situation, that's the best anybody could hope for."

Janusz looked at him and began to wonder where this was going.

"So I have a proposition for you, Sergeant, why don't you extend here for another year. I'll bump you up a rank, you'll get a sign on bonus, and I will see what I can do about getting you some extra overseas pay."

Janusz thought about the prospect of staying here another year, which would allow him to send more money back to Barbara and the family. Finally, he thought about going back to Chicago and what he would do.

The only thing he envisioned back in Chicago was killing Clarence, which would probably land him in prison.

So before the Major could do any more convincing, Janusz said, "I'll do it."

CHAPTER 26

7 MARCH 1972

Everybody was in a sour mood, Janusz included. He and his squad had just returned from a week out on patrol with no break, and now they had to provide extra security for an incoming Distinguished Visitor on base. As Janusz and Major Reynolds stood next to the helipad, they could hear the blades whirling in the distance. Janusz looked at the Major and asked, "Sir, do you have any intel on who this is?"

The Major shook his head. "Not really. Word around the Officers' mess is that he is some asshole politician's son or grandson, I don't fucking know."

Janusz' heart started to race, but he told himself he was being stupid. There was no way Grant could be here. Janusz did the math; Grant would be in his mid-fifties, but Janusz could not kick that thought out of his head that it could be possible. He knew Generals in their fifties.

Just as his thoughts began to take him to some dark places, the voice of the Major pulled him back into reality. "Word is that he is some fucking bean counter doing inventory. I heard he managed to dodge the draft for a while, but then the political pressure on his family became too much, so he got a commission and now he's spending a few hours in the country so he can get his ribbon."

"Of course only in heavily guarded areas," said Janusz.

The Major nodded with a half grin. Both men shielded their eyes as the helicopter prepared to touch down. Shortly after the landing gear made contact with the ground, five men jumped out. One of the men shouted something to the engineer in the helicopter, and the man nodded while the other gave a thumb up.

As the men walked towards them, Janusz began to shake, and his stomach started to feel uneasy. When the men were within ten feet, Janusz could see the Captain's face; clearly, it was Grant. He didn't know how it was possible, but there he was. The entourage of men stopped in front of them and the Major said some greetings.

The helicopter disappeared into the distance, and the voices of the men could be heard. Grant barely acknowledged Janusz, directing all of his attention to the Major. As Grant spoke with him, Janusz noticed something was different. The voice was wrong; it was a bit deeper than what Janusz had remembered. Also, it appeared as if Grant had grown; he wondered how that could be possible. Janusz stared into the face \ and realized it wasn't Grant--not entirely--but it was a part of him.

Janusz stared at the son he had given birth to--a product of rape, agony, and pain.

Grant Jr. looked at Janusz and said something that he could not understand. Grant Jr. spoke again and louder. "Sergeant, are you alright?" He reached his hand out to Janusz' shoulder. As soon as Janusz felt the hand, he recoiled, took a step back, doubled over, and vomited.

The Major quickly moved to Janusz' side. "Are you alright?"

"I'm sorry, sir. Must have been something I ate. Permission to return to quarters?"

"Granted."

As Janusz walked away from the men, he heard Grant Jr. say, "Some men aren't built for war."

CHAPTER 27

8 MARCH 1972

The Major came to check on Janusz early in the morning. Janusz had already been up for quite a while, but had not eaten breakfast; he didn't want to run the risk of seeing Grant Jr. He was still shaken up a bit, but at least he had control of himself again.

"Are you feeling better? What the hell was that out there yesterday?" the Major asked.

"Must be the local food, sir," Janusz replied and smiled.

"Ok, why don't we stick to chow hall food from now on."

"No problem, sir."

The Major was not a man for small talk, and while Janusz did believe he was there to check on him, he imagined there was also some official business as well, and he was right. "Look, Sergeant, I'll be straight with you. We both know this war is unwinnable, but it looks like there is going to be one last big push."

Janusz looked at him and wondered where this was going.

"Starting tomorrow we are going to be sending out patrols to recon some areas, but I know you, as well as your guys, have done more than your fair share, so I want to offer you a light duty which should keep you and your guys safe, at least until they rotate back to the world."

Janusz looked at him and wondered what kind of light duty he meant. "Sir, I'll do whatever mission you need."

The Major put his hand up in the air. "Yes, I know, but I thought I would give you a choice on this one."

"Ok, what is it?"

"Well, you would basically be a babysitter for that shithead Captain you almost puked on yesterday."

Janusz did not like the sound of that at all.

The Major sighed and said, "I'm not going to lie; that guy is a top-notch fucking asshole. He is arrogant and entitled. Just because his grandfather is some senator who ran for president once, he thinks he is in charge of everything."

Janusz was silent for a moment and thought before answering. On the one hand, he could skate out some time, not put himself in any danger, and more, importantly, keep his guys out of danger.

But there was no way Janusz could be around Grant Jr.; it was too difficult, so he asked, "Sir, now may I be honest with you?"

"Of course."

"I figure I'll see enough assholes with hidden agendas when I rotate back to the world, so if it's all the same, I'd rather take the patrol."

The Major nodded his head. "As you wish, Sergeant. You guys hit the road tomorrow morning." The Major got up to leave but stopped at the door and looked at Janusz. "At least with the VC there is no hidden agenda; you know they only want to kill you."

"Roger that, sir."

CHAPTER 28

9 MARCH 1972

The mission pissed off every man in the squad, even the guys who usually didn't hassle Janusz too much. In addition to the low morale, Janusz felt guilty. He was putting the lives of his guys in danger for the simple reason he couldn't stand to be around Grant Jr. It angered Janusz that after all these years, and after the fact that Grant Sr. had murdered him, he was still finding ways to make his life difficult.

As they made their way through the jungle, Janusz wrestled with the idea of whether or not he should tell them it had been his choice to take the recon mission but decided not to. He told himself that it would distract the men from the mission, but in truth, he didn't believe that to be true. It was more because of fear.

The men complained non-stop. Some of them didn't care if Janusz heard and said, "If we had a white squad leader, our asses would not be out here" or "Spineless asshole has no backbone to stand up to the brass." Luckily, over the past 122 years, Janusz' skin had grown pretty thick.

Just when Janusz thought the jungle was never going to end, the squad stumbled upon a small village. The scout went to do a quick stop, and it seemed the village would be a good resting point. No weapons or anything else of danger was in the place, and hardly any men as they were probably all off fighting. He then wondered for which side but decided not to dwell on it.

The squad secured the perimeter, and Janusz gave the order that they would sleep there tonight, and the men happily obeyed. All was calm until he heard some voices speaking, one in broken English, and the other a native English speaker who was one of his men. Janusz got up to see what was going on, and when he turned the corner, he saw four of his men talking to a Vietnamese man with a young woman by his side.

"What's going on here?" asked Janusz.

Pete, one of the guys in his squad, said, "Well, Sarg, we are doing a little bartering for some relaxation time."

Janusz looked at the Vietnamese man with the girl. He seemed determined and was holding on to the girl's arm tightly. Janusz next looked at the woman, her eyes full of fear. She was trying to take her mind to another place, but she must have been new at this because she couldn't do it. Janusz knew that look; he had had it many times before.

"Absolutely not," he said.

"What do you mean? Unless you want to pull rank and go first."

"That's not what we are here for."

Pete started to get angry and wore a look on his face that Janusz also knew, not from having it himself, but from looking up at Grant as he was being violated. "Fuck this," Pete said. "If I am going on some bullshit mission to get my ass shot off, then I am going in with a little stank on my thing." The group broke out in laughter, and Pete walked towards the girl.

Janusz stepped in front of him, grabbed him by the shirt, and threw him to the earth. Pete got up quickly and raised his hand back to hit Janusz, but Janusz held his ground and said, "I'm not some defenseless woman that you can push around, so unless you want me to give you a beating in front of all these people, you will stand down, soldier."

Janusz didn't know if he was talking to Grant right now or Pete. He was unsure of what was going to happen next, but by the look in Pete's eyes, he knew the man was going to back down.

"Fuck this," Pete said as he walked by Janusz, hitting his shoulder with his.

Janusz' entire body shook, but held it together as he said, "Everybody except for those on watch, hit the rack. We head out at first light tomorrow."

Janusz turned to go, but before he did, he locked eyes with the young woman, and he saw relief in them. He only hoped that others would not come behind him and extinguish it.

CHAPTER 29

Janusz and the squad walked along the desolate trail in silence. He couldn't believe how quiet the entire mission had been. They had seen no enemy soldiers, and hardly any villages along the route, and Janusz found himself yearning for a little bit of excitement. Not only would it take his mind off his stolen songs being played across the country, but it also would keep him and the other guys sharp. Too much nothingness led to complacency, and complacency could mean death.

A snap in the bushes caught Janusz' attention, and he froze with his right hand in the air. The entire squad looked around for any signs of movement but saw and heard nothing.

"There is nothing there, just like everywhere else on this fucking bullshit mission," Pete said.

"Keep your voice down," whispered Janusz.

Pete replied even louder, "Why? So we don't disturb the fucking trees?"

Janusz stared into Pete's eyes but said nothing. Tensions had been high since the night in the village, and Pete only spoke to Janusz when he had to, as did the rest of the squad, but as long as they did their job, Janusz didn't care. The problem was that Pete was becoming more and more insubordinate and some of the other guys in the squad were following his lead.

Janusz knew he had to address this, and sooner would be better, but all he could think about was Clarence back in Chicago and his stolen songs. He held the gaze with Pete for a moment longer and said, "Let's get over that ridge, and we will find a place to rest for a while."

"You're the boss, whatever you say."

Janusz told himself he would let Pete get away with the snide comment for now, but he would talk with him when they crossed the ridge to take a break. He took one more look around and motioned for the squad to move again.

Janusz' time in Vietnam had not been quiet, but it hadn't been terrible either. All of his missions had been successful, and he had only been involved in a handful of firefights, but nothing up close and personal. He had heard stories from some of the guys coming back from the field about the hell they faced--the bombs, the hand-to-hand combat--and he felt sorry for them.

So when they were ambushed, Janusz was unsure of what was happening for the first few moments. There were no big explosions, nobody stepped on any landmines; they were just suddenly face-to-face with the enemy. They appeared like ghosts out of thin air and began firing on them. Before the squad could react, two of the men were hit.

Finally, the realization of the situation sunk in, and Janusz returned fire along with the remaining squad. They pushed back the enemy a bit, which gave them a chance to regroup and put themselves in a better fighting position. Janusz could see there were not many of them, and they were not advancing. The enemy didn't have enough soldiers to take them, or they did not want to; either way, they could make a full retreat back.

The only problem was that two members of the squad were down, and he knew for sure one of them was still alive. He could hear cries of pain coming from Stan, and Janusz could not leave him out there. After a moment, he found Pete next to him. The man looked scared, but he was also ready to take action. "What's the plan, Sarg?"

Janusz looked at Pete and said, "I think Mike is gone, but Stan is still alive, so I got to go get him."

"You can't drag him back by yourself and return fire at the same time."

"No, but I might be able to make it if you guys cover me. There is a ridge 20 yards to the left, and if I can get behind that, I am out of their range."

Pete looked over to the ridge, then to his left, and pondered the plan. "Still too risky. We have more than enough guys for cover fire; I think we have them in numbers, or else they would have been on us by now."

Janusz knew Pete was right. "So what do you think?"

"You and I go, that way we can get Stan, and return fire, too. You go to the right and get under that ridge, I take the left and barricade myself behind that tree line."

Janusz then finished the statement for Pete. "Then squeeze them back with the help of the other guys long enough to get Stan and drag him back."

Pete nodded his head, and Janusz brought the rest of the guys into the plan, and without wasting any more time, they were in motion. Janusz admired Pete at that moment; he knew the man was scared, but he was not a coward, and he executed the maneuver flawlessly. Thanks to their position, they forced the enemy to fall back, and that gave them enough time to get to Stan and start dragging him back behind the ridge. Once they got him there, they would be home free.

When the men were a yard away from the ridge, something in the tree caught Janusz' attention. One of the VC had managed to sneak his way up, and he fired on them. Without thinking, Janusz jumped in front of Pete and felt the first stinging punch in his left shoulder. Janusz managed to get off a burst from his rifle, which sent the shooter falling from the tree, but not before he felt another hot blow shattering his knee, sending him to the ground.

Janusz looked behind him and saw that Pete had already dragged Stan behind the ridge and that he was now coming back up for him. Pete cautiously peered over the ridge and Janusz reached his hand out. Pete's hand came around, but he didn't grab Janusz; instead, he displayed his middle finger and said, "Fuck you, asshole." Next, he disappeared behind the ridge and Janusz could hear him retreating.

Janusz tried to scream out, but the pain was making everything turn dark, and before everything went black, Janusz heard Pete say to the rest of the squad, "The Sarg and Mike are toast, we got to get the fuck out of here."

1 APRIL 1972
2 P.M.

When Janusz opened his eyes he was met with that familiar sensation he had experienced three times before; he was confused, his body did not move the way it should, and there was a blinding light shining in his eyes. As with before, there was some yelling and animated talking going on, but this time he could not understand what was said.

Janusz tried to clear his head to make sense of what had happened. But as soon as his vision focused, it became apparent as he looked down the barrel of an AK-47. He was still in the jungle of Vietnam; he hadn't died when he blacked out. As the confusion left him, the pain returned. He could neither move his left arm nor his left leg. As he lay there on the ground, surrounded by faces of VC and an AK-47 pointed at his face, he began to laugh.

Maybe it was delirium, or perhaps it was something else, but he couldn't help laughing at the thought that he had started another "Ride," this time as a Vietnamese baby. What made him laugh was the idea of having to learn the language. During his time in Vietnam, he had done his best to learn as much as he could, but his duties pretty much kept him from really learning as much as he wanted to.

Then a familiar sound snapped him out of his delirium; it was the sound of a round being chambered. He stopped laughing, now thinking he was probably going to get his chance to learn Vietnamese after all, as soon as the man holding the rifle pulled the trigger.

There was some more talking, none of which he understood except for the word "No."

One of the higher-ranking VC discussed something with the others and finally, he put his hand on the barrel of the gun that was pointed at Janusz and moved it away. Although he could not understand, Janusz could tell this made the owner of the weapon very unhappy as he lowered it away from Janusz' face. The higher-ranking soldier said something else to the men, and everything went black again as the stock of an AK-47 came down on his head.

CHAPTER 30

4 APRIL 1972
3 P.M.

When Janusz opened his eyes, he closed them again trying to dip back into the dream he was having. He was with his wife, and they were at their picnic spot along the St. Agnes River looking over to Canada. There were no thoughts of any "Rides" in his head. There was also no Oakbrook, no Grant, and definitely no Vietnam.

The voices finally forced him out of the dream world and back into reality. When he opened his eyes, he was surprised to see what looked like an American man who spoke English to him. "Sergeant, can you hear me? It's time to wake up."

Janusz didn't speak but nodded his head.

"Good," said the man with a tired look on his face. "I'm Colonel Johnson, POW camp representative; I am allowed to make sure you are ok before they take you for questioning."

"Questioning? What do you mean? Where am I?"

There was some chatter from the guards amongst themselves, and one of them pushed the Colonel in the back with the butt of the rifle and said, "Hurry now" in heavily accented English.

"You're at the Hilton," the Colonel said.

Janusz' breath left him.

Everybody in Vietnam knew the Hanoi Hilton, and now Janusz wished he had been killed out there in the jungle. The stories of what happened in this place were infamous, and right now he would rather be taken back to Oakbrook than to be here.

With great care, the Colonel started to check Janusz over; the best Janusz could surmise was that it was an examination. The man began at his feet and slowly checked everything on his body. The Colonel stopped when he got to Janusz' head, looked at his ear, bending it back for a better look, and came in closer.

Quickly, he whispered, "Everybody breaks, just lie as much as you can."

The Colonel stood back up and nodded his head. "You'll live. You'll never walk the same with that knee, and your left arm is going to be for shit, but at least you'll live."

One of the Vietnamese guards then pushed the Colonel away.

The guard then looked at Janusz and said, "You answer questions now."

4:30 p.m.

Janusz lay on that table for more than an hour before anybody else except for the guard appeared in the room. Finally, the door opened, and three men walked in, one of them obviously in charge. He carried a notebook and the two others, who were close behind, each carried a tray. The man behind him to the left had food on his tray and the other to the right, a variety of instruments that Janusz surmised were going to be used to get him to talk. The two men both set down their trays on a desk and stepped away.

Only the man with the notebook spoke throughout the ordeal, and the man took his time before he said anything. He walked over to the trays and gently rubbed his fingers over the one with the cold metal instruments. Every so often the man would stop and look over his shoulder, ensuring that Janusz was watching. After a few moments of this, the man moved his hand from that tray without picking anything up and moved to the other where he picked up a glass and filled it with water.

The man slowly walked over to Janusz, holding the glass of water and looking at him. Janusz figured this was part of the act. He was thirsty and had not drunk anything for a long time. The man took a deep drink of the water and asked, "What were the orders for your squad?"

"Normal reconnaissance," Janusz replied.

"What did you find?"

"Nothing. Everything was quiet."

"Why were you sent on this mission?"

"I don't know."

The man said nothing. He folded his bottom lip in under his top row of teeth and nodded his head. Taking his time, he walked over to the desk with the two trays on it and set the glass of water down. He rolled up his shirtsleeves and grabbed one of the metal instruments.

The man's purposeful slowness drove Janusz insane. He wished the man would hurry up, and maybe even scream or yell--anything but this. Eventually, the man seemed to make up his mind. He said something to one of the guards, who immediately came over and untied Janusz' left arm.

He then came over and pulled Janusz' arm, and a flash of pain shot through his body. Janusz let out a cry, but the man didn't seem to care. Next, right near the incision where the bullet had been removed, the man took the utensil and lightly touched the area. Janusz let out a moan, but more out of fear than pain.

"Why do you fight and keep secrets for a country that doesn't care for you?" asked the man.

"I don't know why we were out there."

"The U.S. military always has a reason."

Janusz took a deep breath and said, "We were only supposed to collect what we saw and report back to the base. I'm just a Sergeant; they don't tell me anything."

The man looked at Janusz for a second before releasing his arm and walked back to the tray of utensils. He let the one he was holding in his hand drop with a loud bang that made Janusz jump, which shot more pain through his body. The man stood over the tray, looking at all the tools there for minutes before he said something to the guards and left.

One of the guards untied his other arm and brought him the tray of food, setting it down in front of him. The other picked up the tray of tools, and then both men left the room, and Janusz heard a metal clang as they locked him in. He sat there for a few moments, certain they were going to come back. He had heard all the stories of what happened here, and he was positive--there was no way that was everything.

Janusz tried to stop himself from looking at the food. But he couldn't help it; he was hungry, and that dominated his thoughts. He kept wondering, *why were they not coming back, and why were they not torturing me?* Also, he wondered if they had poisoned the food, but his hunger won out over the fear, and he ate the food like it was the first time he had ever eaten.

6:30 p.m.

When the door opened again, it was the same two guards, but this time they were walking with Colonel Johnson. Once they were in the room, the Colonel explained to him that it was time to go to get cleaned up and go to his cell. Janusz looked at him and had a thousand questions, but the Colonel said nothing except for asking him if there was any news from the outside. Janusz shook his head.

The Colonel hung his head a little lower and slumped his shoulders and said, "Doesn't matter; this whole thing is fucked."

Janusz could feel the desperation surrounding him and nothing else was said as Janusz walked into his cell, and the door slammed shut.

CHAPTER 31

12 FEBRUARY 1973
9:00 A.M.

As the C-141 aircraft lifted off the ground from Hanoi, everybody cheered uproariously except for Janusz. He was numb; the whole ordeal had been confusing. His treatment at the camp had been somewhat humane. He had never been tortured and had not been starved; especially towards the end where they had been fed decently. Colonel Johnson had told him the NVA knew the end was near, and they used the POWs as a bargaining chip, so it had to appear that the guards treated them well.

Janusz leaned back in his seat and tried to make sense of the past few months. Every day there, Janusz had waited for the beatings, shootings, and anything else, but they never came. His mind had tortured him more than anything else. Then, during the bombing raids over Hanoi, he was sure that was the end for them all; the explosions were deafening, and the walls shook, but nothing had happened. After that, he thought the guards would come in and shoot them all for the actions of the bombings or at least beat them, but that hadn't happened either. Now, after less than a year of being in captivity, Janusz was on his way back to "the world."

The man in the seat next to Janusz slapped him on the shoulder and asked, "What's the first thing you are going to do when we get back to civilization?"

Janusz looked at the man and tried to place him, but couldn't. He must be from another camp. Janusz had trouble finding words. He had no idea what he was going to do. The man next to him must have gotten tired of waiting and said, "Well, after four years of hell, *I'm* going to drink a case of beer and eat enough steak to put me in a coma."

Janusz merely smiled. Soon the man turned around and started to converse with some of the other more talkative POWs. Janusz thought about what the man had said--four years. He looked around the plane and saw some of the POWs from his camp and knew all of them had been there much longer than him. He had no idea why they chose him as one of the first ones to leave. Others, such as Colonel Johnson, had been there for years (six in his case), but the Colonel insisted Janusz should be one of the first to go. His release infuriated some of the other POWs, and he could hear their comments about him; they said he collaborated with the enemy or sold everybody out. None of that was true, but Janusz had been around long enough to know that once a man got an idea in his head, there was little chance of changing it.

So everybody kept their distance from him; the other POWs had never really spoken to him much, and the guards had had an aversion to him too. That was, everybody except for the Vietnamese commander who Janusz had met that first day, and Colonel Johnson. Those two didn't seem to be bothered by Janusz.

But as Janusz sat on the airplane, feeling it climb higher and higher into the air, he could not shake the last words Colonel Johnson had said to him as he left the camp. Janusz had tried to ask why he was leaving so much sooner than all the others. The Colonel, who stood next to the Vietnamese commander, only said, "Sergeant, you don't belong here. Just remember, this is only a minor blip on your long, long journey."

12:30 p.m.

The moment the wheels of the airplane touched down at Clark Air Base in the Philippines, everybody on board cheered again. As soon as the plane parked, the door opened, and a young Major climbed on board holding a clipboard and said, "Gentlemen, let me be the first to welcome you to Clark Air Base and out of Hell."

The Major paused, and the plane erupted in jubilant shouts. After a few moments, the Major motioned for everybody to be quiet and said, "Please follow me and find a seat inside the terminal area. You will be here at Clark for a few days with the primary objective of medical checks and debriefing."

Soon all the men exited the airplane and started to walk toward the reception area. The first bit of air that hit Janusz' face caused him to stop and enjoy the freedom. He closed his eyes, sucked in another deep breath of air, and continued. Along the way, he shook a few hands and finally found his way to a waiting room with a buffet fit for a king and enough beer to fill a pool.

Janusz had no interest in the beer, but the food did catch his attention. During his confinement he was not starved per se, but it had definitely been a long time since he had had a proper meal. Janusz knew what it was like to feel hunger; maybe even more than any of the soldiers with whom he served. And when the hunger hit, he was reminded of painful memories of his youth in Poland and the struggles of his parents just trying to do a simple thing like feed their family.

"Sergeant!" Somebody called to him for the second time.

Janusz looked over toward the voice and realized it was a doctor and said, "I'm sorry."

The doctor's face was grave and his tone stern. "You are going to have to stay over here for an extended medical exam as well as debriefing."

Janusz looked at him and heard what the man said, but his consciousness was still back to when he was a boy in Poland and the sadness his parents felt when they could not feed them.

The doctor asked, "Do you understand what I am saying?"

Janusz nodded his head in affirmation and took the piece of paper the doctor handed him. When the doctor left, Janusz quickly returned to his childhood and reminisced.

CHAPTER 32

17 FEBRUARY 1973

Except for the first, every "Ride" Janusz found himself on seemed to hold a particularly dark memory which stuck out above all the rest. That day, Janusz believed he experienced his dark memory for this "Ride."

First came the debriefing, which wasn't bad. There had been some discussion, which he had not cared for, concerning his captivity and the lack of harsh treatment, to which Janusz had felt they were trying to see if he had conspired with the enemy, but it had been half-hearted. Everybody knew the war was at the end and the treatment of POWs was not as bad during this time as it had been in the early years, but Janusz had felt the man wanted to get him out of there; he was uncomfortable and it had shown.

Then another man had arrived and wanted to talk about his capture. Janusz couldn't stop wondering why they would not have asked about that first, but he had put himself in the right mindset and had answered their questions truthfully, for the most part. Janusz had not thought about that day for a long time.

He had told the story, but he had left out the part about Pete leaving him there on purpose. In the end, it would be Janusz' word against his and Janusz had no idea if Pete was a civilian now or where he was. Janusz had figured enough lives were destroyed and ruining one more, even if it was Pete's, wouldn't have changed anything.

Janusz did find out that Pete was awarded a medal for his actions, although most of the things Pete said he had done were the things Janusz had done, but, once again he had said nothing. Janusz could not have in good conscience accepted a medal as he still felt guilty about getting somebody killed and putting all the guys in danger because he did not want to see Grant Jr.

After all the debriefing, he was directed to an examination room, where he waited for the doctor. When the doctor walked in, he wore a serious face but spoke in a kind voice. "Sergeant Edwards, I am going to be straight with you; the injuries you sustained are serious."

"How serious?"

"Well, to begin with, your leg. You are never going to be able to walk normally again; you will have a limp for the rest of your life."

Janusz swallowed and thought about that for a moment. Having a bum leg with so much life to live was not going to be easy, but in truth, it was something he could deal with. "What about my arm?"

"Son, you suffered major nerve damage. You will have limited movement with your left arm, and you will not be able to grip anything with any real strength again."

The breath left Janusz' chest, and he sat still. "That can't be, doctor; I need my arm for my music. Isn't there any surgery to fix this?"

The doctor looked pained as he said, "I'm sorry, maybe if we could have operated when it first happened, but there is nothing we can do now."

Janusz shook his head. "So it is going to hang limply at my side for the rest of my life?"

"I'm afraid so."

"So what now?"

"Next you will be medically discharged. You are on your way home."

Being discharged from the military did not bother Janusz in the least, but not being able to form a chord again was something he could not bear.

Janusz wanted to scream out loud but didn't. He only raged in his head and cursed God as to why he couldn't have let him die in that place or better yet on the jungle floor. He tried to imagine what life was going to be like without the one thing that made him feel normal, the one thing that kept his sanity in check during this horrible situation of having to come back again and again. He was at a loss and felt more hopeless than he ever had before.

Next came the phone calls home. All of the POWs' families had been notified of their release. Some of them knew their service members were being held captive, but some also thought their loved ones were dead. As Janusz walked into a large room filled with phones, he could see and feel the happiness.

He had just walked into the room when a young man with Captain bars walked up to him. "Sergeant, I'm sorry to tell you this, but your mother passed away last year."

As Janusz stood there listening to the man, he felt guilty. He felt guilty because all he could think about was his arm and not the fact that Barbara had passed away. She had had a heart attack not long after Janusz was listed as killed in action. He felt sad for her, but he still could not get over never being able to play music again. He knew in his situation he was going to see a lot of people come and go and that was something he was going to have to accept.

So he nodded to the Captain and said, "Thank you, sir." As the captain turned to leave, Janusz asked, "Sir, any news about my brother or sister?"

"No idea, sergeant." The man left, and Janusz remained in the room with all the telephones and happiness for longer than he should have. He couldn't force himself to go right away. Maybe he wished some of the joy and hope would wear off on him, but when it became apparent that wasn't going to happen, he turned and limped out of the room.

CHAPTER 33

1 MARCH 1973

Janusz' return to the United States happened so fast he barely noticed it. It seemed one day he was in the jungles of Vietnam fighting, then in a prison camp, and the next, back where everybody acted normal. He didn't believe it possible, but he felt more like an outcast than ever.

He still felt like he was in Vietnam. Or maybe he *wished* he were still in Vietnam as he stood in front of William Sr. and Barbara's house. Janusz didn't know why it had taken him so long to come to the house, but he had finally forced himself to go.

For an hour he looked at the house. Standing in the cold with his hands in his pockets, he wondered how things could change so fast. The house that sat in front of him was not the house he remembered.

When William Sr. and Barbara were still alive, it had buzzed with life and now what sat before him was a depressing relic. There was neither life in the house nor a memory. Almost all of the windows had been smashed in, and the door hung on only one hinge. Although he had not known it at the time, he was as close to being happy as he could have been while living there.

Janusz only hoped the house had fallen into this miserable state after Barbara had passed away. The thought of her living there like this troubled him dearly. Though he had never quite fit in, The two of them had treated him well. He might have gone as far as to say they had loved him and now he felt terrible that perhaps he hadn't loved them as much as they deserved.

He started to walk up the sidewalk and then up the old creaky stairs. When he got to the top, he saw the old rocking chair that William Sr.'s mother would sit in, and for a brief moment, he swore she was there, giving him a look of concern like the one she gave him when the police had roughed him up all those years ago. As soon as he blinked though, she was gone, as was everything else that had filled the house and made it alive.

He continued to walk towards the door but stopped as soon as he got to the threshold as he could see that somebody had been in there and had destroyed what little was left. It was too much for him, and he didn't want to see it in that condition, so he turned around and left.

* * *

Once he was back in the dismal little room he had rented with the little money he received from his back pay in the service, he could not stop thinking how sad the old house looked. He shook his head to clear his thoughts, and the old bed he sat on cried out in realistic agony. He needed to stop feeling sorry for himself, and get back to the task at hand, which was finding a job.

His money was not going to last forever, he knew that, but he'd had no luck so far in finding any type of work. Time after time he would walk into a place and the first thing he noticed was the look. He had come to know the look too well. It was the look of fear and nervousness a white person would give. Then when he did muster up the courage to ask for a job application, they would look at the way he limped and his bum arm and always say, "I'm sorry, we are not hiring." Even at the places where they had a "help wanted" sign in the window it was always the same story, so after the tenth time, he stopped pointing their sign out to them.

He felt helpless and did not know what to do. In times like these, before going to Vietnam, he would grab the guitar, and disappear into the world of music, but that wasn't possible, so, unfortunately, he was left to his own thoughts. He tried to think but he hit a dead end at every turn. Being a Veteran didn't help either. Soon he found out nobody cared and most didn't want anything to do with somebody who had been in the war, not even the government.

After a while, he stood up and thought that while he might not be able to play music, he could still listen to it and that might help, if only just a bit. So he picked up his crutches, decided to leave his pride behind him and hobbled out the door to find some music.

His first and second stops were clubs where his band had once played, but by the looks of it, no more music would be coming out of there anytime soon as both places were boarded up. He kept on his quest, though, and went to another one of his old stomping grounds. He could tell from the outside that this place was still open. He felt his pulse rise a bit and noticed he did, in fact, feel a bit better.

Once he walked through the door the music hit him, but it wasn't the type he had been expecting. It was disco and he hated it. But seeing as his choices were slim, and there was no way he could hobble any farther without a rest, he decided to enter the place and made his way to the bar. As it was still early, the place didn't have many people in it. In fact, there was nobody behind the bar, but he pulled up a stool anyway and waited. When the bartender walked through a rear door carrying a case of beer, Janusz almost fell off his stool.

The moment the bartender locked eyes with Janusz, he too looked like he was going to lose his balance, or maybe drop the case he was holding. Janusz looked directly at his old rhythm guitar player, the one who had stolen his songs and gone on to make a record.

"You look like you are surprised to see me, Clarence."

Clarence said nothing, but finally moved, making his way back to the bar to set the case down. Janusz stayed silent and glared at him. He was so furious and wanted to bust his head open, but knew there was nothing he could do; he couldn't even walk for more than ten minutes without having to stop, let alone give somebody a whooping.

Clarence looked at him, dropped his shoulders a bit and said, "Brother, can I get you a beer on the house?"

"Sure, that sounds fair. You steal my songs, and for restitution, you give me a beer. That should make us square, right?"

Clarence's hands shook as he slowly pulled out a cold beer from behind the bar. The bottle opener clanked against the glass a couple of times before Clarence opened it and set it down in front of Janusz. "Look, Willie, you have to understand, we thought you were dead and we wanted to keep the music alive."

Janusz yelled so loudly the music couldn't drown it out, which made a few people look over, but only for a moment. "That's bullshit, Clarence. I heard the record before I was captured, which meant you didn't even wait for my plane to lift off the ground before you were selling me out."

Clarence hung his head low. Janusz grabbed the beer but just looked at it as the bottle cooled his hand. His heart raced, but he still kept glaring at Clarence. Once he set the bottle down he said, "So why are you here, huh? Bartending, or do you own this place?"

"Look, brother."

"Do not call me brother."

"Ok, I'm sorry, look, I know you got a raw deal and went through some shit, but I haven't had it so good either. After the first record was a hit, they were impatient for a second one and nothing we came up with satisfied them. They said it was shit, and canceled our contract."

"Wow, it sounds like you had it tough. I'm sorry for comparing me getting shot in Vietnam and being thrown into a POW camp to what you went through."

Clarence threw his hands up in the air. "Look, Willie, I don't know what to say right now."

Janusz ignored this and asked, "So what, are you broke now?"

"Yeah, man, in order to get the deal, we signed away the rights to the songs, and when nothing happened with the second album, we were just ass out."

Janusz lost the desire to remain and got up and began to limp out towards the door. Clarence hesitated behind the bar for a moment, before rushing out to Janusz. "Look, I wish I could take it all back, but I can't…but can I do anything else for you?"

"No, Clarence, unless you can pay my rent, we have nothing more to say to each other."

Clarence's face changed for a moment as he thought, and said, "I can't pay your rent, but I may be able to get you a job here, at least on the weekends. The boss is looking for an additional bartender."

Janusz looked at his so-called friend, but said nothing as Clarence kept insisting. "Come back and sit down, man, finish your beer and let me talk to the boss."

Janusz felt his body turn back around and he decided to return to the bar stool while Clarence went back through the rear door. He left the door open, and Janusz could see him talking to a man decked out in disco gear. They talked for a few minutes, and the man looked at Janusz, then looked at the crutches, which were propped up against the bar, and said something before he turned around and walked away.

Clarence stood in the side room for a few moments before returning. Janusz didn't wait though, he had already stood up and was making his way out the door.

CHAPTER 34

1 MAY 1973

Janusz never went back to the bar. He figured there was no use in getting himself all worked up over something he couldn't change. Plus, he had bigger things to worry about, and the main one was rent. After he paid his landlord, Janusz had to admit to himself that he was dangerously close to running out of money and with no job prospects, that left him with only one option, and it was one he dreaded.

Janusz held his head low in shame as he walked through the welfare office doors. Throughout his whole life, Janusz had always believed if a person set his mind to it, and put forth some effort, he could find work. After all, that is why he came to America in the first place. He hated people with excuses, and now, there he was, in the place where he never thought he would be.

He took a number from the ticket machine and looked around for an empty chair. He shook his head; he knew it was going to take a while as the room was full. Finally, he found an open chair next to an unshaven man and sat down. Janusz got the feeling the man next to him wanted to engage in conversation by the way he kept looking at him, but the last thing he wanted to do was talk with anybody.

Janusz deliberately avoided looking at him; instead, he took a look around the room. He could see all types of people. There were men, women, white, black, old, and young. They all had one thing in common:

the desperate look in their eyes. All these people also had folders of paper-work with them, which made Janusz wonder what he needed. It suddenly dawned on him that he had no idea what he was supposed to do, what forms he needed, or what the process was.

After a few minutes, and even though he had never made eye contact with him, the unshaven man spoke to Janusz. "Back in the world for about three months, right?"

Janusz looked at him. "Excuse me?"

"Vietnam. You've been back stateside for about three months, right?"

Janusz' head tilted back a bit as his eyes widened. "Yeah, just about, how'd you know?"

"The look, man. You have the look. The nervous look we get when we are around a bunch of people we don't know. Plus you checked for your rifle two times, only to feel a little stupid when you remembered you don't carry one anymore. Oh, and not to mention, you're banged up."

Now the man had Janusz' attention. "You were in 'Nam too?"

"Yep, fucked up my foot, but that is nothing compared to what goes on in my head."

"Your head?"

The man nodded slowly and looked as if he were in deep thought before he spoke again. "Yeah, if you are like me, the nightmares haven't kicked in yet. They started around six months of being back."

"The nightmares?" Janusz wondered what this guy meant.

"When I first got back, I was so excited, so I guess the adrenaline kept me going. Looking for a job kept my head clear. It wasn't until I real-ized that nobody wanted anything to do with us, and I wasn't getting any work…that was when the nightmares started."

The man looked off into the distance and pondered something for a moment. "Then when I had nothing to occupy myself, that's when it all came back. Mostly at night, they would hit, but sometimes during the day. It was just like I was back there, reliving everything."

Janusz became nervous as he had already had a few anxious moments, but was able to brush them off due to worrying about his bills and most of all, finding a job. He wondered if this might be his future, so he asked, " What did you do?"

The man moved his head around, checking to see if anybody was looking, and pulled out a flask. "The magic elixir, it washes away the G.I. blues, or at least enough of them so I can make it through the night."

Janusz knew he was serious, as he could smell the liquor on his breath as soon as he had sat down. The man unscrewed the top of the flask, took a hit, and held it out to Janusz. "Care for some relief?"

"No, thanks."

The man shrugged his shoulders and said, "As you wish," and put the flask back in his pocket.

Janusz wanted to get off this subject of the nightmares, so he asked, "How does this all work? The process, I mean."

"Well, you get a few months free and clear; after that, you need to start to show proof you are looking for a job."

"What happens if you can't find a job?"

"Well, in your case," pointing to his leg and arm, "you can probably keep getting paid for a while, but eventually they will cut you off."

"What about the VA?"

The man laughed and said, "You will be dead and out on the streets before you get in with them."

Janusz looked forward again and pondered all this information. After a few moments, the man said, "I'm not gonna lie to you. It's fucked up, they send us over there, and we go through all that shit for a reason I'm still not clear about, and then when you come back, they don't want anything to do with you."

Janusz agreed with him on this point and for the rest of the time until his number was called, he listened to the man's advice on the process and other things that could help him get by.

CHAPTER 35

15 JULY 1973

The first nightmare came on a hot July night, or rather early morning. It was almost exactly as the man in the office had told him. Janusz had no leads on any jobs, and there was nothing to occupy his mind; he was left alone with his thoughts.

That day he had been restless and stayed in his room. He had no idea of how long he was asleep, but the dream was vivid, so vivid, in fact, he had no idea it was a dream. He was back on the day of his capture, but something was different. They were heading back to the base, and all the guys were with him.

Janusz was confused as he thought for sure Stan had died out there, but there he was, walking in front of him. Janusz tried to say his name, but no words came out of his mouth no matter how hard he tried to force them, so they kept walking. Something was not right though, it was dark, and they had no light, but they walked on.

As they walked, Janusz could now see people standing among the trees; they were the enemy. Janusz tried to grab his rifle, but his arm wouldn't move, he couldn't get to his gun. He tried to scream, but nothing came out, it was as if his mouth were filled with sand. He knew at any moment they were going to open fire on the squad, and he could do nothing.

They didn't shoot though, they only watched, and Janusz noticed how white their faces were. Everything was wrong, but the squad kept walking, and the enemy with the white faces kept watching. Janusz looked around at the rest of the squad, but nobody seemed to notice the watchers, and they kept moving.

Up ahead, Janusz saw a light. It was a small fire, like a campfire, and they were heading toward it. Something in Janusz feared that fire, and he knew he didn't want to go near it, but on they marched, slowly. Even though the light didn't seem far away, it felt to Janusz that it took them an hour to get to it as the white-faced sentinels in the trees watched them.

Once they arrived at the fire, Janusz recognized it; it was the village where Pete wanted to pay the man for sex with the young woman. Then, before he could look around, he felt his arms being grabbed from both sides. When he looked to his left, it was Stan, but he was disfigured; his face was covered in blood, and Janusz could see that part of his upper head was missing.

He looked away and trembled. Then he saw that the man on his right was also disfigured, but he didn't recognize him; he looked like one of the white-faced sentinels in the woods. He tried to scream again, but only had that slow reaction which prevented him from doing so.

Then he saw Pete standing right in front of him, and Janusz wondered how he had suddenly appeared.

Pete was looking at him, smiling, and said, "You know Sarg, it all worked out in the end. You see, I got to fuck that bitch after all."

Pete pointed to the fire, and Janusz could see the girl lying there, dead, and all cut up with her entrails hanging out. Pete laughed and said, "See Sarg, I fucked her real good."

That is when Janusz woke up. It took him a few moments to realize where he was, but finally, he knew he was back in his rented room, covered in sweat and shaking. After a few moments, he calmed himself, and lay his head back down, but every time he closed his eyes, all he could see was Pete repeating over and over, "See Sarg; I fucked her real good."

CHAPTER 36

18 JULY 1973

After the first nightmare, the floodgates opened, and Janusz had them every night. For the most part, it was the same dream, but variations would be tossed in there too. Sometimes Stan's daughter would ask Janusz why he had killed her father, or the whole village would be slaughtered around the campfire and Pete would be standing in the middle of them, proud of his achievement.

The dreams came regularly now, every time Janusz closed his eyes; they arrived immediately. His sleep, if that was what one would call it, probably totaled less than one hour a night, and by the third night, he felt like he was going to break, and that is when the worst of the nightmares came. This time when the squad arrived in the camp, it was Janusz on the ground next to the fire. When he looked up, he saw Pete as usual, but this time Grant was with him, and he could hear Pete tell him, "You see, throwing this bitch off a bridge doesn't work, you have to fuck her real good."

Grant nodded like somebody would after a salesperson had explained how a lawnmower worked. When Pete finished, Grant turned towards Janusz, and he started to assault him again, just like on the wedding night, over and over, and Janusz was locked in the dream and couldn't wake up.

Finally, after what seemed like hours, Grant finished and stood up. Pete handed him a large knife and said, "It's not done until you put the finishing touches on her." Grant took the blade and plunged it deep into

Janusz' stomach. Janusz woke up the second the knife plunged into him, found himself in his room, and realized it was a dream.

Janusz curled up into a ball on the bed. He pushed his face into the pillow and let everything loose. He was exhausted, but there was no way he was going to fall asleep again and risk going through that one more time, so he remained in the fetal position until he could see the sun crack the horizon and light flooded the room.

Once it was light outside, he got up and went out. He walked for as long as he knew his leg would let him before he took a break. He was determined to find anything of beauty around him to try and erase the horrible visions still lingering from the nightmares. Nothing worked, and every time he sat down, he felt like he was going to doze off, and he did not want to have a nightmare in public.

Not finding what he was looking for--although he wasn't entirely sure what that was--he started to go home. Every step he took reminded him of the dream of the squad walking towards that fire, and he dreaded what tonight would bring. And he dreaded how he would feel tomorrow with another restless and almost sleepless night. He was around the corner from his home when he had to stop for another rest. His knee was causing him agony, and he could not make the final yards to get to his door. As he paused on the street corner, he looked into the window of a building to his left.

There was a big sign in the window with a neon word. "Liquor."

Janusz stood there and stared at the sign; he could hear the words of the man in the unemployment office. "The liquor chases away the G.I. Blues." So without seeing any other option, Janusz went into the store and bought a bottle of cheap whiskey.

When he got back to his room, he did not drink any of the whiskey, at least not right away. He put it on the table and stared at it. He tried to tell himself he was stronger than this, or that he didn't need it, but in truth, he knew he did. He needed to get some sleep without being terrorized throughout the night. So he made a deal with himself. He would drink the whiskey, just for tonight, enough to get some sleep. That way, tomorrow if he was rested, maybe he could better fight these dreams. So he got up and grabbed the bottle, opened it, walked back to the bed, and took a big swallow.

The liquid felt like lava going down his throat, and when it hit his stomach, he could feel the fire spreading throughout his body. It tasted horrible, nothing like the whiskey Grant used to drink, or even the whiskey that Buckets gave him that night in the club. He reasoned with himself that this wasn't to enjoy; he was searching for relief, and he took another swig. Once again he felt the fire, but this time it was a little less than before.

It didn't take long for Janusz to feel the effects of the alcohol. He hadn't eaten anything all day, and the drink went straight to his head. Then he noticed something; he was starting to feel better. The feeling was a lesser version of when he would play the guitar, but at least it was something. He got up off the bed with the bottle of whiskey and continued drinking. But now he was thinking of all the things he could do. He was optimistic; he went over to his desk and started to write down places where he could apply for jobs. All of a sudden, things didn't seem that hopeless.

After he finished writing down the job ideas, he stood up and stumbled. He looked at the bottle in his hand and saw it was half empty. He couldn't believe he had drunk that much, but he could feel it. He was intoxicated. He staggered over to his bed, sat the bottle down on the nightstand, and passed out into a dreamless, drunken stupor.

CHAPTER 37

19 JULY 1973
8:00 A.M.

Janusz awoke the next morning with the sun beating on his face, and he felt horrible. For a moment he thought somebody had punched him in the stomach and followed it with a kick to the head. He got up, went into the bathroom to find some aspirin, but had to make a stop at the toilet first to vomit. He was amazed at how much came up as he didn't remember eating the previous day.

Finally, after everything was out of him, he reached for the aspirin and took a few, chasing them down with some water. He stumbled back to the bed, praying the aspirin would take effect soon. Then it hit him; he had had no nightmares the previous night. He sat up quickly, which made him get sick again, and since he had no chance to make it to the bathroom, he leaned over the side of the squeaky bed and vomited some bile out onto the floor.

10:00 p.m.

After Janusz' headache subsided to the point where he could move without vomiting, he got up and had a good meal. The food made him feel much better, and as he lay in his bed, he reflected on the day. It was the best day he had had since the nightmares had started, and while he probably did not get quality sleep, at least he had slept, and that was all he wanted.

He started to get sleepy again, and this caused him to look over at the bottle, still sitting open on the nightstand. He thought about taking a swig but stopped himself. It was a one-time thing, he told himself, and then wondered why the bottle was still there. But he didn't drink, and soon after he found himself drifting off to sleep.

20 JULY 1973
2 A.M.

Janusz woke up sweating and terrified. He grabbed his pillow and screamed into it when he realized he had had the dream, and it was bad, worse than before. He felt that since he hadn't dreamt the night before, his subconscious had saved up last night's torment for him, and he got a double dose that night. Once again he looked over at the whiskey bottle, but still didn't drink any and after a while, dozed back off to sleep.

Sleep did not hold him long, though; as soon as he drifted off, those horrific images would return, sometimes the same, and sometimes with new twists. Finally, he decided he wasn't going to get any sleep and just lay in the bed looking at the ceiling, feeling the occasional tear roll down his cheek.

CHAPTER 38

22 OCTOBER 1973

It wasn't too long after the second night of nightmares that Janusz succumbed to the pressure of needing dreamless nights. So, little by little, he continued drinking until it became a nightly ritual. In the morning he would feel terrible, hung-over, and ashamed, but he was willing to trade sickness and shame for no nightmares. He also justified it by saying, "Well, at least I don't drink during the day." And that was true, at least until then.

That day was the observance of Veterans Day. Though technically Veterans Day was the eleventh of November, for some reason during the past few years, it had been moved to the fourth Monday in October. So Janusz decided to head out and see the parade--mostly out of curiosity--although he wasn't quite sure how he would react.

Well before he got to where the parade was going to be, he started to see people in uniform. Most of them were old Vets; some wore their full uniform, while others wore just a field jacket. Janusz didn't wear any of that stuff, and he tried to remember if he even had kept anything.

As he walked on, he saw more and more people with their memorabilia, and it started to make him feel uneasy. He stopped, and shook his head, trying to figure out what was going on. After a moment he continued, but the uncomfortable feeling never left him, it only got worse. Then Janusz heard a gunshot and could feel his throat go dry as his body trembled. He quickly ducked behind a big blue mailbox and was looking for the source of the shot, when it happened again.

This time he could see exactly where it was coming from, and he also saw that it was not a gunshot, but a car backfiring. The man inside the vehicle was cussing, and Janusz could tell he was pumping on the gas pedal too hard. Finally, the car started, and there were no more backfires, and then the man looked at Janusz through the window, and Janusz froze. The man was Pete, and he said, "I fucked her real good, Sarg."

Janusz shook his head and looked again, but it wasn't Pete; it was just some guy in a beat up old car. But Janusz didn't feel any better once he realized it; instead, he started to feel worse, much worse. It felt like everybody on the street was now closing in on him and he could hear everybody's conversations at once. He couldn't breathe, and he felt his chest tighten.

He tried to shake off the feeling, but everything started to spin, which was the last thing he remembered until somebody stood over him and asked, "Are you ok?"

After he regained consciousness, he stayed on the ground, trying to figure out where he was. Everything was so fuzzy, but after a few moments it became clear, and he realized where he was. He felt stupid. A couple of people helped him to his feet, and he no longer had any desire to see the parade, so he started to make his way back to his room.

As he walked, he couldn't stop thinking about seeing Pete in that car. His rational mind said it wasn't him, and though he knew it wasn't, it didn't stop the bad feelings. Now he was scared because it was the first time his nighttime terrors had made an appearance in the daytime. It was almost as if they were finding another way to come to the surface since he was blocking them with the alcohol at night.

Janusz was still shaking as he walked through his door and sat on his bed. He kept playing the scene over and over in his head, and it was beginning to make him feel panicky. It was the same feeling he'd had at the start of the scene on the street, and now he worried he was going to go through that again. Though it was only a bit past noon, Janusz walked over to the desk and picked up the bottle and began his nightly ritual early that day.

CHAPTER 39

1 JULY 1974

Janusz paid his rent for the last time. As he spoke to the landlord, he thought about telling him he would be gone on 1 August but decided not to. He didn't want to answer any questions. He still had one more task to accomplish today, and he needed to do it sober, and if he waited too long, the shakes would start to hit him.

Janusz realized he was a full-blown alcoholic, and he was ashamed of himself. The incident on Veterans Day was only the beginning. More and more thoughts and images had begun to seep into his waking hours, and it was more than he could deal with. A reflection in the window would be somebody from Vietnam, or a loud noise would send him clutching his chest, falling to the ground in a sweaty heap.

But the liquor stopped all of that--well, enough of it would. Lately, it had taken more and more to get the job done, and he didn't like that either. It also seemed every morning he woke up was a little worse than the morning before, but he had a cure for that too. A good handful of aspirin and a couple of morning swigs would stave off the hangover, then all he had to do was keep drinking all day and no visions, no panic attacks, and no fear. There was only shame, but enough of the liquor drove it away.

He did not have time to think about that right now though, he needed to get moving, and he was out and on his way. His head pounded, because this morning he had only taken his handful of aspirin, which did not seem to be doing the trick. He was missing the other vital piece, which was the whiskey.

I'll have that soon enough, he thought as he touched his back pocket where his small flask was.

When Janusz took a break from walking to rest his knee, he looked up. A smile splashed across his face as he saw his target right in front of him, so he pushed himself up and continued walking up the stairs to the building. Climbing the stairs took him much longer than he wanted, but finally, he made it to the top and was thankful he hadn't toppled down them.

As he walked through the entrance of the building, the steel on the bar of the door felt cold to him. He thought that strange as it was July, but he imagined he probably had a fever. He knew he was sweating, but he didn't realize how badly until he reached the counter.

A young lady looked at him and asked, "Sir, are you alright?"

Damn, he thought, it was happening already. "I'm fine, ma'am."

"What can I help you with?"

As Janusz said the words, he felt a surge of joy pass through him, which was something he didn't feel much these days. "A one-way ticket to Port Walden, Michigan, please."

"And on which day will you be traveling?"

Janusz swallowed and said, "July 31st."

After he paid the young lady, she handed him the bus ticket, and he was on his way. He hurried as fast as he could out of the doors and as soon as the fresh air hit his face, he grabbed the flask out of his back pocket, opened it, and downed half of it without ever removing his lips. He savored the burn for a moment and was tempted to take another swallow, but stopped himself. He wanted to get back to his place and count the remaining money he had before he became too drunk.

Reluctantly he put the flask back in his pocket, hobbled back down the stairs, and started in the direction of his room. As he walked, he pondered his last visit to the unemployment office. Just as the man he had met the first time told him, they were going to cut off his benefits.

He wasn't too upset with them once he thought about it. He never searched anymore for employment, and when he had gone there last time, he was so drunk he couldn't speak without slurring his speech. So eventually they tossed him out, and sure enough, a few days later he received notice that July first would be his last check.

That was not what bothered him, though; it was the man with the little boy outside the office that cut him. As he had stumbled out of the office, he crashed into a man walking down the street with his son.

The man had pushed him back, causing Janusz to fall to the ground. "Why don't you get a job, you lazy, drunk piece of shit, and stop living off the tax dollars of honest men."

Janusz had wanted to scream back at the man and say he *did* want a job, but nobody would give him one, but he knew it wouldn't make a difference--the man saw what he wanted to see and nothing else. As he walked away, Janusz heard him tell the boy, "You see, son, they're all the fucking same, always wanting something for nothing."

That wasn't the saddest part of the whole thing to Janusz, though. As the man and son had walked away, the boy looked back at Janusz and made eye contact. Janusz could see a bit of pity in the boy's eyes, but that pity would be extinguished in time with more close-minded rhetoric. The boy would grow up, and that would be his truth, and he would never try to see the other side.

As Janusz made his way into his room, he shook the memory from his head. He didn't want to think of that anymore. He needed to count out his money and ration it so he could stretch it to the end of the month. All of the bills were paid, and now he made sure he had enough cash for liquor to last him the month. Once he was done counting, he was satisfied. He had sufficient money for whiskey, and even a bit left over for food. Now, all he had to do was wait for the end of the month.

CHAPTER 40

31 JULY 1974

4 A.M.

Janusz woke up extra early, which wasn't too hard because he was excited. He wanted to make sure he was at the bus station in plenty of time to catch the bus for his trip back to his beloved Port Walden. Once he was out of bed, he dressed and went out the door without a final glance. He didn't want any more memories of this room or this place; he wanted to move on, whatever that meant for him.

He got to the bus station in plenty of time. He even refrained from drinking, as he didn't want to take any chances of not being let on the bus. Once the bus pulled up, he got on and found his seat. As soon as he was comfortable, he pulled out his flask and took a big swig, which immediately made him feel better.

He smiled as the bus pulled out of the station on time, and he was heading back to the place that called him. As he sat and watched Chicago fade in the distance from the window, he reflected on the fact that today was his birthday. He found it humorous, as he usually would tell himself how good he felt for his age. Today was different though; today he felt every bit of his 124 years on this earth.

6 p.m.

The moment Janusz stepped off the bus, energy charged through him. The air was different, and although he couldn't see it yet, he could feel the river in his bones. As he started to walk towards his destination, he became more excited with every step, almost forgetting the pain in his knee. It had been 41 years since he had last been here, but he didn't count that time. All he had seen that day was the luxurious house of the stupid doctor whose name he couldn't remember. To him, the last time he was back in Port Walden, and free, was almost 60 years ago.

He recognized almost nothing. Everything had changed. The one thing that struck him the most was the lack of horses. He knew this was silly as it was 1974, but in his mind, he would always see the streets full of horses and carriages. It was modern, but it still had a feeling of home to it.

Janusz had often wondered throughout the years why he considered Port Walden to be his home instead of Krakow, Poland. Maybe because he had met his wife here, raised their children, built a life together, and died here. He still held a spot in his heart for Krakow, but it wasn't his home.

He had a million things he wanted to do, but unfortunately, lacked the money and the stamina to do them. He wished he could see his wife's gravestone, but that was on the outskirts of town, and there was no way he could walk there. Next, he thought of his children, and his sweet, sweet little girl and this made him smile.

This smile vanished when the thought occurred to him his daughter could be dead, as well as his other children. Janusz stopped in his tracks and sat down on the side of the road. She would be in her 90's and his other children pushing 100. He felt an immense sadness at that thought. In his mind, Button never aged and Janusz then realized that even some of his grandkids could have passed on by now.

He felt ashamed he had not thought of them much throughout the years and that he was too focused on himself. Janusz wanted desperately to know if Button was alive, but what was he going to do? Call her? Get her address and see her? He was ashamed at the thought of her seeing him like this--a broken, good-for-nothing drunk. Plus, he remembered the day when he confronted her on his second "Ride," and there was no way he wanted to upset her if she was still alive and 94.

He took a long hit off his bottle and pushed the thoughts out of his head. Today was about his wife, and he was going to make it to their spot even if it killed him. So he picked himself back up off the ground and kept going.

As he walked, he started to worry that he might be getting lost, so he stopped to ask for directions. The first person he saw was a young teenager on a bike, and Janusz asked, "Young man, can you tell me how to get to the river?"

"Which one?"

"St. Agnes"

The kid looked at him strangely, turned, and pointed. "Yeah, man, follow the bridge."

When Janusz looked off into the distance, his breath seized. Staring at him was a gigantic bridge spanning the yet unseen river across to Canada. He had forgotten about that as the last time he was here, there was only talk of the project being started.

Not long after chatting with the boy, Janusz saw the river come into view. After that, it was only a few steps, and he found his spot. Though the place looked different, he knew where it was. A smile broke out on his face when he saw the place had not been paved over, and, right where he used to sit and picnic with his wife, there was still grass.

He went over and sat down on the ground and took in the scenery. Though the Canadian side was littered with chemical plants, the place was still beautiful. He thought it might actually be a bit more attractive now as he looked up and saw the gigantic bridge off to his left.

His wife would have loved this bridge, and he could almost hear her say, "Isn't it amazing the things they can build now?"

Janusz smiled and said, "Yes, dear, it sure is" as he felt a tear roll down his cheek. He didn't know if the tears he felt were out of sadness or happiness, but one thing he did know was that he was happy. He felt like himself, like *really* himself. He was Janusz--not Roy, not Elizabeth, not William, but Janusz.

He thought more about his wife and wished he could show her all the other things that had been invented or built. She would have loved it. What she wouldn't have loved, though, was what he'd become. As he took another drink from the bottle, he could almost feel her eyes on him.

As the wind blew gently across his face, he listened to the water flow against the bank, and he continued talking to his long deceased wife. "All my life, I stuck to the idea that if you were a good, honest person and worked hard, you would be able to make a decent living and provide for yourself, but that isn't always the case."

He paused only to finish the bottle, and continued, "I tried, my dear, I have honestly tried, but I'm tired and desperate. I guess I'm asking for your forgiveness for what I've done and what I am about to do. I know taking one's life risks eternal damnation, but my love, I'm living in hell right now so I don't see how it can get any worse."

Once he finished talking to his wife, Janusz stood up and walked to the edge of the river, pausing only a minute to take in one last view before he hurled himself in and ended this "Ride."

CHAPTER 41

The boys were waiting for Janusz when he entered the bathroom. His mind wandered, and his guard was down, so he didn't notice them until it was too late. As soon as the bathroom door clicked shut, one of the boys immediately knocked his books to the ground while another pushed him across the bathroom.

The biggest kid, Jake, boxed Janusz in a corner while the other two stood close by.

"What's up, you weird fuck?" Jake asked. "Welcome back to school. I told you last year I was going to beat your ass if you came back."

Janusz said nothing. It was no use. Jake was cruel, and no matter what Janusz said, Jake was still going to beat on him. The problems with him had begun last year when Janusz started middle school. As usual, Janusz was a loner with no friends, and he was an easy target for Jake.

Janusz had seen his type many times before, a kid who was slightly bigger than the rest, but lacked confidence and desperately sought the approval of others. Jake constantly tried to break into the "cool kid" crowd, but he wasn't quite there yet. So he tried to use his size to prove himself as a tough guy. Janusz noted that Jake never picked on people his size: it was always the smaller, skinny kids like Janusz.

"What's the matter, retard? You forget how to talk?" Jake asked, and he punched Janusz in the stomach. The blow knocked the wind out of him, and he doubled over, trying to catch his breath. The other boys ran around Jake and grabbed Janusz' arms, keeping him from falling to the ground as Jake delivered a few more punches.

Soon, Jake tired himself out, and the three boys picked Janusz up and carried him to the toilet where they proceeded to dunk his head a few times while flushing. Luckily, the toilet dunking didn't last long, and soon they were gone, leaving Janusz on the ground, beaten and completely wet.

After a few minutes, Janusz pulled himself up and cleaned his clothes the best he could. He was a mess, and his ribs hurt even though he didn't remember getting kicked or punched there. After he dried off, he picked up his books and noticed his shirt was ripped, exposing most of his side. The people he lived with, or rather, his *parents,* Judith and Ethan, were going to be upset. He exhaled in frustration as he looked at his watch. He was 15 minutes late for his next class, which meant he would not be allowed in.

Dejectedly, he made his way down to the assistant principal's office to say what had happened and to call Judith to come and get him. When he walked into the office, the secretary's face dropped as soon as she saw him. "Oh dear, what happened to you this time?"

Janusz shrugged his shoulders. "They caught me in the bathroom."

There was no need to go into further detail with her; on this "Ride," Janusz found himself becoming even more separated from people. Though the lady was nice, she was from a different era. She, along with most of the other teachers and in particular the administration, still held onto the idea that "boys will be boys."

The woman looked at him for a moment longer before she said, "Have a seat, dear, I'll ring Mr. Sarnaski." After a few moments of speaking with the assistant principal, she turned to Janusz and said, "It will be a few moments."

Janusz nodded and took a seat. While he sat there waiting for the assistant principal, he thought about this current "Ride." His surprise when he came out on the other side after he threw himself into the river was second only to the first time it had happened to him. Of all the times he had died, that had been the first time his death was due to his own hands. Though many years had gone by since he had been in a church, he still held onto some of his Catholic beliefs, so when did not wake up burning in hell, he was relieved, but mostly shocked.

It was the same old pattern he had grown accustomed to, going through infancy, then being a toddler, and so on. He also kept a close eye on his development; he didn't want to appear to develop too fast, just a bit above average. This way he would not be pushed into anything he didn't want to do, or worse, be skipped ahead in grades, which would not be good with how skinny he was now. He already was the target of the bigger kids, and Janusz saw no reason to move ahead and be placed with even bigger ones who could do more harm.

This time he was an only child, and Janusz prayed it would stay that way, which he knew would probably be the case. From what he had overheard from Ethan and Judith, he had been a miracle baby. The chances of them conceiving were slim and there had been complications, too; he was born premature and the doctors said that lowered Judith's chances of having another child even more.

Not being able to have another child bothered Ethan, and Janusz felt the man resented him for it. Ethan wanted a clone of himself to go on and achieve the things he couldn't, which always revolved around sports. Back when he was in high school, Ethan had been the star of the team and had gone to college because of it. The man had excelled at sports, and all signs pointed to him going pro, but just like what happens to many of players, one bad hit and then it was all over.

It was something Ethan could never let go of, and Janusz thought how sad it was to see the man keep reliving a time in his life to which he could never return. So from day one, it was always football or some other kind of sports. He had bought football clothes for the baby, tiny footballs for playing with, and then there were the endless mind-numbing weekends watching football…

As Janusz started to grow, it was apparent his current body was not built for football. But Ethan still pushed him into sports and Janusz failed miserably, not entirely for lack of talent, but mostly for lack of interest. The whole sports thing created a divide between him and Ethan.

But it wasn't all bad. The man wasn't abusive, at least not physically. Also, his job at the factory and the fact he was a successful high school football coach afforded them a comfortable living.

But Janusz was healthy again, and although the time in Vietnam still haunted him, he had his favorite relief readily at hand again, which was music. At first, Ethan had refused to buy Janusz a guitar, but after much pressure, getting perfect grades, and having a paper route for extra money, Ethan split the cost of one with him. In hindsight, the guitar made their relationship better, because it occupied Janusz' time and Ethan saw less of him.

Out of sight, out of mind, Janusz thought and grinned.

As Janusz sat in the assistant principal's office, he thought about music. He was so glad the disco era had ended because he didn't consider that music. Although he felt there was some good music from the '70s, the majority of it, he considered subpar.

The '80s showed promise. Guitars and actual musicians were making a comeback, especially in the hard rock and metal genre. Not the hairband rubbish, though; Janusz thought that was marketing to sell records. He could not wait until he was old enough to leave, because there was a gap in the music and he knew he could fill it.

As he went over chords in his head, a loud voice jarred him out of his thoughts. "Brian! How many times do I have to call your name?" asked Mr. Sarnaski.

Janusz looked up, surprised to see the man standing in front of him. "I'm sorry. I didn't hear you."

Mr. Sarnaski looked annoyed. "Get in here."

As Janusz got up and walked to the man's office, he looked over at the secretary, but she continued to type something on her typewriter. Janusz shook his head and thought again, *out of sight, out of mind.*

As soon as Janusz sat down, the man asked, "So is this why you didn't make it to second period?" as he indicated with his finger to Janusz' wounds.

"Yes."

"Do you need to see the nurse?"

"No, that won't be necessary. If you could please call my mother so she can come to get me, that is all I require."

Mr. Sarnaski scowled. "So what happened?"

"Does it matter? Will you do anything if I tell you?"

"Mr. Richardson," the man bellowed in his deep voice. "You sometimes forget to whom you speak; you talk to people as if you are on the same level."

"I'm sorry, sir."

"I am the vice principal, and you are a student. Know your place."

Janusz said nothing and glanced over at a baseball card in a plastic case sitting on the man's desk. Carl Yastrzemski. Janusz smiled, as he knew Mr. Sarnaski took pride in the baseball player because they were both of Polish heritage, or as Mr. Sarnaski always said, "He's Polish, like me."

Every time the man said that, Janusz had to fight the urge to say something in Polish to see if the man understood, to see how "Polish" he was, but he didn't. The last thing he needed to do was draw more attention to himself.

Mr. Sarnaski continued without a response from Janusz. "So tell me what happened."

Janusz breathed out in exasperation and told the story. When he was done, the vice principal nodded his head. "Ok, I'll talk with the boys, and let them know this kind of horseplay will not be tolerated."

Janusz wanted to laugh in the man's face because he knew what the talking to would consist of: "You guys can't play so rough" or "I know he is weird, but you need to take it easy."

Same old story, thought Janusz. It didn't matter, and he stood up to go.

As he got to the door, Mr. Sarnaski said one final thing. "Brian, you need to toughen up and stop giving people reasons to pick on you."

Janusz looked at the overweight man sitting in the desk and thought, *you mean toughen up like you? Sitting safely behind a desk and never having to worry about anything in life or do anything more than required shuffling papers?"*

But he said, "Thank you, sir," and left.

5:30 p.m.

When Judith had picked him up from school earlier that morning, she hadn't said much. As he waited outside the school, he saw her car pull up and he knew how things were going to go. She would say they would all discuss it when his father got home, and Janusz was right. Then in typical Judith fashion, after she checked if he was ok, she asked him if he wanted to stop and get some donuts. Food was Judith's fix for everything. So to make her feel better, but really so he wouldn't have to talk too much, he said, "Yes mother, I would like that."

Later, when Janusz sat down for dinner, Ethan immediately asked, "So you want to tell me why you got sent home from school?"

Janusz was annoyed with the comment. "I didn't get sent home; I asked to go home."

"Why would you do that? Your mom said it was only a bit of roughhousing."

"They ripped my shirt and dunked my head in the toilet," Janusz replied curtly.

Ethan's face showed a bit of surprise. "Well, what in the hell did you do to those boys to make them want to do that?"

"I didn't do anything."

Ethan slammed his fork down on the table, causing Judith to jump. "You know, Brian, if you didn't piss people off and give them a reason to mess with you, you wouldn't have half the troubles you do."

Janusz had had this conversation many times with Ethan and was in no mood to hear it again. "So what do you suggest I do? Or rather not do?"

"The next time one of these guys messes you with, you knock the biggest one right on his ass."

Janusz continued eating his mashed potatoes while thinking, *yeah, easy for you to say. You were the biggest kid in your class.* As he sat there looking at him, Janusz had the sneaking suspicion that when Ethan was in school, he was probably the bully.

When Janusz didn't say anything, Ethan continued. "You see, if you involved yourself more with sports, instead of twanging on that sissy guitar, you wouldn't have these problems. You'd have guys to back you up."

Janusz hated these talks with Ethan because he only saw the world from the way he had grown up. He couldn't see it from any other perspective. However, Janusz did think there was a speck of wisdom in the statement. He looked up at Ethan and said, "Well...I have been thinking about trying out for the wrestling team this year."

Ethan looked up with the face of somebody who had won the lottery. Janusz didn't know why he had never thought of this before. If he could get on the wrestling team, that would please Ethan and also, with wrestling, he would only be matched up with people his weight.

Ethan smiled and slapped Janusz on the shoulder. "You see, now that's a great idea. You know, I used to wrestle myself, and I can show you some tricks."

Janusz thought to himself, *of course you did*, but only said, "Yes, that would be great, Father."

CHAPTER 42

12 APRIL 1987

Joining the wrestling team didn't make Jake and his buddies stop bullying Janusz immediately. Every chance they got, they would throw a beating on him, and when he did manage to avoid them, Jake would increase his torment by way of psychological means. Lately, Jake had been spreading rumors about him masturbating in the locker room and calling him a fag.

The term *fag* bothered Janusz. He could not have cared less about being called that name--it was the implications behind the word. Janusz knew the term implied that a person was of less worth than others just because they were attracted to members of the same sex. The term also implied the person had a choice and Janusz knew that was not true and he thought about his time as Elizabeth.

Sometimes when it was a group, multiple people would join and say nasty things to him. The name-calling didn't bother him as much as the beatings, though. After all, Janusz had built up a pretty tough psyche with all the other things he had been through, and he knew this was only a "minor blip" on the radar, to quote the Colonel back in the POW camp. In reality, seeing other kids being bullied upset him the most. He felt for the ones who did not have the experience Janusz had and who saw their lives as hopeless, with nobody to help them.

As the wrestling season progressed, Janusz figured out more and more ways to work it to his advantage. Although Janusz was horrible at wrestling, Ethan kept his word and helped him. With the help, Janusz was able to win a few matches, which secured his place on the team. Janusz also credited the coach with making his life a bit more bearable. The coach placed a heavy emphasis on teamwork.

Janusz found this strange at first because he always thought of wrestling as an individual sport. Not the coach, though; he was a Vietnam Vet (which was hard to find, at least in the school system) and insisted everybody treat one another as brothers. He would always say he didn't care if the team won or lost, as long as they did it as a team. So if one person struggled, it was the team's job to lift that person.

So in addition to the help Ethan gave him, he was also getting help from the rest of the guys. But Janusz made no lifelong or deep friendships because of being on the wrestling team; what did the trick was the help *he* gave the team--not help in the wrestling sense, but rather, in the academic sense.

Janusz noticed a lot of these kids struggled in school. And while a lot of bad behavior was overlooked, what wasn't overlooked were grades, especially by the coach. It didn't matter to him if you were the star wrestler; if your grades were not up to standard, you would not be getting on the mat that day.

So after overhearing a conversation in the locker room about how one kid was not going to be able to wrestle if he didn't pass his math test, Janusz saw his opportunity.

He approached the boy and said, "I can help you pass the test, young man."

Everybody stopped and stared at him. For a moment Janusz thought he had made a mistake and they were all going to jump on him and throw him a beating, but after a moment, Chris, the wrestler with the problem, asked, "What do you mean?"

Janusz went on to explain to him what was on the test and how he could help him. All of the other kids were silent, waiting for Chris' move, but he only said, "Ok, you can come over today."

And that was the start of it. After Chris successfully passed his math test, Janusz found himself helping more and more of the guys on the team. Although sometimes it was actually Janusz doing their homework or writing papers for them, he didn't mind. In the end, the kids learned more from Janusz than they did in the classrooms from the teachers.

Ethan and Judith were extremely happy, as they saw this as him having friends. Ethan especially liked it because they were sports buddies. It was at this time that Jake started to lay off Janusz, after a few threats from Chris and the rest of the team.

Janusz smiled as he jumped out of his thoughts and back into the present just in time to see Chris pin his opponent on the mat, which sealed the championship for the state. Everybody was ecstatic and Janusz, even though he hated wrestling, got caught up in the excitement.

After the match was over and the trophies were given, the crowd dispersed. Janusz had not participated in any of the events that day, and because of that, he had volunteered to stay after and clean up. He cleaned up a lot, but didn't mind it one bit, and he had the whole process down to a science. He first cleaned the mats with a solution, and while the mats were drying, he put away the loose ends and piled the towels by the locker room door.

When the mats were dry, he rolled them up against the wall and took the towels down to the locker room and put them in the bin. As Janusz put the last towel in the container, he heard the locker room door slam shut, and he called out, "Coach?"

The voice that answered was not the coach, but rather, Jake and three of his friends. "Nope, no coach or your wrestling buddies. It's just us, you fucking faggot retard."

Janusz spun around to see the group of four boys looking at him. He was panicked as he realized he had nowhere to run and there was nobody here to help him. Out of desperation, he said, "If you touch me, the guys on the team will throw you a whooping."

Jake smiled as he walked closer. "Oh, you mean they're going to come all the way down to Florida and get me?"

Janusz looked at him in horror as Jake walked towards him and said, "Yeah, that's right. Today is my last day of school, freak, and you are the last thing on my list to do."

Janusz tried to run, but Jake was on top of him instantly and the other boys held his arms and legs. Jake rained down punches on his face while the other boys held on tight. "You fucking freak! I told you I was going to beat your ass." The punches caused his head to bounce off the floor a couple of times, but that was it. He blacked out, and by the time he woke up, all the boys were gone.

Janusz remained on the floor and fought back tears. After a moment he tried to get up, but fell back down to the ground and lost his wind. His ribs were in agony, and he couldn't move, and Janusz suspected that once he had blacked out, the boys had probably gotten a few kicks in on him while he was on the ground.

He had no idea why this kid hated him so much, but Janusz could remember the rage and hatred in his eyes while Jake was on top of him punching him. Now it was Janusz who felt hatred--hatred towards Jake, hatred towards Ethan for always blaming him for being bullied, and hatred towards the school system for not giving a damn about how the kids treated each other.

A half hour passed before somebody came. He heard the door open and fall shut with a heavy clang, and a few moments later, the coach stood over him. Janusz was so relieved it wasn't Jake and his buddies that he couldn't hold back the tears anymore and started to cry. There he was, 137 years old and crying like an infant.

The coach sprang into action and called an ambulance. Janusz tried to tell him it was ok, but the coach ignored the statement. He quickly looked Janusz over and said, "Don't move, and don't try to talk." It turned out the coach had been a medic in Vietnam and Janusz guessed his mind jumped back into his training. Janusz knew the feeling well.

When the paramedics arrived, the coach thoroughly briefed them on what he knew as well as what he suspected. Among the paramedics was a police officer and as they lifted Janusz on the stretcher, he could overhear the coach telling the man he suspected it was Jake and his friends as he had caught them after school hours and there was blood on Jake's shirt.

Janusz didn't care about repercussions anymore; all he wanted was to see Jake burn. He wanted revenge, so when the officer asked Janusz while he was being wheeled out of the school if it was Jake who had attacked him, he said, "Yes."

CHAPTER 43

5 SEPTEMBER 1989

As Janusz walked to his first day of high school, he thought about what awaited him. Middle school had been hard, but rumors were flying around that high school would be much harder. He wondered if that would be true. Would there be another "Jake" waiting to take out some misplaced anger on him?

The thought brought him to the memory of the locker room. The incident had led to Jake being arrested and sent to the juvenile detention center. Janusz had heard Jake did not fare so well there; it turned out when he had to fight people his own size, and without an army behind him, things were different.

He also heard Jake's family never went to Florida. Jake's dad had been let go from his job in Port Walden, but had found a new one in Florida. However, with Jake's arrest, the family couldn't go. Janusz knew he should not take any pleasure in the family's misfortune, but he was *glad* this had happened to Jake and his family. Janusz hoped he would never have to see the kid again in his life.

All thoughts of Jake left him as he walked through the doors of the high school. It was huge, much bigger than the middle school, and he was intimidated. Even though he was early, there still seemed like a thousand people milling about the place--and they were all huge.

Janusz had not grown as much as he had hoped over the summer break. He wasn't short per se, but he was skinny. He would have to wait for the "growth spurt" Ethan kept telling him he would get. Also, the people weren't just big; they were adults. He even saw a couple of guys walk by with mustaches.

As Janusz stood in the doorway looking at all these students, a man he recognized only slightly walked up to him. "Brian, I'm Coach Davis, your father told me you were in this year's freshman class."

The man was the high school wrestling coach, and one of Ethan's good friends. Ethan had told Janusz that Coach Davis would find him, but he hadn't been paying attention. His mind had been lost on a new song he was writing, and the last thing he cared about was wrestling or anything Ethan had to say.

"Good morning, Coach."

"We are very excited to have you here."

Janusz thought that funny as he was barely good enough to make the middle school wrestling team, but he went with it anyway. "Thank you; I'm excited too."

The coach then waved his hand in a beckoning manner and said, "Come here, let me show you something."

The coach started walking, and Janusz followed him to the front of the school next to the gymnasium where there was a large display case. Janusz was confused and looked at the coach.

The coach said, "Take a look up at the top, next to the big trophy."

Janusz looked up and saw a picture of a young Ethan holding a football with the words "State Championship MVP" engraved on a plaque at the bottom of the picture.

He should have known, not only was he going to have to put up with seeing Ethan here at the school, he was going to constantly be compared to him.

The coach then said, "Don't worry, kid, once you hit your growth spurt, we will get you squared away, and you will see your name up there too."

Janusz nodded his head and put on a fake smile. "I can't wait."

CHAPTER 44

20 JANUARY 1991

Janusz handed in the term paper a week before it was due. Operation Desert Storm had kicked off a few days prior and was a big topic of discussion in Government class. Therefore, the teacher wanted the students to do an in-depth review on the situation between Iraq and Kuwait as well as what U.S. involvement meant. The topic sparked something in Janusz, and he took the assignment seriously, and unbeknownst to him, the paper was a form of catharsis to release some of the issues he had faced in Vietnam.

The paper consumed him, and he worked tirelessly on it. He included only enough of what he had to about Iraq and Kuwait, but what he focused on were the effects the war had on the U.S. Service Member. As the conflict began to escalate, he became more interested in the events, but he worried about the sentiment he felt the country had.

The country was supportive, but he feared it might have been too supportive. As Janusz wrote in the paper, he expressed the view that the problem with the U.S. was that once the war was over, and all the flags were flown, and the parades a distant echo, it was forgotten. The average citizen would go back to work, talk to their friends about sports teams, and then cookout during the weekend.

The real tragedy was for the men and women who fought in the war. Because for most of them, the war endured long after the memory of it faded for the general public. The war continued to rage in their heads, and for many of them, there was no help. He wrote in the paper how insane it was for the government--and some of the public--to think that one day these military members could be in the middle of hell, and then, once they returned home, they were expected to act normal or forget what happened.

He wrapped up the paper with a scathing reprimand of the non-successful government agencies designated to help service members upon their return. He alluded to some members being tossed aside like garbage or being lost in a sea of paperwork with absolutely no options for help. Before he finished, he also took a dig at the public's disgust of some of the vets who had problems such as drugs or alcohol.

When he typed the last word, Janusz was amazed at how he felt. It was a release; it was the first time he could tell his story, and the words flowed out on the paper. He was proud of the work and knew every bit of it to be true, and so he was surprised when he got a summons to the principal's office about the paper.

At first, Janusz thought they were going to commend him for his raw insight on the effects war had on a service member, but the thought was quickly extinguished when he walked into the office and saw the faces of the principal and the government teacher. Janusz did not even get the chance to sit down before the principal asked, "Do you mind telling me what in the hell this is all about?"

The man's tone took Janusz by surprise. "Excuse me?"

The principal held the paper in front of him, shaking it. "This, Mr. Richardson, this anti-government rhetoric!"

The government teacher spoke in a slightly calmer tone. "Brian, you were supposed to write a paper on the effects that Operation Desert Shield would have on the United States."

Still not understanding the entire situation, Janusz replied, "Sir, that's what I did. The biggest effect, I believe is, what happens to the people fighting the war when they come back."

The principal threw the paper down on the desk. "What do you know about the effects war has on a person?"

Janusz' body tensed, and he gritted his teeth and answered the question with a question of his own. "What do you know about war?"

He had touched a nerve with the principal and the man's face became red. "I don't know what you are insinuating, but I was never called to duty."

Janusz knew the principal's age, and he knew he would have been subject to the draft when he was in college. Janusz wanted a fight, and he wasn't going to back down. He felt the principal was somehow saying that since he was in college at the time, it was almost the same as the men who got drafted. Within seconds, all the catharsis that writing the paper had given him slipped away and was replaced by the memories and images of Vietnam.

"I'm not insinuating anything," Janusz said, "I'm simply saying that it sounds like a better deal to sit in a classroom than going to a place where your life was in danger every single day."

The principal moved forward to say something, but the teacher grabbed his arm and said, "Look, Brian, first off, you have zero references for the claims you make about the soldiers; I could fail you on that fact alone."

Janusz felt like kicking himself. He knew the teacher was right. All of the experiences had come from his recollection, and he really couldn't quote a man who had drowned himself in the St. Agnes River back in 1974.

"Since this is not due for a while, as a favor to your dad, we are going to let you turn in another paper. This time, follow the assignment."

Janusz was still angry and wasn't ready to give up the fight. "So you want me to write a paper saying no matter the consequences, the United States should throw a whole bunch of unsuspecting young men and women into combat, without any regard to them?"

The principal couldn't remain silent anymore. "Mr. Richardson, I don't care how many championships your father wins this school; I will not stand for anti-government statements."

Janusz could not believe he was getting lectured by these two; neither had ever put on a uniform nor looked down the barrel of an enemy's gun, but anger was not going to get him anywhere, so he decided to try reason. "Sir, please, I am not anti-government, but at the same time I am not going to blindly agree with every policy, especially if it puts service members in harm's way with potentially life-long effects."

The principal slammed his fat fist down so hard on the desk that the government teacher jumped. "Let me put it to you this way. You either re-write the paper, or you receive a failing grade for the semester. Now get out of my sight."

Janusz had enough experience to know when a man was not going to change his mind, even if the man knew he was wrong, so he left the principal's office and returned to class.

* * *

When Janusz returned home, he noticed Ethan's car was in the driveway, and that was not a good sign. The man always got home around twenty after five unless there was football practice, and then dinner would be served at 5:30 sharp. He suspected there had been some telephone calls and that the conversation was far from over.

As he walked in the door, he saw both Judith and Ethan were sitting at the table, and the mood was heavy. Janusz did not even get the chance to set his backpack down before Ethan asked, "Do you mind explaining to me what the fuck you were thinking?"

"I just did the assignment from the perspective I felt best."

Ethan stood up. "From your perspective? You have no idea what you are talking about. Do you know how much you have embarrassed me? I lived through the 60s, and you have not experienced shit."

Janusz was in no mood to discuss this topic with yet another man who had sat on his ass in a college classroom during the war, but he had to say something, so he chose his words carefully. "The paper is not anti-government; I wanted to show there is a price when we as a country send people off to fight, and maybe I was trying to say why does it always have to be us? Is the value of a young American less than those of other countries?"

"Jesus Christ," Ethan said as he looked at Judith, "Where does he come up with this shit?"

Janusz became a bit bolder. "I don't think it's fair, that I should have to change my paper because it conflicts with the views of others."

"Oh, you are going to change it alright, or you will never lay another hand on that goddamned guitar of yours, you can bet your ass on that," and then the conversation was over, and Ethan stormed out of the kitchen.

Later that night Janusz sat in front of his typewriter and stared at it for an hour. The only time he would look away was when he would glance over at his guitar. Everything in his soul told him what was in the original paper was right and he should stick to his guns, but how could he keep going if he didn't have music in his life?

Janusz had just started to play in a little garage band over the summer and that provoked feelings in him that he could not describe. So what would happen if he didn't have that anymore? Or worse, what would happen if he couldn't play his guitar? Would the flashbacks return? Would he start having panic attacks again and what would happen if the urge to drink came back?

As he mulled all these possibilities over in his head, he whispered, "I'm sorry," and began to type a new paper. With every touch of the keys, he felt as though he were stomping on the soul of every Vietnam Vet.

CHAPTER 45

31 JULY 1992

Janusz had been counting down the seconds until he turned 18. The past year had been tedious for him, as Ethan and Judith pressured him to apply and go to college. Even high school graduation was mind-numbing; he looked around at all the kids with their parents watching, so full of hope and aspirations. Janusz knew most of them would not fulfill what they were thinking at the moment, but he still hoped the best for them. There was a big hungry world out there ready to smash their dreams and kick them when they were down.

Ethan and Judith were the same way. They forced him to take the college tests, forced him to do the applications, and forced him to commit to a school. He tried to fight it at first, but as a minor, he literally had no control over his decisions. Janusz sometimes chuckled when he looked at kids today. Back in the 1800's he knew many people who had been married and had families of their own by the time they were 18. Back then in Poland, you were considered a man by the age of 15.

He thought of these things to pass the time while he showered. Once he was dressed, he went to his desk and sat down to write a note. When he was finished, he placed it in an envelope and wrote on the front "Mother and Father." He debated whether or not he should write "Judith and Ethan" on it, but he didn't want to be cruel as they were already going to be upset when they read it.

Once that piece of business was done, he did a quick check on the rest of the things he would need. After he was satisfied, he made his way downstairs, where Judith ambushed him with a hug and said, "Happy birthday, Brian!"

To Janusz' surprise, Ethan was also there and had delayed going to work. He walked around the table and put his hand on Janusz' shoulder. "Congratulations, son, you're a man now."

"Thank you," was all he could muster to say.

Judith smiled and said, "I don't know why you haven't quit that job flipping hot dogs yet! You leave for college in two weeks; don't you want to have some fun and spend time with your friends?"

It amazed Janusz that these two still refused to see that he had never *had* any friends. Sure, sometimes people would come over, but that was usually to get what they wanted from him, which most of the time was help with homework. But the time for arguing with these two was over.

"Well, I probably will be too busy with studying and wrestling at school and won't have time to work," he said. "So I want to save up all the money I can right now."

Ethan had a big smile on his face as he pulled out an envelope and handed it to Janusz. "Son, we were going to wait until your party tonight, but let me give this to you now."

Janusz groaned in displeasure. "I told you I didn't want a party."

Ethan waved his hands in a backing off motion. "I know, I know… it's only a few people…but don't worry about that now, open up the card."

Janusz opened up the card and discovered 500 dollars inside, and he slowly looked up. "You didn't have to do this; you've given me too much already."

Judith said, "Now don't you worry about that, this will help at school and besides, you only turn 18 once."

Janusz chuckled a bit and thought to himself, *if only that were true.*

But he thanked them profusely anyway. The situation became extremely awkward for him, and he wanted to leave. "Look, I'm going to be late for the breakfast rush, so I need to go."

Ethan said, "Alright, get out of here, and we will see you tonight."

Janusz made his way to the door but stopped as soon as his hand touched the doorknob. He thought for a moment and turned. "I want you two to know I do appreciate what you have done for me." The statement came from the heart; even though there had been some bumps in the road, overall, it had not been bad. "You two are good people, and I won't forget that."

Ethan and Judith looked at him strangely. Then, Ethan smiled and said, "Buddy, you gotta lighten up and not be so strange."

Janusz took one last look at the house, and went out the door, and jumped in his car. As he made his way into town, he slowed down a bit when he passed the restaurant he worked in. He could see the whole crew in there and could also see that the breakfast rush was in full force. Technically, he wasn't scheduled to work until 11, but the time wouldn't matter, since he was never going back there to work.

He did feel a little guilty about not telling his boss, but he couldn't risk the word getting back to Ethan and Judith. When he was directly in front of the restaurant, he waved softly, but nobody saw him. That didn't matter though as the wave was more of a symbolic gesture for him.

He kept driving to the other side of town until he came to the parking lot near the river. Once he parked, he looked at his watch and decided he still had plenty of time. Janusz got out of his car and walked to the picnic spot. He would come here often, at least once a week; it seemed to give him peace.

He sat down on the grass and said, "Well, my love, I don't want to say this is the last time I'll visit you, but it could be a long time."

After that statement, he was kind of at a loss for words and sat there in silence watching the seagulls fly around, searching for food. He thought about the happy times he had shared with his wife and enjoyed the summer breeze coming down from the lake.

He sat like this for about thirty minutes, then looked at his watch and said, "I will always love you."

Then, he got up and walked to the car. He opened the door and popped the trunk. He took one last look at his car, tossed the keys on the seat, closed the door, and walked to the rear of the vehicle. Inside sat a small suitcase and his guitar case, and he looked at them for a moment. He checked his wallet. He figured he had more than enough money; he had worked all year and not spent anything, plus with the graduation money as well as the birthday money, he would be set for at least six months.

He picked up his suitcase and guitar, closed the trunk, and started to walk towards his destination. He arrived in less than ten minutes. He stopped in front of the building, set his case and bag down, and pulled out the envelope from his pocket. He looked at the stiff card paper inside with the words "Port Walden to Los Angeles" printed on it. Once he figured out which bay his bus was in, he walked towards it, feeling freer than he had in a very long time.

CHAPTER 46

3 AUGUST 1992

Once Janusz stepped off the bus, he could feel the electricity in the air, and he loved it. Although L.A. was seedy, it was also exciting and full of possibilities. He did not want to waste a single minute, so he started to search for a hotel immediately. He figured he shouldn't be in a hotel for too long, but he needed a place to stay, and he didn't want to walk around L.A. with a guitar case and suitcase. Once he found a suitable place, he left his stuff there and set out on his mission.

As he walked down the street, he stopped at a little newsstand and bought a postcard, then found a bench so he could write comfortably. He struggled with what words he should put on the card. For a moment he thought about not even sending one since he had pretty much explained everything in the letter he had left on his dresser, but that wouldn't be fair to Ethan and Judith; they deserved to know he was safe. He owed them at least that. So he took his pen out and wrote,

Mother and Father, I imagine you are pretty upset and not to mention, worried, and that does trouble me. At the very least I wanted to let you know I made it here safe, and I have never been so sure of anything in my life. I hope you can understand this, B.

He licked a stamp, put it on the card, and dropped it in the big blue box. The next stop was the nearest music store, which was not too hard to find in L.A. Once he stepped inside, he saw what he was looking for--the bulletin board with all the advertisements on it. He scoured the hordes of flyers stacked on top of each other until he found ones looking for a singer and guitar player. He ripped off 15 little strips of numbers and put them in his pocket.

Next, he looked on the other side of the board, which listed rooms for rent and people looking for roommates. There was no shortage of these either, and he took about 15 numbers from this side too. Once he was satisfied he had enough, he walked outside to the nearest payphone and started to make some calls.

CHAPTER 47

Janusz didn't have much luck with the want ads in finding a band. Many of them only wanted to be a carbon copy of the 80's hair metal groups, and he wanted no part of that. In fact, he wanted no part of any band wanting to copy somebody else. He had his ideas, and he wasn't going to bend.

There were also already established bands with their own songs, and he didn't care for them either. Many of them just played simple chords, with some flashy vapid lyrics, and the musicians only had basic talent. The day prior he was out on an audition, and while talking to the bass player, he found out the guy had only been playing for a couple of months, had no musical ability, and no ear for tone. When Janusz asked him how he expected to make it, the guy said, "Man, all a bass player has to do is play the root note and look good."

In short, most of them wanted fame and girls. He had not found anybody with a passion for creating something original, something with heart, and he started to get depressed. He stopped going to clubs to see other bands because this depressed him as well when he watched the guitar player fat finger the chords, or be a couple of milliseconds off the beat. But hey, they looked good, and Janusz was starting to think that was what it was all about.

On the positive side, he landed a guitar-teaching job at one of the music stores. Although he was only paid by the lesson, word had started to spread about this guy with "the original sound." Landing the teaching job surprised him a little bit, as guitar teachers were a dime a dozen in L.A., and most of them had formal education. But the people kept coming, and as he walked into the store today, he wondered how many drop-in lessons he would have.

He always showed up to the store a little early so he could warm up and mess around with the store's amps. The amp he had was one chord away from zapping out, and he was doing research and dreamed of buying a new one. Today when he went back to the teaching rooms, he saw a man with short, dark hair waiting for him.

At first, Janusz was a little annoyed; an early arrival meant he would not have a chance to warm up. Janusz said, "Sorry young man, but lessons don't start for another 30 minutes."

The guy looked at Janusz, and smiled strangely, which made him seem even more out of place and not just because his hair wasn't long and hanging down to his backside. Then, the guy said, "I'm not here for a lesson."

"Oh, well if you need something, the sales staff can help you up front."

The guy continued to look at him strangely for a moment before saying, "I'm not here to buy anything, either."

Janusz was not irritated anymore; he was curious. This guy didn't have the kind of aversion to him most people usually had. He seemed at ease and comfortable around Janusz, and that was not something he was used to.

Although Janusz was curious about the guy, he didn't have all day for this staring contest between them and said, "Well, then, lad, why don't you tell me what you want? I have to warm up; I've got a day full of lessons."

The man said, "That's why I'm here, bro. I want to hear the weird guy who thinks he's too good to play in imitation bands and also plays shit nobody else has heard."

Janusz stood speechless for a moment, but he wasn't angry because for some reason, he felt the guy meant it as a compliment. Janusz asked, "Are you in a band?"

"Nope. We can't find a guitar player worth a shit."

Janusz wanted to ask the guy a thousand questions, but didn't; instead, he just walked over, sat down, plugged, in and let the music flow.

While Janusz played, the expression on the man's face never changed. Janusz couldn't tell if he liked it or if it was the worst thing he had ever heard. When he was done, he looked over at the guy who asked, "You feel like coming over and hearing how that sounds with some drums and bass with it?"

Janusz' heart raced a bit, and he said, "Yes."

"Can you sing also?"

"Yes."

"Cool, here is the address, meet us at six." Then the man walked straight out of the store without saying anything else.

6 p.m.

When Janusz went to the address, he discovered it was a practice studio. He saw this as a good sign because he had expected a garage attached to somebody's parents' house, which was what he had seen before. As he walked into the place, the guy he met at the store earlier came up and greeted him. "Hey, you made it. I guess you should know our names since we know you are serious."

Janusz looked at him and shook his hand. "Brian."

The guy took his hand and smiled. "They call me Rack, and that ugly mother fucker holding the bass is Ditch."

Janusz said, "Hello" but Ditch didn't reply. In fact, he looked a bit lethargic, and Janusz wondered if he even had enough energy to play.

Rack motioned for Janusz to follow him. "We don't like to fuck around too much as this place costs money, so let's see what you got." Rack then climbed behind the drums and immediately started to play; a moment later Ditch joined in, and Janusz was awestruck. His former demeanor was no indication of how he could play. Ditch was on fire.

Janusz caught the key and jumped in, and they were off. He felt like he was on cloud nine--these guys were nothing like the guys he used to play with back in Port Walden. These guys were musicians, and they were definitely on his level. After about five minutes of playing, Rack called out to Janusz and asked, "Can you throw some lyrics in there?"

"I believe I can."

They repeated the song, but this time Janusz improvised one of his songs to go with the tempo, and it fit perfectly. When they were finished, Rack was obviously pleased. Janusz couldn't tell with Ditch, though; the man seemed indifferent.

Rack spoke up first. "So what do you say, man? You wanna make some magic happen with us?"

"Absolutely."

Rack looked over at Ditch and asked, "What do you think?"

Ditch shrugged his shoulders and said, "Cool."

Rack smiled and nodded his head. "Couple conditions though; we only do originals, no covers."

"I can deal with that; it's actually what I prefer."

"Good."

"What's the other condition?"

"You gotta change your name man. "'Brian isn't gonna cut it...you need something that grabs people's attention, something nobody else has."

Janusz smiled and gripped the neck of his guitar and said, "Janusz" as he nodded his head. "Janusz Z."

Rack said, "Now that's what I'm talking about."

And Ditch muttered out another "Cool."

CHAPTER 48

1 SEPTEMBER 1993

Janusz waited backstage, and the realization of how fast things had transpired hit him. After he had joined the band, they quickly came up with material, which was a combination of stuff that he had written and things that Rack and Ditch had, and they decided to call the band JRD. He fit with the guys, and their chemistry was apparent from the first show they played in L.A.

Janusz loved the 90s, although the music had become stale; it was a perfect time for something new. By their third show, they already had a massive word of mouth following in L.A., and the fourth show was when the record executives had approached them. When it came to the business part, Rack handled everything. He was older and more experienced and had a good head on him. He also knew that the band had something special and they weren't going to be taken advantage of.

After they had signed a contract, the recording went flawlessly and today was their first day on tour. They were set to be the first opening act for the most popular hard rock band in the country as well as another group. Janusz thought it was funny as JRD wasn't "hard rock" per se, but then again, they didn't fit into any genre.

Rack always liked to say they were a hard rock blues band with soul and classical overtones. Whatever it was, it was working. The album climbed up the charts, and there was talk of it hitting number one. As

Janusz sat there doing a final tune on his guitar, he could hear the crowd outside and his hands started to shake.

Aside from this being the biggest audience they had ever played in front of, it was also the first time everything had been taken care of for them. Janusz wasn't used to all the people buzzing around, or touching his guitars, and the million other things that happened. He also wasn't used to the stage being decorated for them without much input from the band. He complained about this to Rack, who said, "Man, you have to pick your battles."

As he was taking one last look at the set-list, a man with a backstage pass and a hand-held radio came in and said, "Five minutes, guys."

Janusz jerked his head up and thought, *oh my God--this is it.*

He looked around to see where Rack and Ditch were. They were nowhere to be found, and Janusz was slightly annoyed. Those two had a habit of disappearing sporadically, and Janusz could use a pep talk right now.

Another few minutes went by...still nothing. The man who had announced the five minutes now poked his head into the room again and called out, "One minute" and waited by the door. Finally, Rack and Ditch came in through the adjoining door of the next dressing room.

Janusz looked at them and threw his hands up in the air. Rack smiled at him and asked, "You ready to make history, young one?"

Janusz' eyes widened as he nodded and followed Rack and Ditch out onto the stage. His nerves completely disappeared when he stepped in front of the audience and struck the first chord. For him, the crowd vanished along with all the other superfluous stuff. It was just the music, and for the next 30 minutes, he didn't think about the "Rides," Vietnam, Grant, bullies, or anything else that plagued him.

CHAPTER 49

Janusz discovered he didn't care for touring. He loved the part where he played on stage, but all of the other stuff--he wanted nothing to do with it. There were many things that surprised him; the most interesting was the relationship with the other bands. It shocked him how little they interacted with each other.

Right from the beginning, Janusz could tell the headlining band did not like the guys from JRD. The lead singer was a prima donna with just average talent. Janusz knew once the man's looks faded, he would not have enough talent to carry him any further in his career. As for the other musicians, they were good, but Janusz could tell success had gotten to them, and they were riding the wave of their previous hits.

That was fine though; Janusz was used to being alone, but once they got word that their album had reached number one, the relationship with the other bands turned even worse. The singer from the other group would never miss an opportunity to take a jab at JRD, and especially Janusz. One particular time during an interview the singer was asked what it was like to be touring with one of the hottest new bands in the country, and one could see the singer's anger. "Well, first off, they are our opening act, and second, I don't see Janusz much because right after the show is his bedtime."

The singer thought it was an insult, but Janusz found it funny. As he sat thinking, he looked out the window of the tour bus. Their next show was in Detroit, which was a homecoming of sorts for Janusz. The bus he was on now took the same route the bus had while bringing him to L.A., only in reverse. He was more nervous than he thought he would have been. He wondered if he would see anybody from high school in the crowd, but mostly he wondered if Judith and Ethan would be there.

He tried to send them a postcard from every city he went to, to keep them informed. Calls back home did not happen much, mainly because he had nothing to say and when he did, only Judith would talk, since she always said Ethan was away. He knew the man was angry, and he also suspected Ethan had been home most of the times he had called, but there was nothing he could do about that.

Janusz sighed and stretched his arms as a road sign indicating Detroit was 150 miles away flew by the window; he figured they should arrive in less than three hours. Janusz looked at his watch, and then looked around for the guys as they should be rolling out of bed soon. Janusz had discovered a lot about his band mates on this tour as well.

The biggest thing he had discovered was that he didn't click with them well when they weren't playing music. He saw this more in the morning, but at least their attitudes would progressively get better throughout the day. They were completely different people in a social setting than they were playing or practicing.

Janusz rarely hung out with either of them and living in cramped quarters in the bus made it tough. There would be hours where those two would say nothing to him; it was kind of like they were in their own club. Then, when they were practicing or playing on stage, it was like they were best friends and three pieces of a well-oiled machine.

Rack and Ditch were definitely into the party scene that accompanied this lifestyle, but Janusz didn't mind, as it didn't remotely affect their playing. Janusz glanced out the window again and saw another sign, this time indicating Detroit was now 110 miles away. He shook his head in disbelief that he had spaced out in his thoughts for that long. He looked around and didn't see any movement from the guys in the back, so he decided he better hit the bathroom now before they did.

He got up as quietly as he could, which made no difference at all because the guys slept like the dead. When he opened the bathroom door, he was surprised to see Rack sitting on the toilet with a rubber band around his left arm and holding a needle with his right hand.

12 p.m.

The bus parked, and as soon as the band heard the air brakes engage, they all stood up and started to exit. Janusz was dying to ask Rack a thousand questions, but Rack acted as though nothing out of the ordinary had happened. When Janusz had barged in on him, Rack had kicked the door closed, and Janusz had just stood there for a couple of moments before returning to his seat. When Rack had come out of the bathroom, he had only said, "She's all yours."

Now, even as they walked into the parking lot of the arena, they only talked about normal things. Rack looked at him and asked, "So…your big homecoming…how do you feel?"

Janusz wanted to say he felt like he wanted to know why his drummer was shooting something in his arm, but didn't and instead said, "I don't know, feels kind of weird, I lived here for a good while, but never felt at home in this city."

Rack looked at him strangely. "What? I thought you were born and raised in Port Walden; I never knew you lived in Detroit."

Janusz panicked for a second; he was still trying to process what he had seen in the bathroom. He couldn't believe he had slipped up and quickly replied, "Oh, my mistake. What I mean is we used to visit Detroit a lot, but it doesn't feel like home."

Rack gave Janusz a look like one gives somebody when one senses bullshit, but he didn't say anything, and the two kept walking. Since they had a few hours to go until sound check, Janusz was going to hit the dressing room and work on some new material. He had no idea what the other two would do, but right now he needed to clear his mind.

Once inside the building, Janusz had only walked down the hallway for a few yards when he saw Judith. She stood next to the dressing room wearing a lanyard with an access badge attached. Janusz stopped in his tracks and looked down the hall. In his mind, he never thought she would come, and Janusz had hoped she wouldn't. It would have been so much easier that way.

He felt guilty...not for leaving...but for not feeling the same way about them as they did about him. They deserved a child that was theirs, one they could connect with emotionally, and not some 144-year-old Polish immigrant with multiple lifetimes of emotional baggage.

Out here on the road, he could be himself, he didn't have to lie (much) to anybody, and he hadn't realized how good it felt to be relieved of the burden. As he looked at Judith, all the pressure came back. Rack snapped him back into reality and asked, "What the hell is wrong with you, man? Who is that?"

"My mother."

Rack looked at him for a few moments. "Yeah, well, I get you, my parents were shit, and my relationship with them far surpassed shit." He patted him on the back of the shoulder and said, "Good luck, man."

The closer he got to Judith, the tighter his stomach twisted. Janusz could see she had been crying recently, but she maintained her composure now. Janusz stood in front of her; he said nothing, he only looked at her as she did the same to him.

Finally, she broke the silence. "You look well."

"Thanks," was all he could think to say.

"I hope you are not busy; am I bothering you?"

"No, not at all, I have a few hours to spare."

She looked at him some more as if she were calculating her words carefully. "Your dad couldn't make it, but he sends his love."

Janusz breathed out slowly and leaned against the wall next to her. "Look, Mother, you don't have to lie; it's ok."

"You have to understand how disappointed he is. You are so smart and can be anything you want; he hates to see you throw your life away like this."

"Mother, this is what I want, you have to understand, and I'm not throwing my life away."

She either finished calculating her words or mustered the courage to say what was on her mind and let loose. "Please come back; it's not too late. You could pick up right where you left off and start school in the fall." When the last word spilled out of her mouth, tears started to fall from her eyes.

"Mother, when I am playing, it is the only time I feel whole. The only time I feel like myself."

As he finished the sentence, he could see her face tighten and she said, "Well, I'm sorry we couldn't make you feel whole, Brian, or be enough for you."

"That's not what I mean. No matter how much you two tried to pretend it wasn't so, you knew how out of place I was, you knew how hard of a time I had in school."

"Every child has a hard time."

Janusz let out a deep sigh. "You know it was different with me."

"Your dad's heart broke when you left."

"I know, and I'm sorry." Janusz doubted the man's heart was really broken--more like embarrassed and angry--but he didn't want to point that out.

"We were so worried when your boss called that day and said you hadn't shown up for work. We waited and waited, and people started to show up for your party--we felt so stupid."

Janusz was running out of ways to apologize as well as things to say, so he let her go on. "After a while, everybody went out looking for you, and we even called the police. Eventually, we found your car by the river with the keys inside, and we thought something had happened to you. It wasn't until the next day that I found your letter, and we knew where you went."

He knew she was getting some things off her chest that she needed to say, and he owed her that much, so he let her continue. "I wanted to go out to California and get you, but your dad said 'no.' He was afraid he'd kill you."

At this point, her tears escalated, and she was sobbing. Janusz reached in to hug her, not sure how she would handle it, but she let him embrace her and embraced him back.

"And every time we would hear you on the radio, it would upset your dad so much he had to turn it off. We even saw you on the TV once as we were flipping through the channels."

Janusz couldn't take much more of this and grabbed her arms and looked at her. "Mother, I'm sorry, but this is my life, and if you two want to be a part of it, you are going to have to accept it."

Judith pulled her arms out of Janusz' grip and said, "One day, when you have children, you will understand," and she stormed off.

Janusz thought about running after her but decided not to. He stood there and muttered softly. "Judith, I probably understand better than you do."

CHAPTER 50

1 APRIL 1995

The pressure to release the second album was immense. The last tour hadn't even finished yet, and already everybody hounded the band about getting back in the studio for new tracks. It was intense, and there was no downtime. The pressure didn't bother Janusz though, as he was prepared. He had a lot of material he had come up with from the road, as did Rack and Ditch. It amazed Janusz as to when these guys had time to come up with anything because during the end of the second leg of the tour, their partying and drug use intensified.

Before the first leg of the tour finished, the band knew the headliner did not want them back; JRD had outshone both the other groups. So when they got the word that it was official, a second leg with smaller venues was created with JRD being the headliner, and the experience was amazing.

They had about five days of downtime before they were back in the studio and recording. The same magic happened this time as it had the last time and Janusz knew the second album was going to be even bigger than the first.

Then it was back on the road, and this time they headlined a world tour. When the manager proposed the tour dates, none of the locations caught Janusz' attention except one--Krakow, Poland. For the first time in more than 120 years, Janusz was going to be returning to his birthplace.

CHAPTER 51

12 SEPTEMBER 1995
10 A.M.

Janusz had been restless all day. Now, as the tour bus pulled up to the Polish-German border, he became even more agitated. It was silly, he told himself, but he couldn't help it. He didn't know if it was excitement or something else; he couldn't seem to get himself under control.

As he looked out the window, he could see the border guard wave the bus over to the side. Once they were parked, three people climbed into the bus; two of them were border guards, and the other was a young woman who carried a bag and a clipboard. The young woman spoke to them in English and introduced herself as Alina; she was going to be their guide while they were there.

Janusz shivered when he heard her accent, and a million memories came flooding back into his head. He thought of his mother, but most of all, he thought of his wife; it was how she had sounded when speaking English. After the brief introductions, Alina told them the guards needed to check their documents. The bigger of the two came over and started saying something to Janusz in Polish. Alina said, "He is a big fan and…"

"He wants an autograph for himself and his kids," Janusz finished the sentence.

Alina's eyes widened, and she said, "Yes."

Then Janusz started to speak with the guard in Polish and carried on a conversation with the guy. The whole time he spoke, Rack and Ditch looked as if they had seen a ghost. Janusz chuckled because, in a way, that is precisely what they saw.

Janusz couldn't believe how good it felt to speak in his native tongue, and the guard was so happy that he didn't even bother to check the passports. Once they were past the border and on their way, Alina started to explain things to them. She told them it was about a 5-hour trip to Krakow, and they would pass some nice scenery along the way. Janusz paid little attention to her; he was too excited about looking out the window and seeing things written in Polish and checking out the landscape of his birth country.

It wasn't until Rack shouted, "Dude!" loud enough for people outside the bus to hear that he looked over at the others. "Hey, man, Alina is asking you a question."

He looked over to the young lady. "I'm sorry; what?"

"So you have a Polish name, and speak the language. That is very surprising; how did you learn to speak so well?"

Before he could answer, Rack threw his two cents in as well. "Yeah, since when do you speak fucking Polish?"

Janusz was glad that Rack had interrupted her, as it gave him a chance to collect his thoughts and come up with a good lie that was believable. He wondered if he shouldn't have spoken to the man, but really, he didn't have any control over it; it had just come out and surprised him probably more than anybody else.

Finally, he said, "My hometown had a lot of Polish people in it, and a Polish family owned the restaurant where I worked, so they taught me." It wasn't totally a lie, but not entirely true either.

Alina looked at him and smiled. "Impressive, and you will be much more popular here now, although that does make a part of my job unnecessary."

Janusz returned the smile and said in Polish, "Don't worry, these two knuckle heads barely speak English, let alone Polish, so your job is safe" and he leaned back into the chair and continued to look out the window, waiting to get to his birthplace.

5 p.m.

It had taken them a bit longer to get to Krakow than Alina predicted. Janusz was disappointed that he wouldn't be able to go out into the town right away. He especially wanted to see the square; he could remember going there as a child with his father to sell their goods at the market. He was curious to see how much it had changed, and if he would remember anything at all.

Janusz accepted the fact that he wouldn't be going into town until tomorrow. They had to deal with sound check, interviews, and then check into the hotel. He could wait; he knew he would get his chance. He had fought with both Rack and the tour manager to schedule a down day after the show in Krakow. He told them he wanted to go sightseeing, and at first, they had said there was no time. Janusz pressed them, though; he had asked them what the point of touring the world was if they were only going to see arenas, dressing rooms, and hotels. They relented, and in the end, he got his way. He tried not to be arrogant, but sometimes when he wanted something, he had to remind management who the star was. After all, there was no way he could come all this way to Poland and not see his parents' final resting place.

CHAPTER 52

13 SEPTEMBER 1995
7 A.M.

Out of courtesy, he asked the guys the night before if they wanted to go out and explore with him, secretly hoping they wouldn't, and they didn't. He knew Ditch wouldn't want to, but he was unsure about Rack. Sometimes the man surprised him, but Janusz had told him he was heading out at 7 in the morning and Rack said, "Nah, man, I'll probably just be getting to bed at that time."

The only problem was Alina insisted on accompanying him, and their management seconded that as well. They told him he was too well-known, and this way Alina could keep him out of trouble. He gave in, but he had to figure out a way to explain to her why he wanted to see the gravestones of two people who had died more than 140 years ago.

Janusz met Alina at 7 a.m. down in the hotel lobby, and as soon as she saw him, she hurried over. "Where do you want to go?"

He replied to her in Polish, "Let's start off in the Main Square, and then let's see how the day goes. Also, just a warning, it could be a long one."

She looked at him and tilted her head. "Do you prefer to speak in Polish?"

"Yes, it will be good practice for me."

And it was; he didn't miss a beat, although there were the occasional times when she told him the word he used was outdated, or the old dialect, but other than that, it went fine. Speaking in Polish made him wonder about his French language abilities. He had not spoken French for a long time, and wondered how he would do, but doubted he would be any good. Too much time had passed without using it, and French was different; it wasn't his native tongue, and Janusz figured no matter how much time passed, one never lost one's native language.

They made it to the Main Square in no time. The driver dropped them off right on the side of the street, and when they got out of the car, Janusz was awestruck. Of course, a lot had changed, but so much was the same. They walked across the square and stood in front of Cloth Hall. He couldn't believe how it looked; it was magnificent. When he was a child, the place had almost been in shambles. His father had told him this place was once beautiful, a great example of picturesque Renaissance architecture, but since the move of the capital to Warsaw, it had fallen apart.

Janusz wished his father could see it now, fully restored to what he pictured it used to look like, according to his father. The sight would have made the man happy. Janusz then turned and saw St. Mary's Basilica. Without saying a word to Alina, he started to walk straight toward it.

When he walked through the doors, Janusz felt a jolt go through him. The church looked exactly the same, except for the addition of electricity, and it was much cleaner now. Before entering too far, he dipped his hand into the stoup, wetting his fingers with holy water, and made the sign of the cross.

Alina looked at him, amazed. "You are Catholic."

"Yes, but it has been a long time since I have been in a church."

Alina said something else, but Janusz did not hear her. He crept up the middle of the church, running his fingers along the tops of the pews. He was so caught up in the moment that he could almost see his mother and father sitting in one of the pews saying their prayers or his brothers sitting there with their eyes closed, pretending to say theirs too.

He looked up at the paintings and statues of the saints and remembered how much he missed this. There was a timeless sense here, something that could not be found in the United States, where things changed so quickly, that if you left a place for a year, what you remembered was replaced by some cheaply built structure littered with neon lights of advertising.

Alina watched him the entire time with a quiet fascination. As the day progressed, she had become more and more curious about him. He didn't care; he needed this, he needed to quiet his soul. He took another look around and sucked in more of the air, which seemed to have the same smell it had almost 150 years ago.

He looked at Alina and quietly said, "I'm going to need some time."

"Ok, how long?"

"I don't know, but if you want, I can meet you outside or at the café in the square."

Alina looked at him seriously, but said, "Ok," and walked to the back of the church and sat in a pew. Janusz continued walking to the front of the church but stopped at the third pew. He put his right hand on the edge of the wooden bench and knelt before he entered. He slowly walked down the length until he was about a quarter of the way. That seemed about right, from what he could remember.

He bent over carefully and knelt. He closed his eyes and could feel the presence of his gentle mother beside him, almost hearing her prayers to St. Mary. It filled him with warmth that he had not felt in such a long time. It made him feel safe, and he never wanted to leave this church for fear of losing that feeling.

He opened his eyes and took in the image of the Veit Stoss Altarpiece. As he gazed upon its beauty, he tried to remember the last time he had seen something so beautiful. He gazed on all the parts of the piece but stopped when he got to the Assumption of Mary. The sculpture showed Mary being accepted into heaven and being welcomed by Jesus. The scene made him jealous, and the jealousy led to shame. He turned to God in prayer and asked forgiveness for the jealousy, but the feeling was still there, coupled with curiosity.

Why had he not been accepted into heaven? Why was he not with his wife and children right now? Was he going to be doomed like the Wandering Jew who taunted Jesus on the cross and was made to roam the earth until the second coming? Janusz didn't know if he could live with that, but he feared he might not have a choice.

He wanted answers. He wanted to know what he had done that was so terrible he had to keep coming back over and over again. He hated the feeling of helplessness at the start of a new "Ride," he hated feeling out of place all the time, and he hated having to live a lie.

Janusz wondered what he should do. Was he on a path? Or was he being punished? Either way, he felt it was an impossible cause, and this thought made him look at the centerpiece of the Veit Stoss, *The Death of Mary*, and in particular St. Jude, and Janusz thought about him for a while.

St. Jude had told Christians to persevere in times of difficulty, but what if the time of difficulty never ended? He needed strength. He doubted he was going to get any answers, but maybe he could at least find some strength to continue on these journeys. So he bowed his head and prayed to St. Jude, the Patron Saint of Impossible Causes.

When Janusz lifted his head, he looked to the back of the church and saw Alina was not sitting in the pew anymore. He knew he had been in there for a long time, but didn't know how long. Although he yearned to stay in here, he knew he should go, especially if he wanted to get to the graveyard. So Janusz stood up, walked to the edge of the pew, knelt before the altar and made his way toward the exit. Before he left, he dipped his fingers in the holy water, again making the sign of the cross, and walked out the doors.

The moment he stepped into the square, he saw Alina. She sat at a table drinking what appeared to be a coffee, right where he had told her to be. She was engrossed in a magazine, so she did not see him until he was almost upon her. She looked up and began to get out of her chair when he motioned for her to sit back down.

"Finish your coffee," he said. "In fact, I think I'll have one, too."

"As you wish."

Janusz didn't like it when she said, "As you wish." It made her seem subservient, and he wanted her to be at ease around him.

"Alina, I want to have a low-key day, so don't think of this as work. Think of us as two friends out enjoying the day in Krakow."

She relaxed a little, and said, "Ok, no problem."

The waitress came by and stood next to the table. "Would you care for something to drink?"

"A coffee, please."

After she wrote down the order, she glanced up from her pad and stopped for a moment. She recognized Janusz, and her eyes widened. She asked him if he was Janusz Z, and he said "Yes," and signed an autograph for her.

When the waitress left, Alina asked, "Since we are two friends enjoying the day together, may I ask you a question?"

"Sure."

"I've worked with a lot of bands from the United States, but you are different from any of the others."

"Well, that's not really a question, but a statement."

She smiled, slightly embarrassed. "I know, but you don't drink, do you?"

Janusz felt comfortable with her and decided to have some good-natured fun. "Well, I haven't been 21 for that long yet."

She laughed. "You know you don't have to be 21 to drink in Poland."

"I know, but to answer your question, no, I don't drink."

Alina looked at him, pondering if she should ask her next question. "And you don't enjoy the other perks of rock stars...like the groupies, right?"

Usually, Janusz would have been annoyed at this question, but he knew she asked it out of pure curiosity and not with a hidden agenda. He smiled at her and said, "No."

"Why not? Isn't that like, mandatory for rock stars?"

Janusz thought for a moment about how to answer this question and said, "Yeah, I guess it is, but let's say I have personal experience of what the bottle can do to a person...and as for the groupies, well... I guess I haven't found the right one yet."

Alina nodded her head for a moment. "And you don't do any drugs either, like your band mates?"

Janusz' head jerked back a bit. "What do you mean?"

"Come on Janusz, I'm not stupid; I work with enough bands to know who is using and who is not."

"No, as long as I have music, that is the only drug I need." He could tell there was one more thing the curious woman wanted to know, but she was hesitant, so he said, "Anything else? Ask away."

"You are also uncomfortable with your fame."

"Well, it's relatively new."

"Yeah, I know, but it is something else. You are a 21-year-old rock star, but sometimes I get the vibes of an old man coming off you...it's almost as if you don't belong."

Janusz' body tensed up at the last statement. He took a moment to decipher what she meant by it and said, "Well, I've always been an outsider…never really had any friends…so that kind of makes a person more mature."

Alina looked at him for a few moments, which made Janusz feel the slightest bit uncomfortable, as he couldn't read her. After a few seconds of looking at him, she nodded her head and finished the last of her coffee, setting the cup down in the saucer with the slightest of clinks. Janusz too finished his coffee, and said, "So next I would like to make our way over to the Rakowicki Cemetary."

As they left the café, Alina said, "We can catch a cab over there," pointing to a line of them parked, waiting for patrons.

"If it's ok with you, I'd rather walk. If I remember correctly, it should take less than 30 minutes."

Alina looked at him, and Janusz could not believe he had slipped again. He found it difficult not to make mistakes; he was getting caught up in the moment of being here, seeing all the buildings and remembering the talks he used to have with his father. So he added, "From what I remember from my research, of course."

She did not comment on his statement, other than, "Ok."

They both walked in silence. Janusz knew he should be more talkative and ask her a little about herself, but he couldn't. He was reliving too much and walking these streets that he and his father had walked was giving him too much to think about.

The stroll was surreal. Janusz thought it was one thing for a person to see changes happen through time, but it was another to return to a place after so long. There was an essence of modernism along the streets, but it still maintained the "old" feel he remembered. As he passed the Jalu Kurka Park, he looked at Montelupi Palace and was surprised to see how nice it looked. Janusz had to admit; things looked much better now than they did back in the mid-1800s.

Not long after passing the park, they reached the entrance of the cemetery. He remembered the path to his target as if it were yesterday, and within a few moments he stood in front of two gravestones, and Alina said, "This cemetery was mainly used for nobles and people of a higher class."

Janusz didn't look at her when he said, "Yes, but there are also people here who were killed in the Polish uprising against the Russians in the 1860s."

"Yes, yes, that's true," she said softly.

Janusz didn't care at that moment what she thought, or how strange he was. He knelt and reached out and touched the top of the tombstone which read "Jósef Zalewski, 1829-1863." He then looked to his left, reached out and touched another tombstone: "Maria Zalewski, 1831-1863."

Janusz wanted to cry but kept his emotions in check. He was no longer crouching, but rather kneeling in front of the two stones with a hand on each one. He remembered the day he had buried his parents. He was only 13 years old, but he was already a man, and he had two brothers to take care of.

Even though his mother's sister had taken them in after his parents had died, he still had to work every day to bring home food so they wouldn't starve. At the time he hadn't realized how hard it was; it was life. You did the best you could with what you had.

His father had died standing up for something he believed in; he died to create a better life for his children, their children, and so on. Now, looking down at his father's grave, Janusz feared that he would be disappointed. Janusz had no idea about his children or their children, or how they had fared in life; and how many great-grandchildren he had.

Sure, after Janusz took the boat to America, he had worked hard and provided for his family, but what about now? Now, he had the resources to discover the members of his family. So in that very instant, that's what he decided to do. If he would ever meet them, that would be something he would decide at that moment, but now he knew he had to at least find them. His father was in the grave because of a dream, and Janusz did not want his death to be in vain.

Janusz remained at the tombstones for a while longer before he took one final look and said, "Kocham cię," before standing up. He turned around to tell Alina he was ready to go, but she was nowhere to be found. So he started to walk towards the exit of the cemetery and saw her standing by the gate.

When they exited the cemetery, she asked, "Did you find what you were looking for?"

He nodded and said, "I think I found a piece of it at least."

CHAPTER 53

12 OCTOBER 1997

Janusz stood in the hallway of his LA apartment and looked at the wall. He had hung up the platinum album right next to the other one and tried to admire it. He could not understand why he didn't feel a tremendous sense of pride when he looked at it. He had everything he wanted, plus more. The band had sold out every show and the other guys never gave him any problems about new songs he wrote.

He put his hand to his chin and rubbed his two-day-old stubble. Janusz told himself he should do something, but he couldn't figure out what. The band had only finished the tour a week ago, and Janusz didn't know what to do with the extra time. He walked into the kitchen and looked at the calendar on the wall. He flipped the pages ahead to April and looked at the number 2 circled and grimaced. They had six months until they hit the studio and right now, that seemed like an eternity.

Janusz walked into the practice room, picked up his guitar, and strummed it a few times before setting it down. All of the songs for the next album were already written, and without Rack and Ditch, the only thing he could do was come up with some new riffs. He looked at the phone and thought about calling them, but decided against it.

Janusz was doubtful that the guys would want to practice since the break had only just begun. Also, he needed some time away from those two. He walked over to the couch and sank into its depths, and thought about Poland again. He could not shake the feeling he'd had standing in front of his parents' graves.

He stood back up and looked over at the platinum records again and wondered if his parents would be proud of this achievement. He knew the answer and decided it was time to complete the mission that he promised his father at the cemetery. He needed to track down his descendants.

The band manager, as well as Rack and Ditch, had been telling Janusz about this new thing called "The Internet" and how one could find a lot of information about anything on there, so Janusz thought briefly about using this, but then decided against it.

He didn't trust it yet. Maybe he was old fashioned, but he preferred to talk to people face to face as a man should do. Janusz knew that the beginning of his journey was going to have to start in Port Walden, and wondered if he should go back to Ethan and Judith's house.

That was not a good idea, he told himself. He still hadn't talked to Ethan since he had left for L.A., and only rarely spoke to Judith. Besides, she would only complicate matters and not leave him alone to do what he had to do. So he called the accountant and told her that he wanted to buy a house on the river in Port Walden. That would be his base of operations, plus it would be nice to be there and see his beloved river every day

When his accountant asked him how much he wanted to spend, he told her he didn't care. *Just use your best judgment,* he said; he trusted her. The financial security they enjoyed was thanks to Rack, who always talked about bands who got ripped off or got their money stolen, so he made sure that everybody they hired was reliable. The man might be a drug addict, but when the business needed to be taken care of, he made sure it got done. Janusz then thought how screwed they would be if something ever happened to Rack.

CHAPTER 54

14 OCTOBER 1997

Two days later the phone rang, and when Janusz picked it up, it was his accountant on the other end. "Hi, Janusz, it's Janet, we are all set; all we need is your 'ok.'"

"Do it. How soon can I move in?"

"Jeez, don't you even want to know anything about the house?"

"Is it on the river?"

"Yes."

"That's all I need to know."

"Ok, I can have the papers sent over today, and you can move in on 1 November."

Janusz felt his excitement build. "Perfect, will you need anything else?"

"Um, no, but you will...for instance, furniture...and you will need a plane ticket to get there unless you are going to drive?"

Janusz thought about this for a moment. "I've had enough of riding on buses, so yeah, book me a ticket to Detroit."

"Ok, I'll take care of that. I suspect you don't care what is in the house, so I'll handle that too."

Janusz smiled as he held the phone to his face. "You are peaches."

"I know, and who in this day and age calls somebody 'peaches?' But, hey, seriously, why are you going out there, and how long will you be?"

"I just have to take care of some things, Janet. I might be a few weeks or a few months, plus I may have to check out a few other things and travel elsewhere, too."

She was silent for a few moments, but then said, "You know, most guys in your position head off to a tropical island and drown themselves in cocktails and women; they don't go to an icebox in winter." She paused again, then she said, "be careful" before hanging up.

Janusz smiled at her thoughtfulness before hanging up the phone himself. It was going to be an excruciating two weeks to wait, which meant he had to occupy his mind. So after standing by the phone for a couple of moments, he walked over to his guitar collection, picked one up, and started to play.

CHAPTER 55

1 NOVEMBER 1997

Janusz loved the house. It was precisely what he'd wanted, and the back faced the river. Although it wasn't isolated per se, the construction gave him a lot of privacy where he could sit out on the back patio and not have anybody see him unless they were in a boat.

Janet once again was true to her word, and she had everything set up for him. He just walked into the house, and he was home. The convenience made him very happy as he could start tracking down his children right away.

He didn't spend much time in the house--just enough to drop his things off--and then was on his way. He was hoping not to be recognized today, so he grabbed his baseball cap and thick sunglasses and headed out the door.

The trip to the cemetery only took about 10 minutes. Once he got there and parked, it occurred to him that he had no idea where to look. Instead of wandering around though, he decided to start with what he did know, and that was the grave of his wife.

As Janusz started to walk through the cemetery, he realized that he hadn't been there in almost 90 years. He wondered to himself why he'd never made the trip out here before. He never missed an opportunity to go to the picnic spot at the river, but here, the cemetery--he always avoided it.

When he reached his wife's grave, it became clear to him why. As he gazed upon the stone with the words "Marzehna Zalewski, Beloved Wife, Mother, Grandmother, 1853-1905" written on it, he felt his body break. Grief flushed through him, and he fell to his knees. Knowing she was in the ground beneath him was too much for him.

At the river, it was different. When he was at the river, Janusz felt as though she were still alive somehow, or at least with him in spirit. As he knelt there in front of the tombstone, he didn't feel that; he only felt a sense of finality and emptiness.

When he regained his composure, he looked to the right of Marzehna's stone and saw another, and while this one didn't fill him with grief, it did shock him. It read "Janusz Zalewski, resting with the Lord, 1850-1915."

The feeling he had while looking at the stone was a type of aversion. He quickly stood up and backed away as if the grave meant to harm him in some way. After a few moments, he walked closer to the grave again, but felt a sickness in his stomach and backed up again. He didn't want to be near that thing, or even look at it.

Janusz turned his back and walked away from the grave. When he was about 20 feet away from it, he stopped next to a tree and rested his hand on it for support. After he caught his breath, he decided to leave the cemetery. He couldn't bear the thought of how he would feel if he saw the graves of any of his children; it was quite possible that it would have killed him.

So he immediately left the graveyard and drove back to his home. Once he was inside the house, he picked up the telephone and dialed the number for information. The line connected and a pleasant woman on the other end asked, "Which city?"

"Detroit."

"Name or business."

Janusz confidently said, "Private detective agencies."

CHAPTER 56

15 NOVEMBER 1997
10 A.M.

Even though there was a bone-chilling wind coming off the lake, Janusz sat on the back patio holding a large manila envelope the private detective had given him only moments before. He stared at it, especially the letters typed on a white sticker attached to the packet. The words "Geneology of Janusz Zalewski 1850-1915" stared at him.

Inside was the entire history of his family. When they were born, what they did, and when they died. He also had the information on the living descendants. The P.I. delivered as promised, and was working on the histories of the families from Janusz' other rides. Although Janusz didn't know why he was having them tracked down, he thought while he was doing it that he might as well get a complete history. He doubted he would open the other envelopes when they came, but it would be nice to have them nevertheless.

He couldn't understand why he hadn't opened the envelope yet. He was either scared or nervous. Then again, maybe he was just excited. Whichever it was, his hands shook as he held the paper packet and it wasn't from the cold, that much he knew.

"Enough stalling," he told himself and tore open the envelope and began to read.

4 p.m.

By the time Janusz had finished reading the information and re-reading it multiple times, he had made several pages of notes. Janusz was shocked at the sheer number of descendants he had. During his reading, he smiled a lot at some of the things he discovered, such as what some of his family had been or done, but he felt grief, too.

His grandson Robert from his daughter Agata had indeed been sent to WWI, and he had died there. He also had a great-grandson who lost his life in WWII, and he didn't want to think about the anguish the family had gone through. The death, which stung him the most, however, was that of his dear little girl, Agata, his little "Button." As he read the obituary he looked at the picture of an elderly lady; he had a hard time picturing her this old. She had passed away in 1965 at the age of 90, and at the very least, Janusz took solace in that. He prayed she had had a happy life.

Another exciting fact he discovered was that he had gone to high school with one of his great, great, great grandchildren. Janusz looked at the yearbook photo of Stephanie Simmons, but couldn't seem to recall her. She was a beautiful girl, so it didn't surprise him that their paths didn't cross in the year they overlapped at school.

Something else that made him smile was the fact that another one of his great, great, great, grandchildren currently worked at the same restaurant Janusz had. He decided today might be a good day to visit his old place of employment and see if he could get a glimpse of Eric Johnson.

What excited him the most, though, was the fact that one of his grandchildren was still alive--sweet little Edith, whom he could remember holding and playing with many times during regular visits with her mother in the final days of Janusz' original "Ride."

She was 90 years old and in the nursing home not too far away from where Janusz currently sat. He looked at his watch and debated as to whether or not he should try to go over there right now or wait until tomorrow. He knew he should wait, but he was too excited and decided to go then.

* * *

As he walked through the doors of the nursing home, it was about quarter past five. After the lady at reception recognized him and told him how much of a fan she was, he signed autographs for her, and what seemed like everybody else in the facility. Finally, he asked about Edith Stein, and the lady was surprised as to why he wanted to visit her.

He made up a flimsy excuse about being a distant relative and the lady told him they had just finished eating and Edith was probably lying down, sleeping. Also, she told him Edith was not well; she suffered from bouts of severe dementia and most of the time, didn't know where she was or what year it was.

Janusz had come too far to give up, so he asked if he could pop his head in and see if she was awake. The nurse agreed and gave him the room number. As he walked down the halls, the loneliness in the eyes of the residents saddened him. Most of them were wheelchair bound, and some just stared off into space. Janusz wondered if they were reliving a past to which they could never return.

Janusz now pondered if he was doing the same thing. He stopped and thought for a moment if he should turn around and give all this up… maybe return to L.A. and be 23-year-old Rock Star Janusz Z, instead of 147-year-old Janusz Zalweski trying to chase something, which he couldn't really even define what it was. He pushed on though, and stopped when he came to room 31 and saw the name "Edith Stein." He smiled as he saw somebody had drawn a heart underneath her name.

He walked into the room and saw a frail elderly woman lying on the bed, sleeping. He stood there, staring at her for a moment. He couldn't even tell this was the same little girl he used to bounce on his knee — the one who was so full of life and always getting into mischief.

Time was cruel and unfair.

Edith slept, and he did not want to disturb her, so he decided to leave. As he turned, he noticed a scrapbook on the table next to her bed with handwritten script "Generations of Love" and beneath was a heart drawn in the same manner as the one underneath her name in the hall. Janusz suspected that whoever had drawn the heart out there, was the same person who had created this scrapbook.

He spotted a chair at the foot of her bed, so instead of leaving, he grabbed it and moved it beside her bed. He then took the scrapbook and sat quietly, flipping through the pages, which chronicled her life.

The first page made him gasp as it was a picture of Agata holding Edith. Janusz remembered the day well as they had all gone together to get some pictures taken. It was funny how at the time, Janusz hadn't wanted to go. He felt it was too expensive, and had wondered why people's memories weren't sufficient to remember things.

Now he felt differently; he was so happy they'd gone because now he was able to see the people he loved as he remembered them. The next picture was difficult to look at. At the top, in the same handwriting as the cover, someone had written "Grandma and Grandpa," and Janusz stared at a picture of himself and his wife. After he had gotten over his grumpiness that day about spending money on photographs, he'd had fun. Now though, he wished he would have enjoyed the moment more, because a few short months after that photo was taken, he had buried Marzehna.

Janusz continued flipping through the pages, which were in chronological order. The "heart artist" had taken a lot of time and care to put this together for Edith and Janusz could feel the love in it. He was almost to the end of the book when Edith spoke to him in a barely audible voice. "Grandpa, are you here to take me to heaven?"

Janusz jumped and dropped the book to the floor, and his heart started racing.

Her voice was frail, but it had a sense of clarity to it that surprised him, and he asked, "What?"

"Are you here to take me to heaven?"

Janusz' hands shook, and he told himself he must have misheard her when she said, *Grandpa*. He picked up the book again and said, "No, my dear, I was visiting somebody down the hall, and I saw your book when I passed by. It was so pretty I had to look at it."

Now she spoke clearer. "Grandpa, why are you teasing me? I know it's you."

This time Janusz could not dismiss the fact that she had called him Grandpa. Janusz remembered the nurse telling him about dementia, so it could be that, but he had his doubts.

"Edith, why do you think I am your Grandpa, dear?"

"Because Momma told me once that you came to visit her from heaven, but she was scared at the time and got angry with you. She said she slapped you and sent you away."

Janusz felt cold. He couldn't speak and sat there with his mouth open.

Edith continued, "Momma told me she was sorry about that day; she was scared and sad and missed you so much. After she thought about it for a while, she tried to find you, but you were gone, and you never came to visit her again."

Janusz nodded and knew he had to say something as the old lady was now looking at him in anticipation. "Well, dear, I didn't want to make her angry anymore."

"She told me you might come to visit me too, and I shouldn't be angry or afraid."

"That's right, dear, but I'm not here to take you to heaven yet."

"Why not?"

Janusz was now grasping at straws trying to think of things to say. "Well, Jesus told me it is not your time yet, but I should come here and check on you."

The statement elicited no reaction from her, and after a moment of silence she asked, "What's heaven like?"

He reached out his hand and lightly caressed her face and said, "It's beautiful. We are all waiting for you…Grandma, your momma, dad, your kids, and everybody."

Hearing this soothed the old lady and she said no more; she closed her eyes and drifted off to sleep. Janusz remained in the room for about a half hour before he put the chair back at the foot of the bed and exited.

As he passed the nurse's station, the young lady who had helped him before looked up. "How is she?"

"Alright…a little confused."

The nurse nodded solemnly and said, "Each day she is getting worse and worse."

"What do you mean?"

"Well, she sees a lot of her family members who are long dead. Last week it was her mother and yesterday it was her son."

Janusz pondered on this for a moment and wondered if what he had heard were the ramblings of an old lady who had dementia or if it was something else.

The nurse interrupted his thoughts and said, "But I know she loves visitors, so I am sure you made her happy."

Janusz' thoughts were swirling around in his head. He stood outside the door of the nursing home and wondered what he should do next. What did this all mean? The temperature had dropped; the sky was dark and it looked like it could rain or even snow. He told himself he should go back home, play some guitar, and process these thoughts, but he couldn't. He wanted to go to the restaurant; he wanted to see if his great, great, great, grandson was there.

7:30 p.m.

When Janusz walked into his old restaurant, the owner's son, Ben, saw him immediately. "Holy shit, Brian, you're about five years late for your shift. Oh, or should I call you Janusz now?"

Janusz smiled and said, "Anything you want to call me is fine, and I'm sorry about disappointing you like that."

Ben waved his hands in the air dismissively, told him to take a seat, and asked him what he wanted. Janusz ordered, and when Ben came back, he sat down with Janusz, and they both ate together. They caught up on old times and chatted about Janusz' success. Overall Janusz enjoyed himself. Ben was a tough boss, but he was fair, and he'd treated him right, and Janusz had always respected him.

At some point in the conversation, a 17 or 18-year-old kid interrupted them; Janusz guessed he was the dishwasher. Ben looked up at him and said, "Brian, this is Eric, our dishwasher."

Janusz stared at the kid and knew it was him. He sat there looking into the eyes of his great, great, great, grandson. There were a thousand things he wanted to say but was speechless. Then Ben said, "And Eric, of course, you know who this is--our hometown celebrity, Janusz Z."

The kid was unimpressed. He just looked at Janusz with the same expression one might have when looking at a glass of milk. "Sweet," he said and turned to Ben. "So, boss, you think I can get out of here now?"

Ben nodded his head. "Yeah, go on."

When the kid left, Janusz asked, "Kid doesn't talk much, huh?"

"No, but in a strange way he reminds me of you; he is quiet and keeps to himself."

"Really?"

"Yeah. He's gotten himself in a bit of trouble recently, but overall he's not too bad."

Janusz felt there was no more reason to press on about the kid, but he would try to find out what type of trouble he had gotten himself into later. For now, he and Ben continued chatting until Janusz looked out and saw that it was sleeting outside. "Drats, the weather took a turn for the worst."

Ben turned his head toward the window. "Yep, I hope California didn't make you too soft, and you forgot how to drive on Michigan roads."

"Maybe, but I should go anyway. Really, Ben, it was nice talking to you."

"You too, Brian. Don't be a stranger."

Janusz shook Ben's hand and left the restaurant. He was deep in thought as he walked to his car. He thought about Edith, and what she had said. He wondered if he could have been mistaken, and he thought about Eric and what type of trouble the kid was in. What he wasn't thinking about was where he was walking. When he was about ten feet from his car, he didn't see the patch of ice he stepped on, which caused him to slip and fall to the ground.

As soon as he hit the ground, he heard the crack of the bone in his left arm, quickly followed by a shooting pain. He rolled over and grabbed his arm, and tried to move it, but he couldn't; it was broken, and he could only remain there on the ground, writhing in agony.

16 NOVEMBER 1997
1 A.M.

Janusz didn't move at all on the hospital bed; in fact, he barely breathed. When he had arrived in the emergency room he was in excruciating pain, not just from his arm, but his elbow, too. The ER doctor not only confirmed what Janusz had suspected, which was that his arm was broken, but also gave him a new cause for concern. The doctor believed his elbow was also broken and there could be possible tendon damage.

After the initial examination, they gave him some painkillers before he went into X-Ray. Whatever they gave him did the trick, and he didn't feel any of the pain. Janusz thought to himself that he should feel more worried than he did as he waited for the news, but the medicine killed some of that mental pain, too.

When the doctor walked in, Janusz couldn't help but think of the NVA officer back in Vietnam at the "Hilton." Both men were calm and had a "matter of fact" attitude about them, although he didn't think this doctor was going to twist his arm back as the other man had, or at least he hoped not.

"Mr. Richardson," the doctor said, "I have some good news and some bad news."

Janusz noted how interesting it was that the doctor didn't ask him which he wanted first, and began with the bad news.

"Your arm and elbow are going to require surgery, but the good news is that I don't think there will be any lasting damage that will affect your range of motion or dexterity."

Janusz let the words sink in for a moment and asked, "So my guitar playing won't be affected?"

"I don't think so. You were actually fortunate; the breaks and fractures seem to be clean, but I want to make sure about the ligament damage, and we won't know that until the surgery, but I am confident you'll have your motion back in four weeks and should be playing in eight."

This last sentence scared him more than anything, *eight weeks*. Not playing music for eight weeks could be a serious problem. What if the nightmares came back? What if the panic attacks and hallucinations started again? What if he started to drink again?

The doctor must have sensed his unease, and re-assured him again. "Seriously, you should be in and out and on your way to recovery in no time, but I'm not going to lie to you; the recovery and physical therapy are going to be extremely painful."

"How soon before I have the surgery?"

The doctor was back to his serious attitude and said, "The sooner we get in there, the better, as your body is already trying to heal itself with the bones in the wrong position, so we have you scheduled for seven this morning if you agree."

Janusz nodded his head, and the doctor said, "Ok, the nurse will bring in the forms, and you will be all set for tomorrow. I wish you luck, Mr. Richardson." He then left and Janusz had six hours to wait until the surgery.

CHAPTER 57

1 DECEMBER 1997

It took Janusz three times as long to get on the plane and into his seat than it normally would have, due to his arm. The doctor was correct on all predictions he had given Janusz that night in the ER: the surgery had been a success, and there was not going to be any lasting damage, so he hoped he would be able to start playing again soon. There was only one problem; he'd also been right about the pain.

The pain was excruciating. Starting from the day after the surgery, they were moving his arm around and beginning therapy, which Janusz thought was too soon. They had told him it must start immediately so that he wouldn't lose any range of motion.

He was thankful for the pills, though; the pills numbed the pain.

Once he was in his seat, and the plane was preparing for takeoff, that reminded him he had to check how many pills he had left. He took the bottle out of his pocket and could see through the brown plastic that he only had six remaining. He shook his head in disbelief; he wasn't due for a refill for another week, and depending on his pain level, he would be lucky if this would last him through tomorrow.

He put the bottle back in his pocket and rested his head against the back of the seat, making a mental note to call his doctor in L.A. the moment he landed to get this prescription refilled sooner. During the day, Janusz only needed as many pills as the doctor recommended, but it was at night that he had to take more. The first couple of nights after the surgery, his arm hurt so bad he didn't get much sleep, and when he did sleep, he had a couple of nightmares.

It was as if they had been waiting for him under the surface for all those years and once they saw their chance, they crawled their way up and out. So he started to take double the amount that the doctor said he should, and that did the trick. He slept like a baby with no nightmares. Taking the pills allowed him to sleep much better than the liquor ever did, and best of all, there was no hangover in the morning.

Janusz felt the plane lift off from Detroit Airport and watched the ground quickly disappear. He wondered if it had been a mistake coming here. Aside from the accident, had he accomplished anything?

There was one thing though; he felt pretty good. He thought not being able to play guitar would have driven him crazy or made him want to drink, but that wasn't the case; he felt fine, in fact, maybe even a little normal. There was always a period in the morning where he would feel off, but then he would take his medication, get up, move around, and the world seemed to slide back into balance.

Going back to the warm weather should help his arm. Although they still had lots of time before they recorded the new album, he didn't want to take any more chances, so he was going to do everything possible to get better.

Soon, he heard the familiar "ding," which was followed by an announcement that the Captain had turned the fasten seatbelt light off and they would momentarily start their beverage service. When the flight attendant asked him if he would like anything, he told him, "Just some water."

Once he had the water, Janusz reached back in his pocket and retrieved the bottle of pills again. He looked at them and thought, *it's a little early, but I'll take them now so I can sleep and hopefully wake up in L.A.* Then with one flip of the cap, he put the bottle to his mouth and shook out two pills, which he promptly chased down with the water from the flight attendant.

* * *

He woke up about 30 minutes before landing. He had slept deeply and had no dreams, although his arm was a bit stiff and had started to ache again. He knew the trip home from LAX could be a long one, and maybe a little uncomfortable, so he thought it was best to take another pill so he wouldn't be caught in the middle of rush hour in agony. Once again he popped the cap of the bottle and was only going to take one, but two fell on his tongue as he shook the bottle, and instead of spitting one back out, he left it there and washed the pills down with the last of his water.

After landing, the plane taxied into the gate, and he was the first one off. He hadn't brought any luggage with him, so he walked right past the baggage claim and out the doors, where Rack and Ditch greeted him.

As soon as they saw him, they both looked at his arm, which was in a sling, and Rack said, "Fuck... are you alright, man?"

"Yeah, I have some more physical therapy that I will finish up here, but I'm good. It still hurts like the dickens, though, but don't worry, I'll be good for recording."

Rack shook his head and said, "Alright man, let's get you home," and they started to walk out the main entrance. Once they were in the car, Rack asked, "You need anything on the way?"

Janusz could feel the bottle of pills pressing against his chest through his jacket and said, "Yeah, I do. I'm almost out of painkillers, but I don't have a new prescription. You know any doctors that work fast?"

Rack smiled and said, "Dude, this is L.A., there is a doctor on every corner that will give us a prescription," and he put the car in gear and drove off.

CHAPTER 58

AUGUST 1998

As Janusz sat on the tour bus heading to their next show, he looked at his hand and opened and closed it. His arm was perfect--no loss of dexterity. The injury had not affected his playing in the least bit. Also, when it came time to record, they had rolled into the studio and cranked out their magic as usual. So his accident hadn't affected the timeline for the new record, and he was relieved about that. There was one thing he noticed though, and that was his lack of creativity. They'd already been on tour for a month, and Janusz had not written anything new, and this worried him. He also was hanging out with the other guys more and more after the shows, having drinks and partying. Since the accident, he had been finding himself in the circle of playing, partying, sleeping (some) and repeat.

Once he stopped looking at his hand, he opened up his backpack and took out his bottle of pain pills. He shook the bottle and held it up to the light, only to discover there were none left. He checked his backpack for another bottle with no luck.

He started to get irritated, and he also wondered why the damn bus was so hot. He was sweating, and his stomach felt a bit uneasy. He got up and went to his storage compartment to get his other backpack with his extra pills, but couldn't find it. He started to cuss and toss things from the compartment onto the floor in a frenzy. It wasn't there; he must have forgotten it.

He had been forgetting a lot of things lately or letting things slide that he usually wouldn't, but he couldn't believe he had forgotten his pills. He screamed. "Now what the fuck am I supposed to do?"

Rack woke up, and he stumbled off of his cot and over to Janusz. "Dude, what the fuck?"

"I forgot them. I forgot my pills."

Rack took a long, hard look at him. "Shit, man, you're starting to come down."

"What? What are you talking about? I'm not a fucking junkie."

"Think what you want, brother, but it doesn't matter if it comes by way of the needle you bought on the street, or by that doctor with a tie on under his white coat…drugs are drugs, and in a few hours you are going to be full blown."

Janusz looked at him in horror. *How can that be*, he thought, *they were only pills from the doctor*. It was medicine, he had been telling himself over and over as each tablet slid down his throat. And besides, the doctor kept telling him to be careful, so how could he be addicted, he wondered.

Janusz exhaled and ran his fingers through his hair. "I need to resupply once we get to the show."

Rack laughed and tilted his head. "Resupply? Dude, we are playing a show in Utah; we are lucky they are even letting us in the state! There is no way you are going to score some Oxy, and if you tried, your ass would be locked up quick."

Janusz sat on the floor, rocking back and forth and said, "Well, I guess I'm gonna have to push through it."

Rack shook his head. "Dude, you ain't pushing through shit…this is a serious fucking problem, bro."

"What do you mean?"

"What I mean is that in the next few hours you are going to go to shit; what you are feeling now is only going to get worse. You won't be able to concentrate because of your cravings and your head will be pounding bad, you'll be puking up your guts even though you won't be able to eat anything, then it will get worse."

"How long does this last?"

"Depends, but speaking from experience, I usually peak at about 72 hours, and little by little, the physical symptoms start to wear off."

Janusz felt as though the bus was getting smaller and hotter by the second. "So what are we going to do?"

"Are you sure you don't have any pills stashed away somewhere?"

"Yes, I'm sure, I looked a hundred times."

"Well, we have two choices, the first being, we cancel the show, and tell them you are sick."

"What's the second?"

"You ain't gonna like it."

"What are you talking about? I don't like the first choice."

"The second choice is to jump on the horse."

* * *

That afternoon Janusz took his first hit of heroin.

From the time he had had the conversation with Rack, up until about ten minutes before he took the hit, he said, "No way." He thought he could handle it and push through, but Rack was right. The symptoms kept getting worse, and finally, he couldn't take it anymore. So he promised himself that he would take the hit to get through the show and then switch back to pills. When they got back, he would talk to the doctor.

He walked up to Rack and said, "Ok, I'm ready."

Rack looked at him seriously. "Are you sure? Because once you start this ride, there is no getting off of it."

That's what you think, thought Janusz, but he only said, "I'm sure."

"Well, if we do this, we better do it now, so we can see how you react, and have plenty of time to get right before the show."

Janusz sat down on his bunk while Rack went to get his kit. Janusz watched him closely as the man prepared the drug with a mechanical type of precision. Rack explained to him what he was doing, and why it was important, saying twice, "There's no room for mistakes," and "You can't fuck around with this in the least bit."

Janusz laid his head back, and soon he felt the needle prick his skin, but he didn't look down; he just waited for this agony to be over. At first, he felt nothing and asked, "When does it hit?"

"Soon enough."

And then it did hit. Janusz' sickness disappeared the second he felt the rush, and agony was replaced by a euphoria that tripled what the pills had ever given him. He never imagined one could feel that good. He looked at Rack, but only said, "Damn."

Rack nodded his head. "I'll come to check on you in a bit; you are not the only one that has to get right for the show."

CHAPTER 59

4 JAN 2000

Janusz never went back to the pills, and by the end of the tour, though he wouldn't admit it, he was a full-blown heroin addict. Now as he sat in Rack's living room, he knew why Rack had called him and told him to come over, ready to get down to business. Janusz had not come up with any new material during the tour, and now they were two months away from going into the studio, and he had nothing.

Janusz couldn't explain it; he had no creative energy. It was fine on stage, playing the songs they already had, but when it came to something new, he was at a loss. It was weird--since he had started with heroin, and even before with the pills, Janusz never thought about being Janusz Zalewski or any of the other previous names he'd had. It was magic, he only felt like Janusz Z--Rock Star. When he was on the drug, his last rides felt like only memories of dreams, which excited him, but also made him sad in a way. He never thought about his wife or his children anymore. He had even heard his granddaughter had passed away a while ago, and it didn't affect him in the least bit. The only time he felt any of the old Janusz was when he waited too long to shoot up, but once he was "right" again, all was perfect.

He knew Rack wasn't going to stand for the way things were. He guessed one could say Rack was a drug addict with a work ethic. Janusz wanted to get out of there and be alone. That wasn't going to be possible, though, and when Rack walked into the room, he got right to the point. "Look, man, we need to talk."

"I know, I know, I'm working on shit right now," Janusz said.

Rack cut him off. "Janusz, look, you're a young dude, and you had a lot of fame and money put on you real quick, but you can't forget why we do this."

"I'm not," he protested but didn't believe it himself.

"Do you know how long we looked for somebody for the band?"

Janusz didn't say anything but shook his head.

"A year, we wanted to find the perfect fit, and when I saw you play, I knew we'd found it. So be honest with yourself now; do you still feel that?"

"No."

"You see, Janusz, that's a problem, because if you can't find that again, or get back into the groove, what we have here is gone."

Janusz couldn't look at him; he only sat there with his head hanging down, looking at the ground.

"Janusz, look at me, dude, I need to know you understand what I am saying. If you can't get your shit together, you are out of the band."

Janusz jerked his head up and looked at Rack. "What do you mean? You can't kick me out of the band."

"I know it's your guitar and voice that makes JRD what it is, but if you can't do it, then Ditch and I will leave, and believe me, it *will* be hard for us to find another guitarist and singer--but not impossible."

Janusz thought about his words for a moment. Rack was more than a drummer; he was the energy behind the band, and--Janusz had to be honest with himself--he was also the brains behind the whole operation.

While Janusz pondered this, Rack continued. "Dude, trust me, that is the last thing I want, but you have to learn how to balance using and playing. So do you think you can pick yourself up, and head into the studio right now and put some shit together with me?"

"Yeah, let's do it."

Now it was Rack who was silent, pondering something for a moment as if he were working up the courage to say something, and he finally said, "I think I'm at the point now where I need to get clean. I'm in my 30s, and I'm not blind, I know how this story will end."

Janusz looked at him and asked, "Now?"

"We don't have time now, but I'm going to go to rehab as soon as we finish the next tour; Ditch is on board with me, and we would like you to join us as well."

Janusz thought about the prospect of being clean. Maybe he could regain his self-respect and look at himself in the mirror again.

Janusz put his hands on his head. "I don't know how I got to this point."

Rack got up and sat on the couch next to him. "None of us do, man. One day you're partying and having fun, or taking some pills from the doctor, and the next, you're a junkie. No matter how much we lie to ourselves, we are junkies."

Janusz sat up straight and took a deep breath, and said, "I'm in."

"I'm dead serious about this, brother," and Janusz could tell from his tone he wasn't playing around. "We have to keep this under control during this next tour, agreed?"

"Agreed."

"But in the meantime, I got to get right while we are waiting for Ditch. Are you in?"

Janusz thought it was strange that Rack had just given a whole speech on getting clean, and now he asked him if he wanted to shoot up, but they were junkies, and until they walked into rehab, they still needed their drugs. He looked at Rack and nodded his head.

Rack went and got his "kit" and came back and said, "I have some new stuff here; it's a different blend so maybe you shouldn't do as much as you normally do."

Even though he wasn't listening to him, Janusz nodded his head, and they both prepared their needles and shot up.

CHAPTER 60

8 JANUARY 2000

Janusz woke up confused. The first thing he saw was Judith staring at him with Ethan next to her. She had obviously been crying, and he could tell by the look on Ethan's face that he was upset too, although he couldn't tell if it was anger or worry.

Within seconds of Janusz waking up, a doctor rushed into the room, along with what Janusz assumed was a nurse. He realized he was in a hospital, but that was all he could figure out. The doctor soon cleared up all the confusion he had. "Mr. Richardson, how do you feel?"

"What happened?"

The doctor was blunt, but not rude, as he said, "You overdosed, and you've been in a coma for the past three days."

Janusz couldn't believe it, the last thing he remembered was taking the hit, but that was it--nothing, only blackness.

The doctor continued, "Mr. Richardson, you are fortunate. By all accounts, you should have died a few minutes after you injected the drugs into your system."

Janusz cringed when the doctor said that; he was embarrassed to have Judith and Ethan hear it. The doctor wasn't done piling on the embarrassment, though. "Your heart stopped, and we have no idea for how long, plus we thought we were going to lose you in the coma."

"I feel fine."

"The heroin you injected was mixed with another substance, and whoever did it, didn't know what they were doing, as it was much too strong. We are going to have to run a battery of tests to make sure there was no brain damage while you were not breathing."

"Ok," was all he could think to say.

"I'm going to leave you with your parents now, as I am sure you all have a lot to talk about, but I'll be back soon."

Janusz dreaded having the doctor go because that would leave him alone with Judith and Ethan; he was embarrassed and didn't think he could face them. For a while, everyone was silent, until Judith broke the ice. "Brian, how long has this been going on?"

At that point, Ethan spoke up too, but his tone was much harsher than Judith's. "Were you doing this while you were living at home?"

Janusz groaned, as he felt Ethan was going to make this about himself and the public shame it would bring.

"No," Janusz replied sharply.

"Well, it's all over the damn news about how you overdosed. Some reports said you were dead at first, and others said you would be a vegetable for the rest of your life."

Janusz wanted to set Ethan straight, so he started to go on the defensive, but then it hit him. "Hey, wait a minute, where is Rack? If the stuff we took was bad, is Rack ok?"

Janusz felt a sinking feeling when he saw Judith drop her head. "Mother, please tell me what happened? Is he ok?"

More silence. Finally, Ethan spoke up, and his voice was much gentler now. "Brian, I'm sorry, but your friend passed away."

"Passed away? Are you trying to tell me Rack is dead?"

Judith gripped his hands tighter. "Oh, sweetheart, I'm sorry, but your friend is gone. He didn't make it."

Janusz let his head fall back on the pillow and pulled his hands out of Judith's so he could bring them to his face. *It wasn't possible,* he thought, *Rack, dead?* Janusz tried to wrap his head around it, but couldn't. Rack knew what he was doing; he wouldn't make a mistake like that. He exhaled deeply and wondered what he was going to do without Rack.

After a moment, Ethan said, "Apparently he took much more than you did and by the time the paramedics got there, they couldn't do anything."

"How did they find us?"

"Your other friend, Ditch…he found you."

Janusz now remembered. They were waiting for Ditch, and they were going to write some new material. It seemed unreal to him; Rack was always in control and always knew what he was doing. Now--just like that--he was gone.

Janusz started to get angry. He was angry at heroin, angry with the dealers, angry with the doctors who indiscriminately prescribed drugs, but most of all he was angry with himself. He wondered what his wife would think, and also his children.

Judith grabbed his hand again, and this time Ethan held it, too, as she said, "Brian, please, talk to us, sweetheart."

He lifted his head and met their eyes. He had hit rock bottom, and right now they were the only ones he could trust, and he said, "I need help."

Judith gripped his hand tighter. "We are here for you."

"I'm so ashamed," he said as he shook his head. "It's not what you think. After I broke my arm, I was in so much pain, and the doctor gave me pills."

Judith and Ethan said nothing; they only looked and listened as he continued. "Then I had problems sleeping, so I took more. The pain went away, but the urge didn't, and they still kept giving them to me. Next, I found myself in a position where I didn't have any pills, so to calm the urge, I tried heroin, and next thing you know, I'm here."

By the time he finished telling them everything, all three were in tears. Ethan rubbed his eyes and asked, "Where do we go from here?"

"I want to get clean. Father, this isn't me. I'm not the person I used to be, and I need to get my life back."

Ethan glanced over at Judith and back to Janusz and said, "We are happy to hear that, and we are here for you."

"Thanks, I know I don't deserve it."

Ethan got serious again. "But from what the doctor has told me, it's not going to be easy, bud. In fact, it's going to be hell."

Janusz leaned back and closed his eyes and muttered under his breath, "What's new."

CHAPTER 61

10 JANUARY 2000

Janusz left the hospital with good news. He had no lasting damage from the overdose, and he was now on his way to the rehab clinic for a 90-day stint. Ethan and Judith had not left his side for the entire duration, and Janusz had not minded it at all. He had to surround himself with people he could trust.

His spirits were low, though. His face was plastered all over the news, and some of the stories they reported about him were terrible, or not true. Additionally, he had not heard from Ditch at all. He had called him several times but never received an answer. His manager had been to see him several times, but Janusz could tell the only thing he was interested in was getting a new drummer and recording, so they could get back on the road to keep the money pouring in.

Janusz had no idea how he was going to do that. In his mind, it was over. Without Rack, there was no JRD. He couldn't worry about that now, though; the representative from the rehab clinic had told him that right now, the only thing he should concentrate on was getting better, so that was what he was going to do.

As they walked out of the hospital, paparazzi and reporters mobbed them. Somebody from the hospital must have tipped them off, and they could barely make it to the car, there were so many people. Once they were in the car, Janusz turned to Judith. "Are you ok?"

She nodded her head as she sat wide-eyed. "My God, do you go through that all the time? Those people are like animals."

"Not all the time, mostly at shows and when I overdose," he said and smiled, trying to make a little light of the situation.

Ethan then added, "I don't know how you put up with that bullshit." Janusz only nodded his head, and they rode in the car the rest of the way in silence.

Once they arrived at the rehab center, Janusz became panicked for some reason. As everybody got out of the car, he remained. All kinds of thoughts coursed through him, and he wondered if he could do this. Most of all, he wondered why the band hadn't gone to rehab sooner, and why they had to take that one hit.

Judith poked her head back in the car and extended her hand to him, and he took it. As he got out of the car, Ethan put his arm around him, and the three of them walked into the building together. Once they were inside, they were directed to a waiting room where they all promptly took a seat and sat in silence.

It wasn't long before his case manager came in and introduced herself as Darma, and the moment she walked in, Janusz felt electricity jolt through his body. It wasn't because of beauty, although she was attractive; it was something else, and Janusz couldn't put his finger on it. When she started talking to him, he couldn't help but stare into her eyes as there was *something* about them. She was a slender lady who stood about five and a half feet tall with long dark hair that was braided and hanging over one shoulder down to her chest. Her cheekbones were high and above them rested two of the most magnificent eyes Janusz had ever seen. The eyes were so blue that they almost appeared to be projecting light on their own.

She spoke in the calmest of manners, and Janusz felt at ease with her. He told himself that was probably her job, and she had to deal with people like him regularly. He knew it was something else, though; there was something between them, and Janusz was pretty sure she could feel it, too.

"Mr. Richardson," she said as she extended her hand. "Welcome to New Hope; we like to get started immediately here, so I will not waste any time."

As Janusz shook her hand, his attention was diverted from her hypnotizing eyes to a circular scar on her wrist. He then glanced at her other wrist and noticed another scar there as well. He considered asking her about the marks, but didn't get the chance as she said, "As you know, you will be here for 90 days, and during that time, we will go through certain phases with the end goal of you leaving with the tools and the strength to avoid a relapse."

"I don't understand. Won't I leave here without cravings to use again?"

She looked at him pleasantly. "I'm sorry, but that's doubtful. Some people have the desire to use throughout their entire existence. We don't have a magic cure, but our goal is to prepare you for this lifelong fight."

Janusz zeroed in on the word *existence*. He found it strange she didn't use *life*, but let her continue. "Right now, this is the time to say goodbye to your parents; we find it best here if you have no contact with the outside world, including loved ones, for the duration of your stay."

This situation didn't surprise him, as he expected it, so he turned to Ethan and Judith and said, "I am so sorry."

Judith said, "Now stop that, concentrate on getting better and when you get out, we will be here waiting for you."

Ethan smiled and said, "Besides, we are going to enjoy L.A. for a while, and the best part is we get to stay at your house, eat all your food, and make a mess for you, so you know how we felt."

Janusz laughed, stood up, and hugged them both tightly. Once he let them go, he watched them walk out the door and then turned to Darma and stared into her radiating blue eyes and said, "Let's do this."

CHAPTER 62

Janusz sat in the room with everybody, proud of their achievement. He had spent thirty days in the program and looked forward to moving on to the second month. Darma walked in and went behind a podium. She paused and smiled her natural smile and began to talk. She congratulated Janusz on making it through the initial part of the program.

Once the meeting finished, Janusz followed Darma to her office where they had a one-on-one talk. "Congratulations once again, Janusz. At this point your physiological cravings are gone."

"That's great!"

"Yes, but it's also dangerous because the mental cravings can happen anytime, for any reason."

Janusz thought of his Vietnam flashbacks, and how sometimes they would pop up out of nowhere, sometimes for no reason, and this scared him. With the Vietnam flashbacks, he had treated those with liquor, and there was no way he could do that this time. "So what do I do?"

Darma looked at him with a deep, probing look, which seemed to amplify the blueness of her eyes. The look reminded him of staring at one of those pictures with all the dots, hiding something behind the exterior; if one concentrated on it hard enough, sometimes in one spot, one could see something else. That is how she looked at him…like she was trying to see something inside. It didn't bother him, though, as there was something about her, too, embedded in all the colors.

Once both of them stopped their game of staring, Darma said, "Well, you are already doing part of it. Your guitar playing eases your soul."

Janusz looked at her and smiled. "Eases your soul? Not very scientific, counselor."

Now she smiled at him. "Surely you believe in a soul, Janusz, or at least the force which drives this vessel you have--whether you call it a soul, shakra, or simply electrical impulses, if you are so inclined to stay scientific."

Janusz felt the woman was trying to find something out and he was curious. "Yes, I believe in a soul."

Darma looked at him for a moment longer and rubbed one of the scars on her wrist with her thumb before she continued. "The first month was to fix the body, the second is to fix the soul, and the third month of the program is to fix your relationships."

Janusz was disappointed that she was going straight back into talking about the program, but at least during this month, he would find more out about the soul. So he asked, "When do we start?"

"Right now."

"Really?"

"Have you ever meditated, Janusz?"

"Of course, I meditate on a lot of things."

"No," she said, "That is thinking about things, and that isn't the same. I am talking about meditating past what we call this plane of existence."

Janusz never believed in all that mumbo jumbo, but then again, he had never thought a person could die and keep coming back in different bodies, only to have the memories of the other lives, so he figured he could give it a shot.

Their first meditation session did not feel intense, but it changed his life. Darma had him start slowly, but that was all he needed. She taught him how to look at his life--his whole life--and it shocked him.

At the beginning of the meditation session, when she had him meditate on his life, he only looked at Janusz Zalewski, but Darma had suspected he was holding back something, and she was right. He considered his life to be only the years he spent as Janusz Zalewski, but she kept pressing him to look at everything.

She said, "Your life encompasses much more than the things you want it to be; it also encompasses those you don't want to be and maybe even the things you don't even know. They may be different points, but they are all part of the same journey."

Once the meditation session was over, Janusz had a million questions to ask her, but Darma refused to answer and told him that now was the time to let everything soak in and absorb it. So he walked back to his room, confused, but also a little excited at what future meditation sessions could bring. For the rest of the evening, Janusz thought profoundly on his meditation session, and could not get the feeling out of his mind. He also could not forget what Darma had told him about everything being part of the same journey.

He knew that sounded similar to something else he had heard before, but he struggled to recall it. A million things swam through his mind, and he was having trouble separating them. So Janusz lay there and tried to calm himself, tried to be in the moment, and picked all the superfluous garbage swimming in his head away and tossed it out.

Then, plain as day, right there in the middle of his memory, he was able to find it. He remembered where he had heard it before, or at least something similar. He had heard it as he left the POW camp in Vietnam. The last thing Colonel Johnson had told him before he walked out the gates of the prison was "Sergeant, when you leave here, hopefully you have learned to block things, just remember, this is only a minor blip on your long, long journey."

Janusz bolted upright in his bed and breathed heavily. It was almost the same thing. It had to be a coincidence, he told himself, but what if it wasn't? Janusz now made a promise to himself that he was going to watch Darma closely and see if he could find any other similarities between her and Colonel Johnson.

CHAPTER 63

Janusz had packed everything in the room except his guitar. The case lay open on the bed, but the guitar still sat in the corner on the stand. He walked over and picked it up; as he did, he smiled and felt the old familiar charge surge through him.

Over the months, the sensation had come back. He felt the feeling was a force and it had saved his life. During his time here, as he moved away from the drugs, his creativity and desire to play had returned. He had been able to write a lot while he was here. He figured he had enough material for two albums, but there was only one problem--there was no Rack.

He still hadn't come to grips with how he was going to proceed without Rack, or maybe even Ditch, if truth be told. Janusz guessed this was going to be one of the big topics he and Darma would speak about at their final session today. He also hoped he could finally get some answers out of her since he couldn't during his three month tenure. The woman was evasive, only giving a hint here, or a clue there, as to who she was.

She would always shut the conversation down when he probed into her background, only focusing on him. But then again, he told himself, that was why he was here. He kept this thought in his head as he brought the guitar over to the case and set it inside. As it fit neatly in the cutout, it pushed a waft of air up, and the scent hit Janusz in the nostrils.

He had always liked the smell of a guitar case; there was something special about it. The scent was power, but most of all; it was hope. Also, no matter how old the case was, the smell always remained. He closed the lid and clicked the latches shut, and the sound didn't give him a feeling of finality, but rather, of a beginning.

He took one final look around the room to ensure he hadn't forgotten anything, but really, all he needed was his guitar and notebook. Those were the only essential things. Once he was satisfied, he walked down the hall and into Darma's office, where she was already waiting for him.

"Please close the door and have a seat, Brian."

As he did, he sensed something different about her, not particularly bad, or for that matter, good, but something different nonetheless.

After he closed the door, he took a seat and looked at her and said, "Well, here we are, the last day."

Darma smiled. "Or maybe it's the first day?"

He shook his head and smiled in mild frustration at her vagueness and riddles. "Yes, or the beginning."

She wasted no more time and jumped right into the session. "So after today, you are going back out into the world, in a world that is different than how you remember it. What is going to be the biggest difference you think you will encounter?"

"Rack is gone."

Darma looked at him for a moment and probed him a bit more. "Is that all?"

"Well, there may be a change in the band or the attitudes of the people around me."

"Think deeper," she said.

"Deeper?"

"Yes, you are only focusing on one part of your life."

He looked at her. "Well, that is the part which led me to be here."

"Is it?" She asked him and continued. "The one negative aspect of your time here is you refused to focus on your entire life, all of it, and how all parts of it played into your overdose."

Janusz rubbed his forehead with his fingers. "I wish for once you would tell me what you want to know, Darma," and as soon as he said it, he regretted snapping at her.

It didn't seem to bother her, though. "I want to know why you are holding back, why you are leaving out huge chunks of your existence."

"What?"

"Brian, I want you to take a deep breath, and think, THINK about the last time you were honest with somebody else. When was the last time you were honest with somebody about who you are?"

Janusz thought about this for a moment. Darma had asked a good question, and it had been a long time since he had been honest with anybody, probably including himself. Darma prodded him some more. "What's holding you back?"

"Fear."

"Fear of what?"

At that moment Janusz decided to open up a bit, kind of like cracking the door open and peeking into the next room. "The last time I opened up and told somebody the truth, the situation didn't go well," he said, and thought about the time more than 80 years ago when he sat in the church and told the pastor about being Janusz Zalewski.

"Is that same fear stopping you now? Are you afraid I will do the same thing this other person or people did when you told them who you were?"

"Maybe."

"Or are you afraid of how it will sound to yourself when you say it, or maybe you will discover for yourself who you truly are?"

"What?" he exclaimed, "That's ridiculous. I know who I am; maybe I just can't tell other people."

She looked at him with steel laced eyes that shouted a certain confidence and said, "You have to accept yourself for who you are, and until you do that, you will never fully be equipped to fight your addictions. Something else will always come up, and it will divide you, make you vulnerable, and strike when you are down."

Her statement made a lot of sense to him; every time addiction had grabbed him was when he was separated from something he loved or when something had been taken away from him, making him feel less than whole.

He paused as a child might do the first time before jumping into the deep end of the pool, trying to work up the courage to take the plunge. "Fine, you want to hear it? All of it?"

"I do."

He threw up his hands and said, "Ok." He took a deep breath and started. "My name is Janusz Zalewski; I was born in Krakow, Poland in 1850...

2 p.m.

When the last word slipped out of his mouth, Janusz felt like he could breathe for the first time since the whole mess had started. He was so deep into the story that throughout most of it, he had forgotten Darma was there, and it didn't even matter; the more he talked, the more he realized it was for him. He needed to get this out like a splinter caught in a finger; once he pulled it out, he felt better.

When he looked at Darma, the fear came back once he fully realized she was in the room and had listened to everything he had said. She said nothing and only looked at him while rubbing one of the scars on her wrist with her thumb. Something was different, though. He wasn't worried, there was something about her look that told him it was ok.

Then, after what looked like some serious deliberation on her part, she stood up and walked over to a cabinet on the far side of her office. She withdrew a key from her pocket and skillfully put it in the lock and turned it. The door popped open on its own, and she grabbed a silver box with both hands and carried it over to the desk and set it down between her and Janusz.

Janusz had no idea what was in the intricately adorned box or what the woman was thinking. Right now he was glad she had not called for security, and that they were not carrying him away to an asylum. Once she sat down again across from him, she pulled out another key; this one was older than the one she had used for the door. It was decorated in a similar fashion to the box. She inserted the key into the lock and slowly withdrew the contents of the box. Most of the items were pictures, some of which were very old, he noted, but others were objects such as necklaces and various pendants.

"What is all this?" he asked.

At first, she said nothing, but spread the photos out on the table and pulled out an amulet and said, "This amulet was given to a little boy named Pradeep by a stranger traveling a dark road in what you know to be India, almost a thousand years ago."

Janusz sat, confused, and said nothing, hoping some clarity would soon come.

"This little boy, Pradeep, hated the world and hated himself; he was lost, and nobody understood him." She pointed next to a picture of another little boy. "This little boy was named Tilak, another lost boy, but one who was starting to understand his path."

Janusz looked at the picture and noticed the little boy was holding onto the amulet. At that moment Janusz felt as if he were falling, falling and he could not grab onto anything. He stood up from his chair, but the world started to swirl, and for a moment, he did not know where he was.

Darma had gotten up and held onto him while leading him to a couch where he could lie down. He caught his breath and looked over at Darma, who was now sitting on a chair across from him. She said, "Janusz, all of these are stages of my journey, the journey that I have been on now for a little more than 2,000 years."

Janusz was stunned he was not more shocked than he was. Silently, he sat there, not knowing what to say. In a way, he figured he already knew--maybe not exactly but he *knew* something was strange and a bit off about her. There was an understanding between them he could not quite put his finger on. Finally, he managed to say, "So, um..." but even then the words failed him.

"Yes," she helped him out. "I'm like you; I'm a voyager."

"A what?"

"A voyager; it is what most of us call ourselves."

"There are more of us?"

"Oh yes, quite a few."

"So I'm not a...freak?"

"Well," she said, "It depends on your definition of the word, but if you mean what I think you mean, then no, you are not a freak."

Janusz honestly couldn't describe or understand the feelings he had and all he could ask her was "Why?"

She looked at him with sorrow in her radiant blue eyes, she felt his pain, and she understood. "I'm sorry, Janusz, but I can't give you that answer anymore than I can tell you why the sun rises in the east."

"Am I being punished?"

"That, too, I am unable to answer. Many have said what we are is a form of punishment, while others say it is a reward; in the end, it's for you to figure out."

"So like everything else," he said dejectedly, "many questions with no answers."

Darma got up from the chair, walked over to the couch, and took a seat by him. She put a caring hand on his thigh. "I may not be able to tell you why, but I can give you some answers or guidance, which may ease your suffering."

He looked up at her and realized for the first time since she had revealed to him who she was, that this woman knew even better than he what it was to struggle. He did have questions, and while she might not be able to answer all of them, she would be able to tell him something.

"So you have been alive for 2,000 years?" As he said it, the realization hit him. It made his 151 years of existence seem meager, but it also filled him with dread. Was he doomed to walk the earth for another 1,800 years?

The thought made him feel like he was spinning out of control. All at once, he felt like he wanted to drink, to shoot up, and also to kill himself. He threw his hands up to his face. "I can't. I can't do that. I was living with the hope that each "Ride" would be the last."

Now she looked at him and asked *him* a question. "Ride? What does that mean?"

"That's what I have been calling each time I come back. My first life was the original ride, and I am now on my fifth."

She smiled at him and patted his leg again. "Oh, child, you are only at the beginning."

Darma looked at her watch, which made Janusz panic as he wondered if she was going to toss him out or tell him their time was up. He was about to protest when she said, "Janusz, it's getting late, and we cannot continue talking here."

"What do you mean? Do I have to go? But I have so much more to ask you."

"Calm yourself, child. I said we can't talk here. There is more I need to tell you, but I would rather do it at your house, so we will not be interrupted. Is it possible for us to have privacy?"

Janusz quickly thought about what was waiting for him at his house and remembered that Ethan and Judith would be there. "My parents are going to want to see me."

"Tell them to wait. Send them to a hotel, for what I must tell you is important, and you are in a vulnerable and dangerous position right now."

"Dangerous?"

Darma's look became serious. "Yes, Janusz, in addition to you being vulnerable for relapse, your sanity is at stake, and once your sanity is broken, it stays broken throughout all of your voyages."

"Ok," he replied, "I can clear them out for today."

"Good," she said, "I will follow you back to your house and answer all of the questions you have to the best of my ability."

4 p.m.

Darma arrived at Janusz' home only minutes after the cab dropped him off. Her timing was impeccable, and he wondered if she had followed him. He then tossed the idea aside because, in the grand scheme of things, he guessed it didn't matter.

When she entered the house, she looked around for a moment and studied the place. "So this is how a rock star lives, huh?"

"I guess, but I am rather new at it."

He showed her to the living room and offered her something to drink. She refused; she was eager to get started and wasted no time. "Janusz, I imagine you have many questions for me, so feel free to ask, and when you finish, I'll fill in anything you missed."

"Ok," he said, but now that he had the opportunity, he struggled with what exactly he should ask her. "So how old are you?"

"I was born on April first of what you know to be the year of Christ's birth. So I guess that makes me 2,001 years old."

"You were born in the same year as Jesus? Did you know him?" Janusz asked excitedly.

"I came from a different place, but I guess, in a way, everyone knew him, whether they were cognizant of the fact or not."

Janusz wasn't sure what she meant by this, but then asked, "So were you a pagan or something?"

Darma smiled at him. "No, in fact, I come from an advanced society, a society that placed great emphasis on the mind and spirit. My birth name is Saleera, and I was born to a peasant family in what you know as India."

"In India? Were you the first 'Rider' or 'Voyager' or whatever it is called?"

"I don't believe so, but I did not meet another true 'Rider' until 300 years after I was born."

"What did you do then? I have thought I might be in hell or at least purgatory."

"Janusz, you have to understand I was born to a Jainin family."

"A what?"

"Jainin. In that religion, along with some others in India, we believe in reincarnation. We believe after a person dies, based on their Karma, he or she can go to one of four levels of existence. The bottom is the insect world, the next, the animal world, the third, the human world, and the fourth is the spiritual world, which is the ultimate goal as once you are there, you remain there in paradise forever."

"So heaven?"

"Yes, it is what the Christian religion calls heaven. So, in the beginning, I believed everything was normal; it wasn't until later that I knew something was amiss."

Janusz pondered all of this for a moment. "So are we being punished, because we did not treat others well?"

This time Darma sighed. "I don't know, and that is only the belief of the religion I was brought up in. There are others who believe we all must go through a certain number of reincarnations before we go to heaven."

"How many times have you come back?"

"This is my 26th voyage."

"And you have met others?"

"Yes, many of them, of all sorts. You see, once you understand, we can basically *sense* other voyagers."

Janusz immediately thought of the gypsy girl, the blues player in Chicago, "Buckets," as well as Colonel Johnson, or even maybe Alina. As he was pondering this, she continued. "Normally, as you are aware, people feel uncomfortable around us, especially in the beginning."

Janusz nodded his head as he knew the feeling all too well.

"But," she said, "sometimes you come across somebody who feels totally at ease with you and has no problem talking with you or looking you in the eye."

He nodded, thinking of how many times this had happened to him. "So how many of us are there?"

"Good question. I don't know, but I have personally met hundreds, and I suspected you were one even before I met you."

"How did you know?"

"The way you sing and play. You see, we have old souls, and it shows in any of our artistic endeavors."

Janusz dropped his head into his hands. He didn't know if he should be happy or lose himself in despair. He liked having someone to talk to, or at least somebody to understand him. "Have you ever known a rider who did not come back?"

Darma seemed to ponder this question a moment too long for his comfort. She finally gathered the words she wanted and said, "I don't know. There have been people I have been close to for hundreds of years and when they died, I could not find them on their next voyage."

Janusz snapped his head up. "So they made it to heaven, or whatever it was you said a reincarnated soul goes to?"

She nodded her head. "The Celestial Kingdom."

"So are you telling me there is no God, no Jesus?"

Darma got up and walked over to Janusz, sitting down next to him, and put her arm around his shoulder. Her touch felt good, better than anything Janusz had felt in a long time. Something inside him broke, and he collapsed into her arms.

She caressed his head as a mother might do with an upset child. "No, Janusz, that's not what I am saying."

He looked at her. "So there is a God?"

"I believe there is, but I don't think man has all the answers. Maybe God, Buddha, Shiva, or Jesus are one and the same, and we are being tested."

His Catholic training bubbled through to the surface, and he wanted to protest, but he let her continue. "There is one thing I do know from 2,000 years of existence, and that is that God is love. Man creates hate, killing, and suffering."

This was all too much for Janusz to think about. He had a lot of thoughts and didn't know how to handle them. Suddenly exhaustion overtook him, and he just wanted to sleep. He couldn't say anymore and just rested his head into Darma's lap and drifted off into a dream filled sleep.

CHAPTER 64

12 MARCH 2000
8 A.M.

When Janusz awoke in the morning, he felt disorientated but refreshed. He had slept through the entire night, but his sleep was riddled with dreams--not nightmares, per se, but dreams, but when he started to think about it, they were more like memories.

He lifted himself off the couch and looked around. It felt good to be in his house, but then he thought of Darma, and their talk rushed back into his mind much like a river runs into a town after a dam fails. He called out her name, but there was no answer. He rushed from room to room; she was nowhere to be found, and now he began to panic.

"Where are you?" he cried aloud, but he was alone. He started to wonder if he had imagined all of what happened last night, but told himself that was crazy. She was there, and she was a fellow "Rider." The last thing he needed right now was to spiral out of control, so he sat down in the middle of the floor and decided to meditate.

He took in the silence of the house and let it wash over him. After that, he controlled his breathing and tried to clear his mind while he started to chant. Although he really didn't think it was chanting in the traditional Yoga sense, Darma had told him that if it worked for him, it wasn't wrong.

He reached for his rosary and started to pray the beads over and over and soon, just as Darma had told him, he began to feel better and inched ever closer to serenity. Once he felt at peace, he stood up and took a deep breath. He decided to call the treatment center as that was probably where she would be since it was 8 in the morning.

He glanced over at the table and looked at his cellular phone, but decided to use the house phone. He knew he was being silly, but there was something he still could not get used to about using a cellular phone; it was unnatural to him. However, if these last 100 years had taught him anything, it was that you could not stop progress. He imagined phones inside the house would soon become obsolete.

But at least for right now they were not, so he walked over to the house phone and dialed the number. The receptionist informed him Darma was not there, and in fact, she would be gone for an unspecified amount of time. He asked her what that meant, but the receptionist told him that kind of information could not be given out.

As he hung up the phone, he tried not to be dejected, but it was difficult. What did "an unspecified amount of time" mean? He slowly set the receiver down; ironically it somehow seemed heavier than it did when he had picked it up. He decided on his next move. He needed more therapy and knew the best thing he could do right now was to play guitar. He could figure everything out later, after the chords soothed his soul.

As he mentally decided which guitar to play, the doorbell rang. The sound startled him, and he stared at the source of the noise for a moment. *Ding dong*, it rang again, and he was pulled out of his trance and walked towards the door. He reached out and grabbed the handle and paused for a moment, hoping it wasn't Judith and Ethan, his manager, or anybody else that wanted something from him. He wasn't ready yet to face his responsibilities.

Janusz took a deep breath and opened the door to find Darma standing there with two cloth bags in her hand. He was instantly relieved when he saw her. As she stood in the doorway, she looked a bit unsure and said,

"I hope it is alright that I am back and I took the liberty of getting you some food as your cupboards are a little bare."

He didn't know what came over him, but he reached out and embraced her. He was so happy to see her. "Of course, please, come in."

He quickly showed her in, and as if it were magic, he was immediately at ease. "I called your office, and they said you were going to be gone for a while."

"Yes, if it is alright with you, I would like to spend a little more time with you, Janusz. There is more I need to tell you as well as warn you about."

He looked at her sharply. "Warn me about?"

"Yes," she said as he led her back into the living room where they sat down on the couch again. "As I have told you, I have known many 'Riders' as you call us, and not all of them have been able to deal with the experience of going through what happens to us."

"What do you mean?"

"One can get caught in a cycle which can continuously carry over into the next 'Ride,' never decreasing, but only building on the misery over and over."

"What happens to a person who is stuck in that cycle?"

Darma looked at him seriously. "They are reborn into insanity every time, only to get worse and worse."

"So you mean they can never start fresh?"

"I don't know, but I don't think so."

Janusz pondered this for a moment. He could not think of anything more terrifying than to be insane, forever. "Am I on the path to insanity?"

"It's possible."

He stood up and walked around for a moment thinking about what she'd said. He looked around his house and all the items in it. He thought about all the places he had been, and he thought about all of the money in his bank account. All of it meant nothing if he didn't have his sanity intact.

"Help me," he said, looking at her as though a child might look at someone when lost and unable to get home.

Darma stood up and stretched her arm out, offering her hand to Janusz, who took it wholeheartedly.

CHAPTER 65

31 MARCH 2000

Janusz and Darma walked around Skid Row. She had taken him to the darkest and deepest depths of depravity and stopped when they came across a man in the corner of an alley. The man clearly had not showered in a long time as was evident by a stench that turned Janusz' stomach.

Darma pointed at the man. "What do you see?"

Janusz stared at the man lying in his own filth, surrounded by an army of empty bottles and said, "A man in desperation." But the answer was only a guess at what he thought Darma wanted to hear.

"Look closely," she said, "What differences do you see between yourself and him?"

Many thoughts swirled around in his head, but most of them were answers he was sure would not be the ones she would want to hear.

She prodded him again and said, "Be honest with yourself, Janusz, truly honest now."

Janusz stumbled on his words, but finally in a low voice said, "I see a man who disgusts me, one who could not conquer his demons, and one who is weak and has stopped fighting."

After he spat out the words, he waited for some kind of admonishment from Darma, but it didn't come. She put her hand on his shoulder, and he felt the warmth as he had before, and she said, "The first step to break the chains of your soul, the ones holding you down, and the ones that could drive you into perpetual insanity, and it starts with honesty."

He looked at her and wanted to protest and say something like "I am always honest with people," but it wasn't true.

She continued almost as if she were reading his mind. "Many people believe they are truthful and while they may never utter a lie to another living person, many of these people lie to themselves every day."

Janusz thought about this deeply for a moment. It never occurred to him how dishonest he was with himself at times. Darma's voice broke him out of his thoughts. "Janusz, is it possible what you see in this man are also attributes you see in yourself?"

He nodded his head.

"Janusz, the truth here, is this man, or the dozens of others we see, is no different than you or anybody. One of humanity's deepest failures is placing human life over another or the division of classes. So take another look at this man, look at him for what he is--an equal human being--and tell me what you see."

Janusz closed his eyes and said, "I see a man who is struggling but does not have the resources I had."

"Exactly, Janusz, we must treat everyone equally. No matter who you are, everyone makes mistakes, but some people, based on who they are or how much money they have, get redemption while others receive nothing."

Janusz agreed with this point, but only on this "Ride," as he thought back to his previous ride and his struggles with alcoholism, which ended with him throwing himself in the river.

"Darma, but that hasn't always been the situation with me. I have been raped, beaten, murdered, betrayed, left for dead, and imprisoned."

She listened patiently and waited for him to finish. "You have indeed suffered. But take a look at yourself now; where are you?"

He looked back at the man and thought of himself again. He knew he was in a better position than the man, but he was having a hard time getting past the fairness of everything.

"I feel as if God is punishing me, and I have done nothing to warrant such treatment," he said as he felt anger build inside him.

"Janusz, maybe it is not what you have done, but what you have failed to do."

"What do you mean?"

"At what point in any of your existence did you use any of your gifts or fortunes to help somebody else?"

This statement pushed his anger even further. "I worked my entire life to ensure my children had a good life! That is what I have done for others."

His anger did not seem to bother her. "Did you do that for you?"

Now he felt as though Darma was playing games with him. Of course, he didn't do it for himself; he had sacrificed everything to make sure his children were fed and clothed.

She prodded him some more. "Think about this--would you agree that parents are supposed to take care of their children?"

"Of course."

"Yes, of course, you and your wife created them, so they were your responsibility, but what if you thought of everybody as your children? What if taking care of your own is just the starting point?"

Janusz pondered this for a moment; he was always taught that a man was supposed to take care of his responsibilities. As he knew from his previous rides, that was not always possible. Not everybody had the same opportunities.

She stopped and looked at him. "What about your father and his sacrifice?"

A touch of sadness flowed through him as he thought about his father. "My father sacrificed his life so that his children could have a better future."

Darma reached out and touched his shoulder and said, "No Janusz, not entirely. Your father sacrificed himself so that everybody could have a better future, not only his children."

Pieces of the puzzle began to fall into place as he thought about her statement and he asked, "So do you mean that my father viewed everybody in Krakow as his children and died for them?"

Darma didn't answer his question, but rather posed another one of her own. "What does your religion say about caring for others?"

Janusz reflected on his religion and thought about how Abraham was going to sacrifice Isaac. This led him to the basis of Christianity and ultimately, Jesus. "It says caring for others is above all."

"Yes, in your religion, God sacrificed his own son for the wellbeing of others."

They started walking down the alley again now which gave Janusz a moment to reflect on her words, and after a few moments of silence, he looked at her. "How do I know who is right? Who should I follow?"

Darma knew he was talking in terms of religion. "Well, in Jainism, how you treat others influences your Karma, which determines where you go when you leave your current body; the same is true with Hinduism. In Christianity, Islam, Judaism, and almost all others, it is similar. It is how you act on earth that determines if you go to Heaven or Hell."

Janusz didn't quite grasp the point she was trying to make and wished she would stop speaking in riddles. "So, they are all right?"

"Imagine what would happen if we all stopped focusing on the differences or who was right and wrong and only focused on the essence of the meaning instead of the words written by man."

At this point, they were halfway down the alley and came across a woman sitting against a wall with her knees pulled up to her chest. Janusz looked at her, and when their eyes met, he knew the look. He didn't even need to see the track marks on her arm to know this woman was a junkie and she was coming down and would need a fix, sooner rather than later.

The woman on the ground straightened out her legs, reached out a shaky hand, and looked up at them. "Spare some change?" The woman wore a shirt so short that it exposed her entire stomach, and he could see she had stretch marks, and Janusz guessed she had given birth at least two times. Darma and Janusz looked at her and the woman asked again, but became more desperate. "Please, anything, I'll make you feel good, or you can watch me with your lady, but please, I need 10 dollars."

Janusz recoiled, but Darma grabbed his arm and pulled him back with surprising strength for a woman of her size. "If your Jesus were here right now or watching, which do you think he would rather see? Do you think he would favor the person who goes into a church, lights candles in the correct order and says empty words of prayers long ago memorized, or do you think he would favor somebody who shows kindness to this woman, even if that person had never stepped foot in a church?"

Janusz quickly reached into his pocket to withdraw his wallet, and the woman's eyes widened, but Darma stopped him. "Money alone will not fix this problem; it is merely a tool that is far too often misused."

After hearing what Darma said, the woman realized she was not going to allow Janusz to give her any money and said, "You fucking bitch" and spat at them. Janusz jumped back, unsure of what the woman was now going to do, but Darma didn't flinch. Instead, she walked towards the woman, who shied away a bit, and leaned down in front of her. Darma reached in her pocket and pulled out a card, leaned forward and whispered something into the woman's ear.

Darma stood up and motioned to him to start walking. Janusz waited for her to say something and when she didn't he asked, "What did you say to her?"

She didn't immediately answer his question but instead posed one of her own. "Janusz, if you were standing on the corner of Rodeo Drive in Beverly Hills and a man wearing a 2,000 dollar suit came up to you and asked you for directions, what would you do?"

"I would help him if I could?"

"Then why wouldn't you help this woman? She is lost like the man, but the only difference here is that she has taken the wrong path in life, but we can help her all the same."

As they continued walking, it all became clear, and Janusz understood the lesson she was trying to teach him, or at least he thought he did. "You gave her a card to the rehab center, didn't you?"

"Yes, but that was only a sliver of the total. I gave her directions to get back on the right path and shined a light for her to follow."

"But what if she doesn't take it, or takes it and relapses?"

"Then we try again, and again, and again."

Janusz marveled at her patience and kindness. He looked back at the woman as they walked away and saw she was looking at the card. He wondered briefly how everything would turn out for her.

"Janusz, the path to keep you out of perpetual insanity is not what you do for yourself, it is what you do for others, and the path is paved with Love, Kindness, and Charity."

CHAPTER 66

14 OCTOBER 2000

Janusz had asked Darma to join him today because he wasn't sure how he was going to react. When they arrived at the door, Janusz paused for a moment and thought if he was ready for this. He felt Darma's grip on his arm, which was comforting and somehow gave him the strength to go in.

As he walked through the doors of the recording studio, he could feel the electricity buzzing around him. It felt good to be back, but Janusz was also a bit scared. The path to get to this point had not been easy, in fact, far from it. With help from Darma, it was possible, though. Janusz had gone through a change for sure, a change that he considered to be in three phases. The first stage was knowing, the second was believing, and the third phase was putting it into practice. The last step he found to be the most difficult and a stage he might be in for the rest of his life.

Janusz knew he needed to use music to help people. That was clear to him, and at first, he didn't exactly know which path to take. He had written some good material for JRD and had constantly reached out to Ditch, but it was a void. When he had finally gotten ahold of Ditch, the man had been listless and strung out.

Janusz had thought that maybe this was the first step in his path, to help Ditch, so he put everything on hold and devoted all of his energy to help out his band mate. That was a rough road for Janusz, though. No matter what he did, he could not get through to Ditch and Janusz had started to believe he would probably never play music with this man again.

Then, one day after Janusz had done his morning meditation, he sat down on the couch to try and figure out a new way to reach the man. He was coming up short, and it frustrated him, so he turned on the TV to try and clear his thoughts. That is when he saw it. It was right there on the news with the headline "Bass Player of JRD found dead of a suspected drug overdose."

He remembered the sense of overwhelming failure he had felt as he sat there on the couch. That sense of failure made him angry, the anger had consumed him, and out of the blue, he had an incredible urge to use. A vision popped into his head of him tying his arm off, plunging the needle into his arm, and shooting a dose of heroin into his veins.

Janusz tried to shake off the vision, but he could feel himself beginning to sweat as if he were going through withdrawal. He knew that was impossible, but the feeling was real. He felt hopeless and decided to make a phone call. He found himself standing up and going to call his dealer. He was just going to see if his dealer would answer, that was it, he told himself, and if he did answer, maybe he would hang up or perhaps he wouldn't. Janusz decided he would cross that bridge when he came to it.

He was already off the couch and halfway to the phone when the doorbell rang, and it stopped him in his tracks. He looked at the door, then over to the phone, and back to the door when the bell rang again. But now it wasn't a bell, it was a beacon, drawing him in, and he felt himself walking towards the door instead of the phone.

Soon he found himself standing in front of the door with his hand outstretched, but not yet touching the handle as he still thought he could go back to the phone and make the call. But the doorbell rang again and all of a sudden he wanted to open the door more than make the call. He shook his head and knew it was more than a want; he *needed* to open the door. So he did, and behind the door, he saw Darma standing there.

Now as he stood in the studio, she was with him again, his "flashlight," as he thought of her, shining the light down the path he needed to take. She had talked him down that day; she had showed up at his door in the right moment. He knew what would have happened if he had made that phone call.

Now he needed her help again today. As he looked around the studio, he noticed several familiar faces, but also some he did not recognize. He did not see the one face he was dreading, though.

His manager walked up and shook Janusz' hand and said, "Janusz, even though I don't understand what the hell is going on, it is damn good to see you in here."

"Thanks, it's good to be back, and don't worry, you are not alone. I'm not entirely sure what I am doing either, but I have it on good authority that this is the right step." He glanced at Darma and winked.

"If you say so," his manager said, "But I am still not sure about the musicians. The guitar and bass player look like they are one step away from the nursing home. Are you sure they can play?"

Janusz shrugged his shoulders. "I guess we will find out. Are they here?"

"Yep, they have been here for a while now; everybody is in there waiting for you, looking as confused as the rest of us."

"Ok, can you tell them I'll be in soon? I need a few moments."

"Sure thing, Janusz, take your time."

The manager walked towards the recording room and pulled open the door and walked in. Before the door shut, Janusz caught a glimpse of the man he was dreading to see, but only for a moment. That was all it took for the thousands of emotions to come barreling back to him.

He felt his breath become rapid, almost as if he couldn't catch it, and the room started to spin. He sat down for a moment, and Darma came over to him and put a hand on his shoulder and said, "You can do this, the only way to expel hate from within is through forgiveness. Without forgiveness, there is no moving forward, no matter how deep down you shove those emotions."

"I didn't realize it would be so hard. Every fiber of my being is urging me to go in there and wrap my hands around his throat and squeeze. And why do I want to drink when I see him?"

Darma sat down next to him and said, "This hate keeps you in prison. This prison is preventing you from fully showing kindness and love to others, Janusz, and it is the kindness and love you show to those who have wronged you the most that truly matters. Forgiveness is the key to the world, because, without forgiveness, there can be no love."

He looked at her, nodded his head, and stood up. Taking one more deep breath with closed eyes, he pushed his feet forward and entered the recording room. The three men looked at him with wide-open eyes of awe and admiration. After a brief moment of silence, the guitar player came over to Janusz, held his hand out, and said, "It is such an honor to meet you, Mr. Z, my name is Clarence."

"Johnson." Janusz interrupted as he shook the hand of his old guitar player from more than 30 years ago. "I am a huge fan of your band and your album."

The moment Janusz touched Clarence's hand, the guitar player's eyes changed a bit. It wasn't necessarily good or bad, but there was energy, and Clarence could feel it. Clarence then said, "If I didn't know any better, I would say that I have met you before."

Janusz smiled as he let go of the man's hand. "I get that a lot. I think it's because so many people see me on TV, especially lately...you know, with the overdose and everything..."

Clarence nodded his head. "Well, Mr. Z, I am in no position to judge another man; I have had my fair share of demons and done things I am not proud of."

Janusz looked at Clarence and could see the man was honest. "Thanks, Clarence, and please call me Janusz."

"Ok, Janusz, so I must tell you that I was curious when I found out you bought the rights to the album from the record company, and when I got the call that you wanted to record it again with the original band members, or what was left of them, it almost floored me."

Janusz looked deeply into the man's eyes. The years had not been kind to him, but Janusz could still see the young 20-year-old with the flashy clothes and the constant cigarette hanging out of his mouth in there and said, "I am glad you still play."

Clarence nodded his head. "Yeah, well I never really stopped playing throughout the years, same with Johnny over there on the bass."

Janusz picked up a guitar, but not to play yet, only to hold it. Holding a guitar was kind of like a shield for Janusz; it protected him and made him feel safe. He then sat down on a stool and motioned for Clarence to sit as well.

"Clarence, can you tell me a bit about the inspiration for the album, how did you guys come up with it?" Janusz was obviously testing Clarence to see if he would tell the truth. His anger for the man had not completely fizzled, and even though he should let it die and record the album and get on with the mission, that was something he couldn't do yet.

"Well," the weathered man said, "It was a pretty magical time, but I must be honest with you, Janusz, it was Willie that was the lifeblood of the group."

"What do you mean?"

"He wrote all the songs, he was the talent, that's why we only got out one album. When he left, the magic left with him."

Janusz admired Clarence's honesty, but still needed to hear more and asked, "He went to Vietnam and got pretty banged, up right?"

"Yeah." Clarence looked down, unable to look Janusz in the eyes, but continued talking. "We did him wrong."

"What do you mean?"

"We were on track to record, make it big, we all thought, but Willie got drafted and went over. The record company man said he wanted to still proceed with the album, even without him. We protested at first, but they told us it was 'now or never' so in a way, we told ourselves we would record this one, and when he came back, we would pick up from where we left off."

Janusz glared at him and asked, "But that is not the way it went down, huh?"

"No, sir, we got word he was killed, which he wasn't; he was in a damn prison over there, but we were still thinking about ourselves, I can't lie."

Now Janusz had one more final question for Clarence, a sort of moment of truth. "So, Clarence, why are you doing this now?"

"To be honest, I didn't want to do it at first, but I listened to all your music for hours on end, and I'll be damned if it wasn't like listening to a ghost sing. I could feel Willie when I listened to your music and I thought, maybe with you, we could do the record right. I guess you can say I owe my old friend."

Janusz stood up and walked over to the man. He reached out and placed a hand on Clarence's shoulder and said, "I am positive he would be happy." Janusz looked at the old man some more and felt something change within himself; he let go of the anger. It didn't serve any purpose, and it was liberating. So Janusz looked around to the rest of the group and said, "So what do you boys say we make some magic happen?"

And magic they made; they recorded for seven days straight, playing the old songs they used to, and Janusz put every ounce of his soul into the record.

CHAPTER 67

2 APRIL 2001

Janusz walked off the stage feeling better than he ever had. Before the show he'd had second thoughts about starting the tour in Chicago; he wondered if it would have brought up too many painful memories, but in the end, he knew it had to be there. Chicago is where it started; it was the place where he was truly turned on to music, and this was the place the tour had to start.

As he walked backstage with Clarence and the rest of the guys, the noise from the crowd was deafening. Janusz turned to Clarence. "What do you think?"

Clarence rode a euphoric high and for a moment, Janusz thought the man would be unable to speak, but he said, "I ain't never experienced no shit like that."

"Yeah, well it happens when you have the number one album in the country."

As they continued walking to the dressing room to meet the press and, most importantly, Darma, Clarence said, "I still can't believe all these people are excited over an old album; most of them out there were not even born when it first came out."

Janusz nodded his head. "I wasn't sure how it was going to go either, but we just won over Chicago; it is the wind to our backs from here on out."

Before they entered the dressing room, Clarence stopped him. "How many record sales do we have now?"

"I don't know exactly, but it is more than any of my others for sure."

Clarence stood stoic as the realization hit him. Janusz slapped him on the shoulder and put his arm around him. "You are going to be set for life, old friend, and that is after all of the other proceeds that are going to the soup kitchens and the schools."

Janusz then opened the door and walked into a flurry of reporters and multitudes of other people, all wanting to talk to him and the rest of the band. He tried to avoid everybody and find Darma, but it was futile. There was a line of reporters between them, and he was going to have to talk to some of them before he got to her.

The first two reporters only wanted to ask about the overdoses, and any other dirt they could think of, but Janusz dismissed these guys quickly enough and said, "That part of my life is over, and I am on a new path now. There is nothing more to learn about that dark period; sorry guys, you will have to get your dirt from someplace else."

The next reporter tried to pry into the relationship between him and Darma, and he quickly shot that down too. "I hate to disappoint you again, but Darma is my rehab counselor and spiritual advisor."

"So there is no woman in your life?"

"Just Lady Music," and he pushed his way through to the next reporter.

This man asked, "Is it true you will be donating all the proceeds and working in shelters in between the shows?"

Janusz looked around at all the reporters. "Finally, a good question. Yes, in between shows we will be hitting the streets and spreading goodwill. In fact, that's where we are going now. Outside we have set up a soup kitchen, so join us if you care to."

Janusz pushed his way through the crowd and found Darma. He looked at her and saw hope. Without her, Janusz did not want to think about what might have happened and said, "Thank you."

She smiled at him with that warm smile and radiating blue eyes. "You are welcome, Janusz; I am happy you see your path."

He now looked back over to Clarence and watched him talk with a reporter. None of this would have been possible if he'd still held onto the grudge over what had happened all those years ago. He turned back to Darma and said, "I never thought forgiveness could be so liberating."

She continued to smile, but her eyes took on a serious look. "Forgiveness not only cleans the soul but it allows us to achieve many things, but I warn you, Janusz, forgiving a remorseful person is easy, forgiving those who have no remorse or are bound by hate, is more difficult. It is the forgiveness of those which is the most important."

Janusz looked at her and thought deeply about the statement. He knew that in 2,000 years, there must have been many people who had wronged her and probably some who felt no remorse for their actions. Now he wondered how he would have reacted if Clarence had not been remorseful.

As they walked out of the room, he pushed this thought out of his head. He was excited; he could not wait to get outside and start helping people. He looked at Darma, and said, "My hands are shaking; I am so excited."

"I'm pleased to hear that, but please keep in mind you may not be able to reach everybody, so don't be discouraged when that happens, and above all, do not give up. No matter what happens," she said, "Do not give up."

"I won't; I promise."

Darma stopped walking and grabbed him by the shoulder and said, "Please remember this."

He said nothing and only smiled as they walked out the door. Her words stuck with him, though. He wouldn't give up, he told himself. He was thinking about this exact thought when the man yelled out to him, and at first, he didn't understand what was happening. It was fast and loud, and a tad dreamlike. A man screamed at him, and the voice seemed familiar.

"You think you are some fucking hotshot, but you ain't nothing but that same skinny little faggot you always were!"

He looked at the man yelling and recognized him; it was Jake from school, the one who used to bully him. Janusz wondered why he was here; it made no sense to him. He stood there dumbfounded with his mouth agape, even when the man pointed a gun directly at his face. He couldn't move, and he could not understand why Jake would be so angry.

Janusz heard the gunfire, but he didn't remember being pulled to the ground or any of the commotion for the next few minutes. His sense of awareness only came back to him when he asked Darma what had happened. She was lying on top of him, but she didn't answer him, and she didn't move. He reached out to her and shook her, calling her name, but she wouldn't answer…something was wrong…and then she was being pulled off of him and taken away.

CHAPTER 68

9 APRIL 2001

Janusz remained in the cemetery long after everybody else had left. He was devastated, and also ashamed. He was devastated such a beautiful person was gone, at least in this form. She was gone, and it was because of him. She had thrown herself in front of the bullet, the bullet meant for Janusz, a bullet that came from a person he had not seen in so many years and had forgotten about. He was devastated because a person whose only goal in life was to help and love other people was gone.

He was also ashamed because he had hatred in his heart. He hated Jake for what he had done now, and also in the past. He was also ashamed he had canceled the next show as well as the trips to the shelters, because that would have broken Darma's heart. She would have wanted him to continue with the work.

Continuing was something he knew he would do, but he feared it might be for the wrong reason. He knew how easy it would be to slip back into his old habits, start drinking or using, and brood over what happened. He knew that would eventually destroy him, and he could slip into perpetual insanity, and he was not going to let Jake do that to him. So he would go on, but for now, he needed to mourn for just a bit.

CHAPTER 69

31 JULY 2001
9 A.M.

Janusz was silent on the way to the courthouse. Today they were going to sentence Jake, and Janusz would get to say to the court what he would like to see happen. Before that, he would get to talk to Jake, and Janusz wanted to know the answer to one question--why?

The police had told Janusz much about Jake. After he had been arrested back in school for beating Janusz, his life had gone downhill. Jake's father never got the job he had hoped for, and their family life deteriorated. His father became an abusive alcoholic, which landed him in jail, and later his mother committed suicide. His mother's death led to Jake being placed in foster homes and then in and out of jail.

The police had also shown Janusz pictures of Jake's apartment. The man had been obsessed with Janusz; his walls were plastered with photographs and magazine articles about him. Over most of them, Jake had written various threats or messages of hatred directed at Janusz. Jake had been obsessing over Janusz for years and took his shot when he had the chance.

The driver's voice jarred him out of his thoughts. "We are here, Mr. Z."

Janusz looked up at the driver and said, "Thanks, Jim, I don't know how long I'll be, but I'll call you when I am done." As Janusz got out of the car, he stood in front of the courthouse and looked at the entrance for a few moments. He did not want to go in there, and he certainly did not want to talk to this monster who had removed from his life the most selfless person he had ever known. He slowly forced his legs to move and walked through the doors.

Jake was in the room, waiting for Janusz, when he arrived. He sat behind a table where his arms were shackled to the top, and his legs to the floor. Janusz took a seat and looked at the man for a moment. Jake also just sat there, glaring at Janusz, and finally spoke.

"So what the fuck do you want?" he asked. "Let me guess; you want me to cry or beg and tell you how sorry I am for what I did, right?"

Janusz couldn't answer; rage clouded his thoughts.

Jake continued, "Well, I'm not, so fuck you. You ruined my life, and then I had to see you flashing all your fame and success around everywhere, and everybody loves you, but I know you…you are still that skinny little shit who didn't know his place."

More silence, but Janusz knew he should say something. "I'm sorry you feel that way."

Jake laughed, and said, "Fuck you. Don't feel sorry for me. You know, at first, when that bitch threw herself in front of you and ate the bullet, I was pissed. I was mad I didn't get to blow your fucking brains all over the ground."

Janusz' hands trembled and he now thought this was a mistake. This man had no remorse; he was just inflicting more hurt. So Janusz got up and motioned to the guard to open the door; there was nothing else to say here.

"Wait," said Jake. "Don't you want to hear the best part?"

Janusz knew he should not stop, he should go, but he looked back at Jake.

"Yeah, then I realized shooting that bitch was even better, because now you will have to live with it for the rest of your life, you fucking faggot."

Janusz closed his eyes and walked through the door, trying to remain in control. He was trembling, but kept walking. He could hear

Jake's maniacal laughter quite clearly even after the door to the room had been shut.

11 a.m.

As Janusz sat in the courtroom waiting for Jake to be brought in, the only thing he could hear was the cruel laughter over and over in his head. He was told the sentencing would go relatively fast after the people gave their statements. And Janusz had a lot to say, so he was anxious for his turn.

After what seemed like an eternity, the judge called out Janusz' name and asked him if he had anything to say before he passed judgment on Jake. "I do, your honor." Janusz walked to the front of the court and took a seat looking directly into the hateful eyes of Jake.

Janusz took a deep breath, closed his eyes, and thought of Darma. He thought of all the good she had done and how that was ruined. Finally, he exhaled and said, "Your honor, I believe the accused is a hateful man with no remorse. He took away a woman whose only goal in life was to help other people, and the bitter part of me wants to see this man rot in a prison cell in the worst conditions possible."

He paused, took another breath and continued. "But something keeps ringing in my ears, something Darma told me and that was 'forgiveness is easy when the other person has remorse; it is much harder when they don't. But that is when it counts the most.' That was the motto she lived by."

Pausing again, he knew this was going to be the hardest part, but he continued. "So first I would like to say that I forgive you, Jake, and I would like to ask the court for the lightest sentence possible and that counseling and treatment be given to this man, so he gets a proper rehabilitation."

The judge's face showed no emotion, but he did pause for a moment before he said, "Are you sure about this recommendation?"

He nodded. "Yes, your honor, there has been enough hate, and vengeance won't fix anything. Sure, it may make me feel better for a moment, but in the end, the hate will come back stronger, and that would be the worst thing I could do for Darma's memory. So if you can, please take pity on this man."

The judge nodded at him and said, "Thank you, Mr. Richardson, you may take your seat now."

Janusz got up and walked back down to his seat. The judge announced a 30-minute recess to the court and said that after that, he would give his decision. The bailiff announced in a deep baritone voice, "All rise," and Janusz watched the judge walk out the door and off to the left.

Most of the people sat down then, some left, and Janusz could see Jake's lawyer talking to him. Janusz stood there for five minutes, just thinking, before he walked into the aisle and out the doors. He exited the courthouse and called Jim, who picked up on the first ring. "Hi, Jim, I'm ready, and out front; there is nothing more for me here."

While he waited for Jim to arrive, Janusz reached in his messenger bag and pulled out the large unopened packet containing the family histories from his other rides that the PI had given him years ago. He looked at it and knew that inside he would find all the information of what had happened to his multiple sets of other parents, brothers and sisters, and his offspring, and even Grant.

Janusz was not entirely sure why, until now, he had never opened it. As he held the envelope, he saw Jim pull up in the car and wave to him. Janusz took one last look at the unopened envelope and tossed it into the trashcan beside him. He then walked to the car, jumped in, and closed the door with a satisfying click.

Jim looked at him and asked, "Where to, boss?"

"Forward, Jim, down the path."

CHAPTER 70

31 OCTOBER 2077

Janusz was pretty sure today was the day he was going to die. He was tired and ready to let this body go. He had managed to stay active until this "shell" was almost 100, but eventually, Mother Nature had taken over. His fingers wouldn't move the way he wanted them to, which meant he couldn't play his guitar. That didn't bother him too much though, because over the years, he realized his guitar was only one of the tools he used to forge the path.

In total, he had been on this earth for 277 years, but the best ones, the ones that mattered, were the last 75. He had achieved more than he could have dreamed; his kindness and love had spread all over the globe, and that made him proud. There wasn't a day that went by that he didn't wake up and ask himself how he could make Darma proud, how could he continue her work?

He followed her examples. He let things go, he forgave, and he loved unconditionally. Well, there was *one* thing he never let go of, and that was his search for her. After she died, he had hired a private investigator and researched all of the babies born in the Chicago area around the time of her death.

That was how it worked, or so he thought. He seemed to always come back to whichever baby happened to be born the closest to his time and place of death. But he found nothing; he had followed those children throughout the past 75 years and had never seen any sign of Darma in them.

Not finding Darma had pained him a bit, and he wondered if she had come back or not. And if she had, why hadn't she reconnected with him? Strangely, he thought he would see her today as he lay on his death-bed, but there had been no sign of her. Maybe she had found her "Celestial Kingdom" or "Nirvana" or "Heaven."

Janusz didn't know, but he never let it distract him from his work. Now he began to think about what his next "Ride" would be like. He had been an old man for so long, he had forgotten what it was like to be young, and at least that was something he could look forward to. He was also thankful for the moment of peace he had at the moment.

There had been a steady stream of visitors, all of whom he loved and who loved him based on his work, but he was so tired. He didn't feel like talking and needed a little rest. He set down the tablet he had been reading with the files on all the people who he thought could have been Darma and looked out the window. The big tree that stood guard right outside no longer had any leaves on its branches. Janusz tilted his head in thought; he could have sworn just moments ago there had still been a few clinging to the branches.

Janusz closed his eyes. There was no reason to think about the leaves anymore; he felt strange and at first, didn't know what was happening, but he quickly remembered. He was dying; he was slipping out of this body. He remembered the feeling now, although he wasn't in pain or anguish. He let himself slip away as he had done many times before.

The last thing he heard was the steady tone of the machine mon-itoring his vital signs and thought to himself, *oh calm down you damn machine; I'll be back.* And then Janusz Zalewski drifted off into death for the 5th time in 277 years.

EPILOGUE

As the young woman with the long dark hair and the unnaturally radiating blue eyes walked through the cemetery, she noticed how beautiful the day was. Her braided hair bounced against her chest with every step she took. It was bitterly cold, but the sky was blue, and the sun shone bright, spreading hopeful warmth over everything it touched.

No matter how many times she stood in the sunlight, it never ceased to amaze her--the power, the warmth, and the magic. Because of the sun, she strolled through the cemetery extremely slowly; there was no need to hurry, because the person she was going to see was not going anywhere.

Finally, she arrived at her destination and looked down at the stone. She smiled and rubbed one of the scars on her wrist with her thumb as she read the words inscribed on it:

Brian "Janusz Z" Richardson

July 31, 1974 - October 31, 2077

Forgiveness Lights the Path to Kindness and Love

The woman smiled as she knelt in front of the stone and reached out her hand. As she did, her blue eyes radiated even more and she said, "Rest easy, my child, you did well."

The End

Photo by Jessica LaGassey-Simpson

Charles Simpson was born and raised in Michigan but left home at the age of 17 to join the United States Air Force and see the world. He credits his international lifestyle with opening his mind and giving him an appreciation for different cultures. He has lived in Japan, Korea, Italy, Germany, and Turkey and has traveled extensively on five of the continents. Even though he is now retired from active duty, he continues to call the world his home. He is a man of many passions: music, surfing, languages, motorcycles, biking, aviation, and art. Charles currently lives in Hawaii with his wife Jess, who shares his love of travel, and their two Chihuahuas. "The Rider" is his first novel.

.